# GOD'S INFLUENCE IN THE POWERFUL 7

——————— A NOVEL ———————

Something Special about the Number Seven as
Influenced by God and Shared in Writing

By

## J. ANDY WELCH

ISBN 978-1-64191-300-3 (paperback)
ISBN 978-1-64191-301-0 (digital)

Christian Faith Publishing, Inc.
832 Park Avenue
Meadville, PA 16335
www.christianfaithpublishing.com

Printed in the United States of America

# CONTENTS

# FORWARD

I found the book, *God's Influence in the Powerful 7* to be informative, eloquent, fluent, emphatic and just plain fun to read.

Strange occurrences involving the number seven begin to reveal themselves to the main character, George Belten. Research in the number seven brings a theological perspective of completeness, creation, and divine perfection. George Belten uses the number seven to break an addictive habit he had for over 25 years. He later uses the number seven to help people with financial budgeting and addictive behaviors.

In the story, George's Christian ethics are challenged when he becomes a victim of criminal mischief by a person whose attitude is synonymous with the crime. Can he forgive? Can he persevere?

Since reading this book, I am more aware of the number seven in my daily life and I consciously now think about the seven and use it often.

God Bless! Seven Up!
AGB

# INTRODUCTION

George Belten begins to understand that his experiences involving the number seven are not coincidental. It was unusual for George to lay awake during his nights. He would normally check the time on a nearby clock before going back to sleep. Generally, he prayed for his needed rest, then close his eyes. Night after night, the clock read 2:32 a.m. "I lay awake until I pray for the Lord to help me get my rest, and then I almost immediately go back to sleep." "Why am I awake at the same time nightly". "Something strange is going on here, for certain." he thought.

And, it came to him, 2 plus 2 plus 3 equals 7. "Why is the number Seven becoming so significant to me?" Turning to the Bible, he discovers the number Seven is in referenced over four hundred times. God sanctified that number and it became sacred as a sign of success, of completion.

Many life changing events turned to success as George prayed and leaned on the the number Seven. He began guiding others as they conquer finances, relationship confrontations, excessive weight, and other problems as they empower number Seven.

There is a time of suspense, a time for laughter and, a time for your eyes to water in this writing.

# CHAPTER ONE

George Belten and his wife Carol live in Spring Creek Glen, a quiet neighborhood outside the city limits, in Lane County. Spring Creek Glen is a small community with one way in and one way out, and with only forty-four homes. George and Carol have lived here over twenty years and know almost every family in the Glen. They have watched as newborn babies grow up and become adults.

George is fifty-six years old, 5'11", average weight; and he makes no effort to hide his graying hair. People at church tell him that he married up when he latched on to Carol. Carol is 5'2", pretty, and most people believe she is still in her mid-thirties. George has three sons from a previous marriage that resided with him until they completed their education and established their own career paths. Carol never had children of her own, and she loves these boys and their families as if they were her own.

George would not allow himself to be serious about any lady until his boys were almost grown. Ladies would often ask him, "What are you looking for in a wife?" He would never tell anybody as they would attempt to portray themselves to possess those qualities. Carol had the character, morals, and integrity that George was looking for. He always felt that those qualities would get you through a lot of marriage hurdles.

Carol was visiting her sister living in Texas, and George wrote her a letter, asking for her hand in marriage. Why would anybody propose by U.S. Mail? It allowed her the time to consider marriage, talk with family, and respond without pressure. Carol accepted, and Seven months later, they were married.

Four years ago, they decided an addition to the family would be good. So they searched for over two months for the perfect puppy to bring into their home. One Thursday afternoon, they drove to the next small town to see a six-week-old Shih Tzu/Maltese mix. It was love at first sight! The puppy was solid white with soft hair associated with Maltese breed. So they brought him to live with them, and he was so small that he fit in George's hand perfectly. "Barney," Barney Fife, became his name. Today, Barney weighs eleven pounds and is amazingly smart, a result of being around Carol and/or George twenty-four seven. He even sleeps on their bed at night. Barney welcomes all visitors with excitement, even strangers. He is definitely part of the Belten family.

Carol's day normally involves volunteer work at their church and with seniors in the community. She is ideal in that function as her energy and love for others is obvious.

George has been an independent consultant, representing a well-respected and recognized corporation that provides products and updating guidance to businesses, large and small. His region covers approximately 150 miles in all directions from his home. The area is not protected from other consultants intruding. However, with his longevity representing the company, there is an honor system in place that encourages other independents to avoid infringement of his area.

Monday morning and George has awakened to the whirling blades of a low-flying helicopter in the near distance. *What is that thing up to this time of the morning?* he mumbles.

He looks at the clock, and it's only 6:15 a.m. *Oh, what the heck.* He groans while he looks over at Carol as she remains in deep sleep. He then sits up on side of their bed, lights up a cigarette, climbs out of bed, stretches, and heads outside, still in his pajamas and robe. Barney trots along behind him as he heads to the deck. Barney goes through his morning routine; he goes out in the back yard, pees, and runs back to the deck. There, he stares at George. It's his way of communicating to George: "Hey, I did my business. Where's my treat?"

George reaches in his pocket and drops a treat on the deck as Barney's reward.

He pulled the treat from the container as he walked by the kitchen bar on his way to the deck.

Standing on the deck, he listens. The helicopter has faded off in the distance. It is unusual to hear a helicopter hovering in the area. He wonders, *Were they searching that area for a criminal? Is there a dangerous animal in the area? Or was it some kind of a practice maneuver by the chopper? Oh well, whatever the reason, it seems to be solved now that it's gone.* George considers.

The sun is rising in the east. The morning is so quiet he can hear every little chirp of birds and the barking of a squirrel. The temperature is perfect, just cool enough to make it enjoyable outside.

The first cigarette of the morning is always the most enjoyable. Especially while relaxing outside, it seems to make the early morning more enjoyable.

After several minutes in the fresh air, he lights up his second cigarette of the morning. He coughs a few times, looks at the cigarette between his fingers, and again thinks, *I wish I could give up this horrible addiction to cigarettes.*

He has quit many times throughout his thirty years of smoking but always lights up again within a few days. Once, he quit smoking for almost a week. *Someday, I'll quit smoking for good,* he thinks.

After a few minutes, he extinguishes the cigarette in an ashtray. "Barney? Are you ready to go back inside?"

Barney jumps up with delight and runs to the door leading into the house. George slides the door open, and Barney makes a mad dash for the bedroom to wake Carol. George picks Barney up and places him at the foot of their bed. He runs up to Carol and begins squealing, as if to say, "Get up, get up, I'm here now. Wake up, Carol!"

George asks Carol, "Did you hear that helicopter early this morning?"

"I don't think so. When was that?"

"A few minutes after six. I believe it was nearby, but I believe it was over on the other road. Sounded like it was hovering, searching for something or somebody. I would estimate it remained for about two or three minutes, and then it left."

George's normal early morning passion is a good hot shower. Slinging a fresh towel over the shower door, he steps inside and adjusts the water temperature to his liking. He gently pats a mole-like growth on his chest and thinks, *This mole, or whatever it is, on my chest is growing too big, too quickly. I wonder what it is. It started out a few weeks ago as a small flat mole like growth. Now it appears to be about three-quarter-inch diameter and sticking outward about a quarter inch. I'm concerned.*

While towel drying, he observes the growth again, this time in the mirror. This thing is not normal and needs medical attention. He steps in his shorts, pulls an undershirt over his head, and reaches in the closet for a pair of Levi's and button-up shirt. He seldom wears golf shirts anymore.

Carol walks over to George with a cup of coffee. This is an ongoing service by each, George and Carol. Whoever goes to the kitchen first makes a cup of coffee for the other. George reaches for his car keys, wallet, cash, and a pen from atop the jewelry box in their bedroom, and then walks toward the kitchen as he continues sipping the coffee.

Morning breakfast is normally oatmeal for George. Carol normally prefers cereal flakes for her morning meal. This morning, however, Carol turns to George and mentions that she would like an egg and pork sausage with gravy and biscuits.

Cooking is a hobby of George's. He seems to have an extra sense for cooking and seldom follows written recipes exactly as outlined. He seems to just throw things together that always turn out perfect in taste. So as George volunteers to cook, Carol knows this morning's breakfast will be delicious. He starts out with four frozen biscuits on a pan and put it in the oven at 350 degrees. Frying sausage offers the foundation for making gravy, but that comes after frying the eggs. Then it only takes a couple of minutes to make the gravy using flour, water, and milk. He browns the flour in the sausage grease, adds cold water and milk, and stirs it to the right consistency. Carol remarks how hungry she has become by just looking at the dish containing eggs and sausage, browned gravy, and sliced tomato.

They seat themselves at the dining room table, and George asks the Lord for blessings. They now enjoy their favorite breakfast, seldom eaten because of the fat and calorie content.

"Anyway, Carol, I'm going to call Dr. Morris this morning," he says.

"Why? What's up?" she responds.

"You know that small spot on my chest? It is growing and looks kinda strange, so I want Dr. Morris to look at it and probably have a surgeon remove the nuisance."

Carol asks, "Do you want me to go with you?"

"No. I'll be in and out quickly. It's no big deal."

George checks his schedule to make certain he has no outside sales appointments before calling Dr. Morris' office. His flexibility as an independent consulting representative has its advantages when time off is needed.

The telephone rings, "Carol, will you get that?"

"Who is it?"

"Barbara."

"She says Dan is out of town and she needs a plumber. Who can we recommend?"

"Hold on. I'll look up Bucky's company. They are dependable and not too expensive."

"Okay, tell her to call this number I've written down."

George walks toward the door and onto the deck. Sitting in one of the outdoor chairs, he thinks, *What a peaceful morning*, as he lights up another cigarette *The first cigarette after any meal is always special, very soothing and tasteful*, he says to himself.

Carol opens the sliding door going out on the deck, "George! I wish you would give up that awful habit! Don't you want to be alive to enjoy our grandchildren as they grow up? Don't you?"

Silence. George has heard this conversation before. He agrees with Carol, but she has never smoked cigarettes and doesn't understand how tough it is to stop smoking. She knows of others that have given up the habit and assumes he can do it too. *I can't seem to get through to her and convince her on how impossible it is to stop smoking; she does not understand,* George thinks.

He puts out the cigarette, starts to reach for another as chain smokers normally do, and stops. Thinking of conversations with friends and clients, he has heard them remark that smokers have an offensive odor coming from their pores and breathe. Sometimes, nonsmokers actually stay clear of smokers because of the offensive smell. He ponders that the tobacco odor can even have an effect on his client relations and his sales income.

Ex-smoker associates and friends have all said the same thing. You'll give up cigarettes for good when you make up your mind to do so, and not before. You don't want to stop. "They're nuts! I do want to quit," he mumbles to himself.

"George! Billy is on the phone for you."

"Hello. Good morning, Billy. What's on your mind this great morning?"

"Greetings," replies Billy.

"Did you hear that helicopter earlier this morning?"

"I did. Do you know what it was up to?"

"No. I was hoping you knew something."

"I have no clue."

"So what are you up to today, George?" Billy asks.

"I'm going to call for an appointment with my doctor and then make sales calls around that schedule."

"Are you okay?"

"Sure. I just need him to look at a mole or something on my chest area."

"Oh, okay. Yeah, you're smart to deal with moles that change in any way and get to it in early stages. My dermatologist surgically removed a very small pre-cancerous growth on my left back in January. It, of course, was benign. Well, Joan is calling me to help her do something. I'll bet she wants me to reach something in the utility room for her. Sometimes, I wish she were taller than me.," Billy says with laughter.

"I'll talk to you later. Let me know if you find out anything about that helicopter, and I'll call you if I know anything."

"You got it. See you soon. Take care," says George.

It's 9:05 a.m. as he dials Dr. Morris's office number.

The receptionist answers, "Dr. Morris's office, this is Sue. How may I direct your call?"

George briefly shares his ailment. "Sue, I've got a growth that has become much, much larger within the last three or four weeks. I need Dr. Morris to look at it for me."

"Please hold, I'll see when his first available is. I know he is booked up for the next four months, but let me look a little deeper for you."

"Thank you, Sue."

"Aha. Mr. Belten, can you be here at 10:15 today? I know that's short notice, but he had a cancellation and I can plug you in for that time."

"I'll be there! Sue, you're wonderful."

George relaxes and updates Carol on the appointment.

"George, are you absolutely certain you don't need me to tag along?"

"No, hon. All that is taking place this morning is he will look at the growth, and if surgery is needed, he'll refer me to a surgeon. I'll return home and await the next step. However, I can be persuaded to drink another cup of coffee if somebody will volunteer to make it for me."

Carol wastes no time in responding, "George Belten, you're a rascal! Do you know that?"

"Yeah, but I'm a lovable rascal."

The drive to Dr. Morris's office is less than twenty minutes. George peers at the wall clock and its 9:45, time to go. "Hon, I'll be back in a few."

"Okay, dear."

The drive to Dr. Morris is almost a straight drive down Micco Road, and then turn left and left again. As follow-up, when George arrives in the medical parking lot, he looks at the time. It's 10:07, right on time for his appointment in eight minutes.

"Good morning. I'm here for my 10:15 appointment."

"And I'll bet you're Mr. Belten."

"George Belten. And you're Sue? I really appreciate you going the extra effort to work me in today. Dr. Morris has been my doctor for over ten years."

"Have a seat, Mr. Belten. I'll let the nurse know you're here. Dr. Morris was sidetracked for an emergency earlier, so it may be a few minutes before you are called back."

"That will be okay."

In the waiting room, he recognizes a mutual acquaintance, Ralph Sewell. He can hear some of Ralph's conversation with an airline or travel agent. He must have had a bad experience in his travels.

George first looks around for any changes in the waiting room since he was last here. Everything appears as it has been over the last few years. Then he picks up a National Geographic magazine and starts flipping through the pages. An article on wildlife in Alaska gets his attention. Alaska is a favorite area he enjoys visiting from time to time. He recalls the Seven-day cruise he and Carol went on last year. They left out of Vancouver, British Columbia, and went up the inside strait. The scenery was spectacular. All the cruises they have taken to the Caribbean islands in no way compare to Canada and Alaska.

As he flips through pages, he sees a photo of a coyote walking along the snowy coast. He recalls seeing a very similar scene. The glaciers were different in appearance to the picture he had seen, but they were beautiful. Then he turns away from the Alaskan articles and is reminded of their train ride. After the cruise, they returned to Vancouver and headed to the train station. They boarded the train for a long ride across the Canadian Rockies on to Edmonton, Canada. *What a delightful trip*, he recalls.

Their train would periodically pull over for freight-hauling trains to go by uninterrupted. By doing so, the trip was twenty-seven hours of spectacular scenery. At one point of travel, they were in the upper dome of the train, and George looked down the edge of the mountain they were traveling around. He recalls looking down over the edge of the mountain, and the snow-covered pine trees below appeared so small they resembled blades of grass. Had he alerted Carol to view the scene, she would have gone into a panic because the train was so close to the outer edge of the mountain.

Ralph is off his phone and turns to greet George. "George, how have you been? I haven't seen you in ages."

"I'm doing quite well. And you?"

"Good, I guess. I got bumped twice on my airline in Chicago as I was trying to get back here for an important meeting. That's the third time in about two years that I have been detained flying through O'Hare, and in the future, I will put forth extra effort to avoid that airport again."

George responds, "I too will avoid travel through and change planes in Chicago. It seems O'Hare is jinxed or something."

"So what was your experience as you flew through and out of Chicago?" asks Ralph.

"As Carol and I flew back from Edmonton, Canada, O'Hare had a fire alarm alert in the flight tower. No planes could land or take off from Chicago, so they were diverted to Milwaukee. Milwaukee is not an international airport, so they could not deplane.

"Finally, they were able to land at O'Hare. Inside, lines were extremely long with people attempting to fly out. Some were there from cancellations on the previous day because of storms and were on standby along with us, hoping for any way to get out of Chicago. Our friends Jim and Joan were traveling with us.

"It wasn't just our airline. All planes were off-schedule and the travelers on standby was extensive. They didn't seem to know how to deal with it. Jim and I stood in line Seven hours just to reach a service desk and be placed on standby for a 1:00 p.m. flight the next day. Carol and Joan were seated, and from time to time, I could see Carol praying. She knew I was experiencing terrible lower back pain from standing so long.

"We finally were nearing the service desk. All they were doing was put people on standby for a future flight. All hotels were full. No rental cars were available in the area. I had determined that I would have the service agent put us on any flight out of Chicago, and I would then fly from any city on to Jacksonville. The young couple in front of us was discussing their options with the service desk. We were finally, after Seven hours, next in line.

"A young lady appeared at the roped off area on our left, motioning for me to walk over. I asked Jim to see what she wants and I'll maintain our place in line.

"Jim came back to me. 'She wants to talk to you. She says she can get us on a plane out of Chicago.'

"I walked over to the lady. She told me to follow her over to kiosk 64, and she will get us on a plane to Jacksonville, Florida. I said, 'We've been in line for Seven hours and we're next for the service desk, and you want us to go with you. How did you know we're going to Jacksonville?'

"She didn't answer my question. She simply repeated, 'Please meet me at that kiosk 64,' and pointed to the computer at a station. For some reason, I felt I should go to that kiosk.

"I turned to Jim, 'She says she can get us out of here with a flight to Jacksonville. If we stand here, all the flight attendant will do is put us on standby for the 1:00 p.m. flight tomorrow. Let's see if this young lady can live up to her statement.'

"At kiosk 64, within about Seven minutes, we had tickets in hand; and she told us, 'You're flying out of a particular gate number and out of another concourse, and you have fifteen minutes to get there. So, please hurry!' she said.

"Jim and I made our way to that concourse and gate. It took us twenty minutes. I just knew we had missed that plane. As we arrived at the gate, the flight was an unscheduled flight they had set for people flying to Jacksonville, and they were waiting on the pilots and crew to report for duty.

"I have often thought, *Who was that lady? She appeared to be a native from another country. How in the world did she know we were flying to Jacksonville? Why did she select Jim and me out of hundreds of people in line?*

"All this happened about two years ago, and it's still a puzzle. I do believe it was in response to Carol's and Joan's many prayers."

Ralph then follows up with, "I believe your experience at Chicago's O'Hare is tougher than mine. My biggest problem at the time was that I really needed to get back here in time for my meeting, and I failed. I have seen on the news several disruptions flying through Chicago, so I decided to avoid that exchange whenever possible."

"Mr. Belten, Dr. Morris will see you now. Follow me down the hall to the third room on the left," says the nurse.

"Ralph, it's nice to see you again. It's been a while. Maybe we can have lunch one day."

"That will be great. I'll look forward to it."

"Have a seat and I'll check your vitals," the nurse tells him.

She rolls up the sleeve on his left arm and places the blood pressure wrap around it. On his finger, she attaches the monitor for his oxygen level; and beneath his tongue, she inserts the thermometer.

"Your oxygen is 97, temperature is great, and blood pressure is slightly elevated. However, that can happen with some people when visiting their doctor's office. Dr. Morris will be with you in a few minutes."

George looks around the room at some illustrations of the human anatomy posted on the wall. "I often wondered why medical offices and hospitals are always cold. Somebody told me that germs thrive in warm temperatures, and maintaining a cool facility wards off germs. I guess it makes sense." He reaches to his chest and mildly feels the growth, as if to make sure it still exists.

Dr. Morris enters. "Good morning, George. What's up with you this morning?"

"Doc, I've got a mole or something on the left side of my chest that I want you to look at."

"Okay, open up your shirt and let me see."

George unbuttons his shirt and pulls it up.

Dr. Morris takes a close look at the mass and tells George, "Man, you've got a full blown cancer there! I'm going to get you in to see a surgeon. Do you have a preference for a surgeon?"

"I guess not."

"I'll be right back," Dr. Morris says as he leaves the room.

"Oh no! Not cancer," George says to himself. He continues to think, *I really did not consider hearing that diagnosis. I just never thought I could have cancer. That means I've got melanoma cancer, and it's incurable especially when it gets to the advanced stage. The size of this thing indicates to me that it is definitely in an advanced stage.*

Dr. Morris re-enters the examination room and takes a seat in front of George. "I've got you an appointment with Dr. Hughes, a surgeon. The earliest he can see you is next Wednesday, July ninth. His office will call you with the time to be there. He'll perform the surgery on that same day."

"Any questions?"

"I guess not. I'm having a crowd of friends and relatives over for a cookout tomorrow, July fourth, so I'll try to shake this shocking news off by then."

"Well, you'll be in good care with Dr. Hughes. He's a well-respected surgeon, one of the best."

George walks back out to the receptionist and hands her some paperwork, then pays his co-pay. Ralph is still waiting to see Dr. Hughes.

"Well, how'd it go? You gonna live?" says Ralph in a joking tone.

George always looks at the bright side of issues when he is around others and seldom shows his emotions. "Oh yeah. He is referring me to another doctor that will remove this spot from my chest."

"Good for you. My ailment is a sinus issue, probably some infection."

"Okay, I've gotta go now. It was great to see you again, and I look forward to our lunch meeting."

George knows very little about skin cancer. He relies on what he has heard about melanoma, which he has been told that it is usually deadly. His mind is real active on the way home, thinking he may not survive this disease.

"What did Dr. Morris say?" asks Carol.

"Let's have something to drink and I'll tell you about it. If you'll pour us some iced tea, I'll meet you out on the deck."

"Here's your tea. What did Dr. Morris say?"

"He looked at the growth, looked at me, and said, 'You've got full-blown cancer.' I never even considered that cancer was involved. I have surgery scheduled for next Wednesday with Dr. Cranston Hughes. I am told he is a good surgeon."

"Oh George, you'll be okay. We'll just pray about it."

"I'm going to take the day off and start getting the smoker and grill ready for our cookout tomorrow."

"I'll help you," says Carol.

"That's not necessary. There's not that much to do. Next, I want to cut the grass, then edge around the road and driveway."

"Okay, dear. Let me know if I can do anything." says Carol.

Many things are racing through George's mind. When should he tell their sons? The will is up-to-date, but Carol doesn't have a clue about their finances, investments, bill paying, and financial matters in general. The amount of life insurance should have been increased; now it's too late because the diagnosis is on record. *I just need to get away and think everything through, but I can't cancel the cookout for tomorrow,* he thinks.

"Carol, can you come here for a minute?"

"Sure."

"What do you need me to do, hon?"

"Nothing, really. Why don't we drive down to the coast Saturday and spend the night? I just need to break away from everything here and spend some quiet time, just you and me."

Carol agrees, "I think that will be a great time to relax and enjoy the weekend. Let's do it."

"I still wonder what that helicopter was up to. It woke me up circling around and then seemed to get lower to the ground or closer to our house. I just couldn't tell which," says George.

21

"I didn't hear anything. How close was it?"

"Not real close, maybe over around the Jacob Road area. I assume it was law enforcement because I can't imagine any individual pilot coming in that close to a residential area."

Carol changes the subject. "George, why don't you stop smoking now?"

"Carol! I have tried, and I just cannot stop. You never smoked, and you don't understand how hard it is to quit! Believe me. I would if I could! And you're wasting your breath trying to get me to quit. It's something I must deal with. Nobody can make me quit cigarettes."

Today is July fourth, and George is out of bed at 5:00 a.m., gets dressed, and goes out back to start the smoker. He uses a large smoker with the fire offset on the left side. A pan of water is placed over the fire. That allows the steam, heat, and smoke to go across the meat and out through the small chimney. He allows the smoker to reach the determined temperature. It's now 5:45 a.m. as he places several slabs of pork ribs in rib racks, then he places two pork shoulder roasts on the rack, closes the door, and walks back in the house. From this point, and for the next Seven hours, he will monitor the water level and temperature at the smoker.

Guests begin to show up with their side dishes at 11:30. Carol's brothers and sisters-in-law are first to arrive. By 12:30 p.m., there were seventeen relatives and guests, all hungry, there to enjoy the feast. Carol was serving boiled ears of corn, fresh green beans, and potato salad along with all the other side dishes. For dessert, Carol's brother and sister-in-law always request George's homemade banana pudding. He makes the pudding from basics as featured in his mother's old cookbook dated in 1948.

Mid-afternoon, Carol told the group that George is having a skin cancer growth removed the next Wednesday. And immediately before any respond with questions and conversations, she changed the conversation to the fireworks they could hear in the distance. There were a few questions and comments later in a one-on-one chat with Carol. The ladies began to clean up after the feast, some preparing dishes to take with them later for their dinner. The guys were gathered on the deck, talking politics and news.

Carol's sister-in-law tells her they need to be home by 6:00 p.m. so her husband can watch a special program on television. She offered to them that she's available if Carol and George need anything during his surgery. As they leave, others begin to give hugs and make their way out for the drive to their home.

Saturday morning, George and Carol throw some clothes and essentials in a bag as they head to the coast and for an overnight stay at Carol's sister's beach cottage. Traffic was moderately heavy as they travel down the two-lane highway to their destination. Carol likes antiques and always wants to stop at an antique shop near the beach area, so they briefly stop as Carol looks through the store. She spots a set of glasses she has wanted for some time. George collects old ashtrays, and he looks around for that little treasure. They pay for the glasses, and he makes room in his trunk so they will not move about and break.

Arriving at the cottage, they unload the clothes, essentials, and food they will prepare while there. Sun is beginning to set, and temperature outside is expected to reach a high of 96 degrees today. This is a day of relaxation. The back deck is screened in and faces the gulf waters. That is an ideal setting for relaxing in a pair of straight-back wooden rockers.

In the early evening, George grills two thick filet mignons while Carol prepares baked sweet potatoes and a salad for dinner. After dinner, the sun is setting with a beautiful red and orange tint as George says, "Hon, let's go out and walk on the beach."

"I like that idea," she says.

Still, George is not up-to-date on the type cancer he has and the probability of a full recovery. He believes he has melanoma, and the probability of survival is not so good. He and Carol walk along the beach, hand in hand, enjoying the sounds of waves splashing as the tide rolls. They are quietly walking and George tries to be positive, but his concerns generate tears in his eyes, unknown to Carol at the time. Their walk along the water takes them a good half mile away from the cottage, then they turn back. There is very little conversation between the two. They are just enjoying each other, hand in hand, slowly walking along. Their conversations have gradually drifted away from the illness at hand and more toward how they have seen God's healing for others.

George walks out to the car and retrieves his metal detector that he put in the trunk just before they left home. He wants to rise early tomorrow morning and use the detector along the beach area. "You never know what you'll find buried or laying on the sand," he tells Carol.

As they retire for the evening, Carol turns to the Lord in prayer for a good night's rest. George is now less concerned about the cancer as he knows it's now in God's hands. He leans over to Carol, says, "I love you," and closes his eyes.

He slept well and wakes later than intended; it's 7:10 a.m. "Hon, I'm going to the beach with the metal detector and shower when I return."

Carol sits up in bed. "Okay, let me make coffee real quick. And I'll watch for you to come up the path and start breakfast."

As George walks down the path toward the beach, Carol is perched on a stool at the deck, still in her pajamas, watching George. She sees him begin using the detector as he begins to slowly walk along the beach. Soon, he is beyond her sight with all the palms and bushes in the area.

*I'm glad he brought the metal detector and is using it on the beach area. That helps to occupy his mind and get it off the upcoming surgery,* she thinks. Her coffee cup is almost empty now, so she goes back to the kitchen for a refill. "I'll go ahead and get my shower now. A shower will be the first thing George will do when he returns to the house," she considers.

Afterwards, now fully clothed, she returns to the screened deck, sipping her second cup of coffee. Looking at her watch, George has been gone almost an hour. "He must be finding some interesting items out there." The sun is up and no clouds appearing, just a beautiful day for relaxing. "We really enjoy the beach areas, but neither of us wants to live at the coast. This particular area is not convenient to shopping, hospitals, and so forth."

In the distance, she hears a helicopter and thinks, *It's probably a tourist flight. They generally fly around the more occupied beach areas, but it may be that the tourists want to view this coastal area specifically. George had fixed-wing lessons and went up in a helicopter with another pilot once, but I have never flown in a helicopter. I'm not certain I have a desire to be up in something without wings.*

She listens as the helicopter becomes louder, getting nearer. Then she sees it flying by. "That's a medical unit from our city hospital. It's flying low and along the beach in the same direction that George walked. Oh no! Something has happened to George!" she screams out as she runs out the door and down the path toward the water. She is in tears as she feels something awful has happened. She runs out on the beach, near the water, and looks toward the direction George walked. Then she sees George walking toward her, and she begins running frantically toward him.

"What's wrong, Carol?"

"George! I thought something had happened and that helicopter was for you!"

"No, it landed further down near a small boat with people on it. There must have been an injury or other emergency with somebody on the boat."

"I was so upset! I could just imagine that you were the intended transport for that chopper.

Did you find anything interesting?"

"Only some small pocket change that I kept. I did find a wedding ring, but three people in the immediate area seemed to be looking for something so I inquired; and fortunately, they were searching for a diamond wedding ring. Their description matched the one I had picked up, so I handed it to the young lady. She hugged me almost as meaningful as you do." He laughed.

Back at the cottage, they enjoy breakfast, not the usual oatmeal and cereal. George grilled steaks while Carol mixed six eggs, cheese, and a small amount of milk, and then scrambled the egg mixture. Whole-grain toast is always their favorite bread. Before leaving home, she picked some fresh tomatoes from the vine and sliced one as a breakfast side item.

After breakfast, they spent the day leisurely, sitting while viewing others strolling along the beach. Mid-afternoon, they walked along the beach one more time before leaving for home.

Time flies and it's now Wednesday, July 9. Dr. Hughes's office called yesterday, and surgery is scheduled for him. He needs to be at the surgery center at 6:00 a.m. today. George is out of bed and showering at 4:15 a.m., anxious to get this surgery over with. Carol brings his coffee and asks, "Hon, do you want oatmeal this morning?"

"No. I can't eat or drink anything before surgery, so you drink the coffee. Let's go to the Waffle House, and you can enjoy breakfast there. You'll have time to eat and still be at my scheduled appointment by six."

At the restaurant, Carol is uncomfortable eating in front of George who can't eat anything. But George insists that she order her favorite—a pecan waffle, grits, and coffee. He reaches across the table to Carol, holds her hands, and prays.

It's quiet at their table. Both George and Carol have a lot going on in their minds.

George is thinking, *What if I never pull out of the surgery. Will Carol be okay on her own? Will the boys help her through tough times? I can't bear the thought of all the pain and anguish my family will go through if something happens to me. Oh well, my life is in God's hands, and He will see them through any adjustment. And the medical profession is so much more advanced than it was even ten years ago. Surgery like mine is an everyday event for those doctors. I'll be fine.*

"What are you thinking?" Carol asks

"Oh nothing, really. I'm just wondering how long the surgery will take. Are you ready to go?"

"I am," Carol responds.

The surgical center is an outpatient facility and that means they should be in and out quickly.

In the lobby, he approaches the check-in area. "Good morning. My name is George Belten, and I have an appointment for surgery."

"Yes, sir. If you will complete this paperwork, the nurse will take you back."

The normal medical forms need to be completed. George, however, never writes his date of birth or social security number on forms. He will provide it verbally for them to verify against the insurance data on their computer. He will not allow a photocopy of his driver's license. They are only allowed to take a picture of him and include it in the file. He understands that medical data is the most widely shared for identity theft and compromise. Medical offices understand that some patients are more protective of personal information and are aware of how to work through that.

A young lady steps through a door and to the waiting area. "Mr. George Belten?" He answers and walks toward the nurse. "Follow me, Mr. Belten. We'll go to this first room on your right."

In the surgery preparation area, the nurse says, "I'll check your vital signs now and then we'll get you comfortable and ready for surgery."

George knows the routine. After the vitals, he will be given a gown to slip into after removing his shirt.

Dr. Hughes enters the room, "Good morning, Mr. Belten."

"Good morning, Dr. Hughes."

"Let me look at the mass we'll be removing. Okay, that's a basal cell carcinoma cancer. The good news is that it's a midrange cancer and never a problem for you when removed in this early stage. You're a smoker?"

"Yes."

"How much and how long have you smoked?"

"More than thirty years, two packs a day."

"I studied your chest x-rays, and after listening to your heart and lungs, I seldom observe lungs so clear after smoking that much. In fact, I'm impressed."

George thinks, *That's good to hear. I'll tell Carol about that report when this surgery is over.*

In the surgical area, George adjusts on the table and becomes comfortable for the surgery. The nurse positions a folded sheet between the growth and his face, preventing George from seeing the actual surgery process. Dr. Hughes walks up. "Okay, this will sting a bit. I'm going to give you several shots to numb around that area, and we'll get you out of here shortly. You do have somebody to drive you home, don't you?"

"Yes. My wife is in the waiting room."

The nurse lays towel-like cloths all around the chest area. She makes a final adjustment to the folded sheet between his face and the surgical area. During surgery, he can feel some tugging of the flesh and hear instructions given to the nurse as Dr. Hughes begins working on the chest area.

"Are you okay?" asks Dr. Hughes. "Can you feel any pain?"

"No. I only feel some pressure at times and tugging on the flesh."

"That's normal," replied Dr. Hughes. "We have now removed the cancerous tissue and will send it out to the lab to make certain we got it all. I'm now putting sutures in place, and we'll bandage the area. You'll be ready to go in a couple of minutes."

The nurse helps George put his shirt back on. "I have some details to go over with you now. Do not allow this bandage to get wet for the next twenty-four hours. After that, you may wash the area with soap and water, and put on a fresh bandage daily from this packet. And I am giving you written instructions to use in caring for the area until you come back in. Dr. Hughes wants to see you again in one week to remove the stitches. Any questions?"

"I don't believe so."

"Okay, we'll see you on the sixteenth." The nurse rolls George to the lobby in a wheel chair.

"How'd it go?" ask Carol

"It's all done and the cancer is gone. That of type cancer is not life threatening"

She stands up, gives him a hug, and they proceed to the car already near the door.

During the ride home, George tells Carol, "I've got some good news. Dr. Hughes told me that he has never seen lungs as clear as mine after smoking as much and for as long as I have. Can you believe that?"

"Hey, that's good. You need to stop before your lungs begin to deteriorate."

Carol pulls in the driveway, and before entering the garage, with George still weak, she helps him through the house and to the deck where he wants to sit and relax. There, he lights up a cigarette, his first one since early this morning. Immediately, he is reminded of Dr. Hughes's report about his lungs.

*Based on the condition of my lungs, I can smoke another thirty years without any problem,* he thinks. *Or I can quit while I'm ahead? That would be good, but I can't quit. I've stopped many times, and I just cannot stop smoking. And everybody tells me I would gain about thirty-five pounds if I quit. And I'm not in favor of that.*

"George, what would you like for lunch?" Carol asks.

"A ham-and-cheese sandwich would be good."

"Okay. I'll take care of it. You have a telephone call, George. Do you feel up to a call?"

"Who is it?"

"Sounds like Billy from over on Lamar Drive."

"Hello?"

"George, my man. You're home already. How'd your surgery go?"

"Very well. I feel like I'll live another hundred years, maybe more."

"You know that helicopter we've been hearing? It was over there again just after daylight this morning. Did you hear it?"

"No, I had probably already left the house on my way for early breakfast and the surgery center."

"Well, of all things, while the chopper was hovering, I could hear two or more cars roaring in to that general area and then what sounded like voices on a speaker system. Something strange was taking place over there."

"What do you think was going on?"

"I have no idea," says Billy. "But I think I'll be nosey and drive over in that area. Want to go with me?"

"No, I better not. An afternoon of rest will be good for me."

"Okay, glad you're doing well. I'll talk to you later."

"Thanks for checking on me, Billy."

As George ends that call, another call comes in.

"Hello?"

"George, this is Paul Barr at Barr Lincoln dealership. My sales manager tells me you had surgery. How are you?"

"I had a cancer removed from my chest area this morning. Right now, the area is still somewhat numb, so all is good for me at the moment."

"Did they remove all the cancer? What kind of cancer was it?"

"Dr. Hughes said it was a basal cell carcinoma and that we got to it in time so it will not be a problem for me."

"Well, that certainly is good news, George. I know the skin cancer is not of any relation to smoking, but I've gotta ask you as a friend; why don't you quit smoking? Just stop today!" Paul says.

"Paul, I've tried and I just can't stop. I have quit, and it lasts anywhere from a few hours to a couple or three days. I'm truly addicted to cigarettes."

"I smoked for about twenty-five years and stopped about ten years ago. It takes commitment. It's tough to stop, but it is worth it. One thing I remember doing that helped, I stayed home for the first week and refused to leave the house for several days. I would want a cigarette so badly that I probably would have given big money just for one cigarette. When the strong urges came on, I would go take a hot shower, even several showers throughout the day."

"I sure wish I could quit," George says.

"I'll say this to you, George. You can quit smoking once you make up your mind to do so, and not before. You will quit when you decide to quit. I've got another call coming in. Take care of yourself, George. Come by to see me when you're in this area. Call me ahead of time and we'll have lunch over at Captain Ross's seafood."

"Thanks, Paul."

*Wow! Paul smoked and quit? If he quit, I can quit!*

Carol calls out to George. "Lunch is ready. Would you like to eat out on the deck?"

"I'd like that," replies George.

Biting into the sandwich, George is thinking, *I'm in a fork in the road of life. I can continue smoking with little health risks, or I can quit while I'm ahead. Hmm.*

"Want some chips?" asks Carol

"I'll have a few."

It's quiet outside as they both enjoy their lunch. Stopping cigarette smoking is starting to weigh heavy on George's mind. He can identify three of his close acquaintances that were heavy smokers and stopped completely. "I am no different to those guys. I have to bear down on smoking and stop. If I keep those guys in my mind, maybe it will help me stop."

He thinks about previous times he has quit for short times and then went right back to the habit. *I don't want to spend the rest of my life craving a cigarette every minute of every day.* Then, *Wait a dad gum minute. The human brain plays tricks on us at times!* he thinks

His mind races through the deep mindset. *Others that gave up cigarettes seem to no longer think about smoking after a few weeks. They no longer crave a cigarette. Why do I assume I'll be miserable for the rest of my life if I stop smoking? Each time I try to stop smoking, I unconsciously reach for a cigarette every few minutes and continually have the urge for a nicotine fix. I've never thought of it that way. The human mind misleads smokers to believe we will be miserable for the rest of our lives without nicotine. That is very misleading. I think I'll call Paul again and pry into how he quit smoking and what steps he went through.*

He dialed the dealership number and gets through to an office person.

"My name is George Belten. May I speak to Paul, please?"

"Hold, please."

"Hello, this is Paul"

"Paul, George here. Have you got a couple of minutes?"

"Absolutely. What can I do for you, George?"

"When you gave up smoking cigarettes, how did you do it?"

"I just got up one morning and never smoked again. Ha. I'm kidding. Let me think for a moment. I set a stop smoking date about three weeks in advance, right down to the hour. I guess I prepared for that hour and date so strongly that I stuck to it. It was tough at first."

"How long did the urge for a cigarette last?"

"I'm not sure now, but best I can recall, the nicotine craving lasted about a week; and the habit began to taper off after several weeks, maybe three, and continued tapering off until I no longer even thought about smoking."

"Paul, you're a motivation to me. If you can do it, I can do it!"

"I hope I can be an encouragement to you. I have noticed that some people have an easier time with the stop-smoking ordeal than I did. I was hooked big time. So you may experience an easier or maybe tougher process than I did. But just be prepared for the worst-case scenario and stick to it. You can do it."

"Thanks. I'll let you go now."

"Call me if you need encouragement. Any way I can help, call me."

George walks in the house and reaches for a pen and paper on his way to the back deck.

Carol asks, "Are you feeling okay?"

"Oh yeah. I'm okay. Just enjoying the summer air outside. I want to sit and relax."

"Dr. Hughes prescribed some pain meds, but so far, I don't need anything. I feel certain I'll not need any of that crap. I just do not like taking any prescription pain medicine, and when I did in the past, I had to take an allergy pill to ward off the itching that followed. I prefer two Aleve tablets for pain. If by chance I do need the medicine, I may ask you to go up to the pharmacy and pick it up for me. The pharmacist knows the two of us well, and I'm sure he'll allow you to sign for it."

"Let me know," Carol says.

Out on the deck, George leans back in the chair and collects his thoughts toward devising a step-by-step approach to giving up the tobacco addiction.

With pen in hand, he begins to position the notepad for some notes to aid in his approach. The remark by Dr. Hughes that his lungs are clear and his thoughts at the time about living another forty-five years as a smoker came to him. *Giving up smoking will extend my life tremendously, I am sure. I'll use forty-five years for my mind-bending calculation*, he thought.

*Let's see now. Forty-five years with fifty-two weeks in each year. That totals out to 2340 weeks. Wow! And here I am, allowing myself to believe I will crave cigarettes for the rest of my life. Am I nuts? This is great stuff. I'm probably going to be miserable for a week, reaching for a cigarette that is not there for another three weeks, and have an occasional desire to smoke for another few weeks, maybe up to three months or so. I am willing to be miserable and uncomfortable for a few weeks up to twenty-one weeks out of 2,340 weeks. Why haven't I considered that equation before? Amazing! I can accept that!* he thought, happy with his theory of conquering the misery of giving up tobacco.

His thoughts continue, *Now, how should I go about setting my stop tobacco date. For some reason, I want the date far enough out that I have plenty of time to prep myself for a final cigarette. Five weeks. That's it. And I'll schedule a week's vacation at that time.*

"Carol, you got a minute?" he calls out.

"Sure. What do you need?" she replies.

"I'd like for you to come out here and have a seat, dear. I don't want you to fall out. I've got some developing news to share with you."

Carol was in the process of pulling dishes out of the dishwasher and putting them in the cabinets. She stopped, dried her hands, and walked out on the deck. "Okay. Unload it on me."

"I'm going to stop smoking!"

Carol quickly responds, "Again? No. I'm kidding. Well, that deserves a big, big hug! Come here! I love you!"

"And I love you too."

"So what brought this on?" Carol asks.

33

"It's a foolish addiction and habit, and I have firmly decided it needs to go away for good this time. Forever!"

"George, you don't know how happy that makes me. And you sound convincing this time. Like you really mean it."

"Here's my plan. I'll smoke my last cigarette on Sunday night, five weeks from now, and take that week off from work with no travel in order to change my normal routine during that first week. In fact, I'll plan to stay home and not even leave this house for the first few days. After that, I'll never smoke a cigarette again!"

And your week off is when Barbara wants us to visit them down at the coast.

"Darn! You're right. We may need to cancel that visit. As I think about it, there is a corporate meeting at about that time. I'll check out the dates and may revise my quit-smoking date."

George considers himself worthy of bragging rights as a result of coming up with a plan the way he, as a smoker, hit on a plan to simply alter the way his brain normally handles the task.

Carol answers the phone, "George, Dr. Hughes's office is on the phone for you."

"Okay, the nurse is probably checking in on me to make sure I'm doing well after the surgery. I'll take the call."

"Hello, this is George."

"Mr. Belten, this is Sandra at Dr. Hughes's office The lab report came back, and there is still some cancerous tissue around the border that needs to be removed. Dr. Hughes wants you in the surgery center on Monday the fourteenth at 7:00 a.m. Is that schedule okay for you?"

"I'll be there."

He turns to Carol. "Gotta go back in. They didn't get all the cancer and more surgery is needed."

Carol responds, "Well, it's good they caught it early. You're in good hands with Dr. Hughes."

Monday morning, George and Carol are both up at 4:15 a.m. and anxious to get the surgery over with.

34

He showers as Carol makes a cup of coffee for herself and starts to make one for George but realizes he can't have any food or water before the surgery. While George dresses, Carol showers and puts on her normal makeup. Both are walking around at a leisure pace, getting ready. George glances at the clock on the nearby stand, and it reads 5:33 a.m.

"Carol, why don't you have your morning bowl of cereal, and we'll then go on over to the center? They open up at six, and maybe I can get this over with earlier than anticipated."

Carol agrees. She pours out a bowl of flakes and adds milk. As she begins to eat, George is pacing the floor, not with anxiety about the surgery but his decision to quit cigarettes. He goes from being happy with his decision to asking himself, *Who am I fooling? I can't give up cigarettes! That's stupid to even think I can do it.* Then back to, *You darn right I'll stop smoking because I now have a plan that makes sense.*

"Aren't you ready, George? What are you doing?"

"Coming," he says.

At the surgery center, George provides his name, and the receptionist asks him to have a seat. Local morning news is on the waiting room television.

Carol is paying attention to the morning news. "Hey, they were reporting something about that commotion over in our adjoining neighborhood. The helicopter had been used for something, and then it showed a young man being loaded in the squad car. I just caught the tail end of the news. Did you catch that news?"

"No, Carol. I guess I was daydreaming about the smoking issue. Maybe they'll cover it again in the next half hour. You can watch for it while I am in the surgery room."

"Mr. Belten?"

"Yes."

"If you'll come with me, we'll get you ready for surgery."

After changing into a surgical gown and cap, the nurse inserts the needle in the back of his right hand for use with the IV. Things are busy right now in the room. One young man introduces himself as the anesthesiologist. His job is to keep the patient alive and pain free.

While the nurse covers a portion of George's face and eyes so he doesn't see the actual surgery being performed, Dr. Hughes explains, "According to the lab analysis of the cancer tissue sent to them from the surgery last week, some cancer remains in the outer rim. So this time, I'm going to remove a tissue and have it hand-carried to the lab in this building where it will be studied. We'll continue that process, if necessary, until they tell us we have removed all the affected tissues."

Dr. Hughes worked for a few minutes. He placed the small portion of flesh in a sterile bottle and handed it off to a nurse waiting to take the sample to their lab. Everybody in the room was in general conversation until they heard back from the lab.

"We have almost got it all but need to go deeper in one small area. Are you doing okay, Mr. Belten?"

"I'm just resting while you folks work," George says with a little laugh.

What seems weird to George is with all the effort they made to prevent him from seeing the actual surgery being performed; they didn't give thought to the huge stainless steel light holders and arms that allowed him to see the reflection of the doctor's detailed work. At first glance, George thought he shouldn't be viewing the procedure and should turn his head away. However, watching everything didn't bother him at all.

Dr. Hughes sends the nurse back to the lab with another sample.

"Mr. Belten, are you hanging in there? Doin' okay?

"I'm fine as frog hair," says George.

"Good boy. We'll be through here shortly."

The nurse returns from the lab and hands some paperwork to Dr. Hughes.

"All right, my man, we got it all this time!" says Dr. Hughes. Then Dr. Hughes tells George, "Okay. The surgery was deep enough this time. I'm going to put sutures inside the area and then surface stitches on the outside area of this incision."

George had anticipated this surgery to be a major deal, going on for an hour or two maybe, but now it's over, all in a matter of a few minutes.

"Okay, you're good to go. My nurse will go over some instructions with you," says Dr. Hughes, and then he leaves the room. She takes over and helps George put on his shirt and then places his left arm in a sling of some type that has extensions that loop around his body to secure the arm so it will not move.

"Dr. Hughes wants you to come back on July 24 and we'll remove the stitches. In the meantime, you are to wear this sling twenty-four seven in place and strapped to your body as I have it in place now. The surgery required a rather deep incision and some stitches are below the surface. If you were to lift your arm outward, you could rip out the inside stitches. You must keep this sling on at all times, other than while showering. Do you have any questions?"

"I don't believe so at this time."

George is dressed and placed in a wheelchair to be rolled outside. Carol has already gone to the parking lot and drove their car to the door for George to transfer from the wheelchair to the car. He's still partially out of it from the anesthesia. Traffic is moderate as she drives toward home. Looking over at George, he is semi-alert, dozing off from time to time.

Arriving at home, Carol helps George out of the car and into the house. He heads straight to the bedroom and collapses on the bed, almost instantly asleep. Barney follows them closely, keeping his eyes on George and then whines as he stares at Carol. She knows he wants to be on the bed with George, so she picks him up and lays him on the vacant side of the bed. He immediately goes to George and lies across his chest area. "That little guy knows George is not well, and he wants to do his part toward comforting him. I've never seen Barney do that before. He's a smart dog."

Carol relaxes out on the deck, sipping on a glass of tea. It was such a beautiful morning, so quiet. She can only hear the normal singing of various species of birds that is music to her ears. She missed most of the local news this morning, so she walks back in the house to pull it up on her laptop. Specifically, she wants to see news about the happenings nearby, but she finds no further details beyond a sketchy article earlier today.

*Whatever has been going on over there is worth knowing about especially with it being so near to our house. It all began with the helicopter hovering and then law enforcement placing a young man in their car,* she thinks. *I'm going to be nosey and call Judy. She lives in that area and probably knows the details of the event. Her phone number will be listed in the homeowner's association directory.*

Walking through the family room and on to the small office, which is really the fourth bedroom that has been converted to an office, or man cave, as George refers to it. She reaches for the directory, and the first page she opened to had Judy's listing. While reading the phone number, she dials it on her cellular.

After five rings, someone answers, "Hello?"

"Judy? This is Carol Belten."

"Oh hi there, how have you been?"

"Good. George has been in surgery twice in the last few days. But he's doing fine. Sleeping at the moment."

"Anything serious?" inquired Judy

"Just a skin cancer, and they got it all. I'll tell you why I called. Recently, a helicopter was hovering over some property near you, and the police were on the scene. Do you know what was going on? I'm just being a little nosey, I guess."

"Yes, I certainly do. That is the Henderson family residence, and apparently, their sixteen-year-old son had dug a huge hole on their property and then covered the hole in an attempt at making it appear normal. I'm told he had an entrance so he could go in and out easily. He had electricity to the hole by using an extension cord, stretched out just below the surface of the ground and from the house to his hole. Evidently, he was growing marijuana plants down there under a special lighting system.

"You're kidding. But how did the sheriff's department detect the plants?" asks Carol.

"Our daughter Susie said he thought having plants growing underground would prevent any detection by law enforcement. Even Susie doesn't know how they picked up on the ingenious plant-growing system. We saw police taking an armload of plants to the trunk of their car."

"I wonder what the parents' reaction was."

"I kinda kept an eye on the situation from our house, and Mr. and Mrs. Henderson spend considerable time talking with law enforcement out in their front yard. About all I could do was pay attention to their body language. I'm assuming they were totally surprised with the event. I don't believe they had a clue that illegal plants were being grown on their property."

"Amazing! We never know what our neighbors are up to, do we? George is resting now, but when he wakes, he'll be anxious to know what all that commotion was about. Take care, Judy. Tell Frank we said hello."

"Will do," replied Judy

The next morning came on early. George thinks as he wakes, *Man, I slept forever, it seems.*

# CHAPTER TWO

George greets Carol, "Good morning, dear," as he heads out to the deck and walks out to light up his first cigarette of the morning.

"Any soreness or pain?" Carol asks as she peeks out the door.

"Some pain. Slight discomfort along with the pain."

"Do you want me to have the pain medicine prescription filled for you?"

"No. While in the bathroom, I swallowed two Aleve with a large glass of water and that should take care of any exaggerated pain."

Sitting in a deck chair, he turns his thinking back to tobacco. "I'm going to quit smoking. I'll make it happen some way," he vows to himself.

Carol sits and says, "Guess what all that police activity was about over near Frank and Judy's"

"What?" responds George.

"The young Henderson boy had spent weeks and a lot of his energy digging a huge hole out back of their house, apparently covered it with boards or something, and sodded over that. He had an opening so he could get in and out of the hole and ran an electrical extension cord from the house. Now, guess what he was doing in the hole without the knowledge of his parents."

"I have no idea," said George

"He was growing marijuana plants. He even had a lighting system set up that imitated sunlight for his plants."

"Are you serious? That kid had some imagination. I wonder if that helicopter had equipment that could detect the plants even underground. I believe there is a means of detecting the heat from those lights. As a result, they may have raided the area. Or he may have shared his little project with another youngster that further shared it with the law. Who knows?"

George looks down at his half-smoked cigarette and turns to Carol. "I'm still going to stop smoking," he says.

Carol responds, "I sure hope you do," in her tone of half-belief. She has heard this before many times.

"Hon, I am going to need your help with this sling and bandaging before and after my shower."

"Are you ready now?"

"I am," he said as they make their way through the house and to the bathroom.

Carol commands, "Turn and face toward me so I can remove the sling and the bandage. Good grief! Dr. Hughes did a lot of work here! Just look at all those stitches!"

"He wants me to hold my left arm in place as if it were still strapped across my upper stomach area and shower as usual while using caution in soaping the stitched area."

"That seems awkward. How will you shower with your left arm held in place as if the strap was still on your body?"

"I'll manage it as best that I can."

The shower feels great, so relaxing he could remain under the mist of water for hours, but after about ten minutes, he emerges.

Carol is standing there with a warm towel to dry him off. She understands to pat dry the left chest area and dry it thoroughly in preparation for the fresh bandage. She applies a salve provided by the doctor's office, and then applies a bandage and tape. She then slides the left arm into the sling and straps it around his body, holding the arm in place. She remembered George telling her that Dr. Hughes's nurse cautioned for him to not pull back his left shoulder or to open the left arm outward as it may rip out the stitches located deep inside the surface of his cut.

Carol assists on putting his shirt on, then George walks toward the deck with a fresh glass of iced tea in his right hand. Their deck is his favorite place in early mornings and late afternoons, unless of course the weather is bad. It's always quiet out here. *Gives me a good time to think deep thoughts,* thinks George.

*I don't believe Carol buys into my stop-smoking commitment. After all, she has heard it numerous times before. But this time, I'm really going to do it! It will happen. I'll call my office and schedule a week's vacation. Five weeks from now gives me plenty of time to firm up my commitment. I'm going to stop smoking this time,* he thinks.

George reaches for the phone and dials his office. The answering system allows him to enter the extension of Ralph, his "go to" person at the company.

"Hello, this is Ralph. How can I help you?"

"Ralph, George here; how are you today?"

"Hey, man I'm great. I'm glad you called. I wanted to ask you about the duplicate order for Bud's Wholesale. Did we ship the same order to him twice?"

"Nope. He placed the order, and then called me later to double the order and have it shipped to him two days later."

"Okay. That makes sense. I saw what appeared to be duplication and just wanted to know. I was about to call you. So what's on your mind?"

"Ralph, I'm finally giving up cigarettes, and for good this time. My plan is to lay them down on the weekend of August 30. That's five weeks from now, and I want to take a week off beginning on Monday, September 1, which is actually Labor Day. My plan is to modify my daily routine during that week as help with the commitment to quit."

"Let me look at those dates. Hold on for a moment, okay?"

"Sure."

"Is that week absolute? Is it written in stone?" asks Ralph.

"Uh, not really. I can consider other dates."

"How about it if we adjust that schedule because the entire sales team will be in a three-day meeting in Nashville and then set up the trade show for that weekend and on to Tuesday of the following week. You don't want to miss that, do you?"

"Absolutely not. So how about the week beginning on Monday, September 15? That will give me extra time of seven weeks for preparation."

"Done."

"Hey, George. Marcus is calling me to his office for a staff meeting. I've gotta go now. Is there anything else?"

"No, sir."

"Carol? Can you come here for a minute?"

"I'll be right there," she replies.

"I have scheduled my vacation for seven weeks from now and with that, I will absolutely give up smoking on Sunday night. During that vacation week, I will be here at the house or around and about. I will not be in any portion of my normal routine."

Carol looks him directly in the eye, "You are serious this time, aren't you?"

"I am. Here are my motives: When smokers stop tobacco, they experience misery for about a week, and the human brain, subconsciously, is continually telling them, 'You are going to be like this and live miserably for the rest of your life, always wanting a cigarette.' In my case, I decided that I must reprogram my mind to reality. The urge to smoke does go away.

"And here's what I did. I believe I will live another forty-five years, minimum. That's 2340 weeks. So I figure I will be miserable for about a week, still desiring to smoke for another three weeks, and uncomfortable with occasional urges for another couple of months.

"Bottom line is that I'm willing to be miserable for one week with the habit remaining three weeks, desiring and uncomfortable for up to another twelve weeks; that's up to twelve weeks of the 2340 weeks! It's a no-brainer!"

"George, you're amazing! How did you come up with that formula? I've never heard of it before. I am proud of you. We both need to be in prayer about this," says Carol.

Holding hands, George and Carol bow their heads as Carol opens in prayer.

"Well, there is one other phase that must take place between now and my quit date. Part of my self-commitment is that I intend on announcing to all our friends that I will stop smoking on that September date. You can help by alerting all our friends and relatives that I am giving up tobacco after smoking up to two packs daily for over thirty years. The more friends that know of my commitment for that exact date, the more committed I must be. If I commit to enough people, it will be even more difficult to fall back on my commitment."

"You've got it all planned out, don't you?"

Weeks rush by and his sixth week is present. George opens up his only available pack of cigarettes. He looks at the full pack as he says to himself, *I've got to do this. I've got to stop, completely stop, when this pack of smoke is gone.*

He lights up the first cigarette from that last pack and inhales the smoke deeply, almost as if he will never have another. But today is the day, and a large group of friends and relatives are cheering him on. *These people believe in me,* he thinks. *I'm going to do this!*

It's Sunday afternoon, and after church, George accompanied friends out to Summerland golf course for lunch and some practice on the three-par course. George arrives home at 5:45 p.m., walks in, and delivers a kiss to Carol. She says nothing about the normal smell of smoke all over him and his clothing. She hopes that will soon be a thing of the past. He has three remaining cigarettes in his trouser pocket, and before Carol can ask if he has any remaining cigarettes, he announces, "Well, I'm through. I may as well stop that stupid habit a few hours early."

Yet he knows he has a few backups as he begins to curb the habit between now and Monday, tomorrow morning. "That's just in case the urge gets too tough between now and Monday morning, my stop date."

Carol rises early before George on Monday morning. She will make him a cup of coffee and then wake him. George sits on the side of their bed as usual, and Carol hands him the coffee. Suddenly, it hits him! He reaches for a cigarette and discovers there is none available! "Honey? Do you notice anything different in the house?"

He had to notice something to fulfill her need for a compliment on whatever she did today.

"It seems the house is especially neat and clean," he replies

"Hmm, that's involved, but I emptied all ashtrays inside and outside, washed them out thoroughly; and they are now in the trash can out near the road!"

"Then, I guess my stop-smoking jolt is for real," he says laughingly.

Throughout the evening, George fought off the urge to smoke, pacing the floor, reaching in his pocket for a cigarette. "This is going to be tough! But I can and will do it."

He wakes early Monday morning, sits on the side the bed, wiping his eyes, and then as usual, for the last several decades, he reaches for a cigarette only to find an empty pocket.

"I know where there is a cigarette, and I've got to have one. I'll go outside the house and light up." Slipping on his house shoes, George quietly heads through the house, careful not to wake Carol.

Outside, he puts the one cigarette he has to his mouth and holds the cigarette lighter in the right hand. The lighter fires up and he moves the left hand that holds his last smoke toward his mouth. "No way! No way will I give in to this habit." He stomps the cigarette in the dirt and returns to the house.

Throughout this Monday, he is away from work and all normal daily activity. George sets out to keep himself busy, very busy. Careful to not do normal chores or to drive anywhere using the normal route and to normal stores. By the end of this day, he had washed both cars, cleaned the tires, wheels, and waxed both. After dinner, he insisted that he and Carol play a game of cards. Carol is eager because she knows he needs to keep his mind and hands occupied.

George continually reaches to his pocket, and Carol recognizes that he seems to be irritated that no cigarettes are available. And she notices that he is snappy and short tempered about everything, even toward her. After a game of rummy, George takes a shower and turns to bed earlier than normal in hopes of sleeping early and warding off the urge to smoke.

Next morning, after breakfast, Carol leaves the house early as she is volunteering at the church today and tomorrow.

*I must be disciplined enough to not leave this house. If I get in my car and go anywhere, I will buy a pack of cigarettes. That's for certain! I cannot allow that to happen*, he thinks.

His morning is spent pacing the floor. "This is tough. But it's only a few short weeks, a small portion of my anticipated life span of some 2340 weeks. I will do this!" George says to himself.

It's now 11:15 a.m. and his cellular phone rings.

"Hello, this is George."

"George! What are you doing? This is Irv from the company's credit department."

"Hey there! You know I'm on vacation this week, right?"

"Yeah, you told me. Still not smoking, right? So whatcha doin' this morning, George?"

George answers, "Well, I've been out back climbing trees."

"Do what? Why are you climbing trees?"

"I know dad gum well a squirrel found a cigarette butt in my yard and has taken it up on a tree limb, so I'm trying to find that half-smoked cigarette."

"You're hilarious, man! You know I have never smoked one cigarette, but I do know of people that want to quit and can't. I admire you for stopping. Don't you dare let anything come between you and your commitment. Well, as you might know, I've got a couple of calls coming in so I need to answer them. I'll talk later. Good luck with the non-smoking deal," says Irv.

"Thanks."

*This is tough, very tough. I don't know if I can do this. Maybe I will be better off to just slow down instead of stopping cold turkey. The nicotine patch didn't help me to slow down last week. I wore the patch and still smoked! That was stupid and probably dangerous. What am I saying to myself? I will not turn back to smoking!*

*Paul mentioned that taking a hot shower, even several times in a day, can help. He said it helps get rid of the nicotine lingering in the body by sweating it out through the pores. I'm going to try it!*

George gets in the shower with the water spraying as hot as he can tolerate. *Aha! This feels good.*

After almost fifteen minutes, he steps out feeling fresh, and at least the urge for a cigarette is gone, temporarily anyway.

Now fully dressed, George reaches to his shirt pocket for a cigarette. *Oh crap! I have been told that I not only have a nicotine addiction but I will also experience the habit of reaching for a cigarette. I wonder how long this will go on. Got to stay busy,* he thinks as he drags out the blower in preparation for cleaning off the driveway.

Today is Tuesday. Carol is out running errands. As this day goes on, he has already been in the shower three times! He watered the fruit trees twice, dug up and relocated three shrubs, walked around the neighborhood twice, and numerous other chores to keep him active and his mind off the habit and his addiction.

On the computer, George decides he will set up a spreadsheet as his daily activity calendar extending through three months. Using a green ink pen, he begins to mark each day with a smiley face to indicate another day completed as a non-smoker. He believes the calendar will help him stay on course and highlights the seventh, fourteenth, twenty-first, twenty-eighth, and thirty-fifth day.

He acknowledges, "At least I seem to sleep well at night. Mornings are real tough. Fortunately, I am told that within seven days, my addiction to nicotine will be gone, and the habit itself will begin phasing away."

Wednesday!

*Today is Wednesday, my third day of vacation and no cigarettes. I only want one cigarette, just to ease my anxiety and urge. But I will not go to a store today! I will not leave this house today! I will not go anywhere today! I've got to keep my cool and remain committed. This is really an hour-by-hour task! I've already got two whole days invested.*

*Why would I want to go back and start over, going through these three days again?*

Finally, after dinner, he tells Carol, "This seemed to have been the longest day of my life! I have kept busy today as my way of avoiding the urge for a cigarette, but it has been tough. I probably almost gave up and decided to go out and buy a pack of cigarettes at least twenty-five times!"

"I know, dear, but look at the almost three whole days you have already invested in kicking that horrible habit. To even smoke one puff from a cigarette now, you would have to start all over and go through these few days again. Just stay on course, my dear."

"It has been a tough week, and now it's Monday. I have fought it and have Seven days invested in my commitment. I can tell that my urge for that tar and nicotine is gone."

Today, it's back to the normal business routine. Every day has been a little easier as he looks back on his last Seven days. This is the real test for a continued commitment to remain a non-smoker. Travel routes, people he will be around, businesses he will visit in daily sales calls, all are part of his old habit of reaching for a cigarette.

Throughout the day's activities, George finds himself reaching to his pocket for a cigarette. *I'm now experiencing the physical habit I've had for many years. How long is this going to go on?* he asks himself. I guess the nicotine addiction may be out of my body now, but the habit is still quite demanding on me."

George approaches the receptionist at one of his biggest clients and asks to see Mr. Judson.

"I'm dialing his extension now," the receptionist tells him.

"Mr. Judson will be right with you, Mr. Belten."

"Thank you."

Barret Judson appears, "George. Come on back. How are you this morning?"

"I couldn't be better if I tried," George responds with a moderate laugh.

"You recently stopped smoking, didn't you? How's that going for you?"

"I'm now on my eighth day and hangin' in there."

"That is great. I admire anybody that stops that messy habit. I tried to smoke one cigarette when I was about sixteen years of age. It tasted awful. George, May I be open to you and say something about and for you?"

"Please do."

"I immediately noticed a difference. I'm not the only person out there that is bothered by the yucky body odor and smoke-in-the-clothing smell of smokers. Smokers reek of an odor. Many of us non-smokers try to avoid close contact with smokers for that reason, and I'll bet it affects the smoker's success in their career. Anyway, thought I would share that with you along with congratulations for giving up the habit."

"Man, I appreciate that. I never realized I had an offensive odor."

"Just keep it up. Don't ever light up again. Now, on to business. Will you schedule the consultant from your office to come in and train three new employees we have in our telephone department?"

"I'll be happy to do that."

"Just schedule it with Sarah in our human resources department and have them report to her when they come in."

"I'll take care of it."

"Good to see you this morning, George. Whatever you do, stick to your non-smoking commitment."

"I promise I will do that!"

George bids farewell to the receptionist on his way out, and then reaches for a cigarette in his shirt pocket on the way to his car only to realize there is no cigarette. "Dad gum! I wish this urge would hurry and go away!" he says to himself.

It's a leisure twenty-minute drive to his next client, Sam, owner of Packers automobile dealership.

Fortunately, George stopped smoking in his car a couple of years ago, so that helps void any urge for a cigarette while en route.

George is greeted by a sales representative. "Good morning, sir. What can I show you today?"

"I'm here to see Sam."

"May I tell him your name, sir?"

"George Belten."

"Thank you, sir."

This dealership showroom is always very colorful and neat with five new vehicles displayed. The sales team appears quite professional as they remain ready to help their customers through the car-buying process. Observing their techniques, they do not seem pushy. I notice there are always two white vehicles strategically positioned in the showroom in the mixture of other colors. I find that interesting when associated with the other color of flooring and walls. Everything is positioned for effect.

"Mr. Packer says for you to come on back. Do you know where his office is?"

"I do. Thank you."

Sam steps out of his office into the hallway and sees George walking toward him. "George Belten! It's good to see you today. Come on in."

"Sorry to barge in on you without notice, but do you have a couple of minutes to spare?"

"Always for you, George. How was your vacation? Where did you go?"

"Oh, I just hung out at home and caught up on some honey do's and chores."

"That's fantastic. Vacations that involve airports, hotels, and travel are not vacations in my view. You don't really fully relax and unwind."

"Is there anything my team can do for your business at this time?" asks George.

"Let's step outside and I'll tell you what I'm going to be interested in doing soon. I'll have a smoke while we talk."

George ponders to himself. *No way! I cannot expose myself to him smoking a cigarette near me! Should I tell him no? He's a client of mine. Well, I guess this can be my first real test. I've got too much time invested to turn back now; I've got to honor my no-smoking commitment.*

"Wow! Sam, I didn't know you smoked!"

"That's a story within itself." He reaches for a cigarette and lights up.

Watching Sam inhale that first draw and exhales the smoke makes George almost ask him for a cigarette, and he opened his lips to say so, but he stops the words before they were expressed. "I stopped smoking for ten years. Last month, I took the sales managers out for a beer. Bobby, my used-car manager, lit up, and I told him I wanted to try one just for the heck of it.

"George, when I finished smoking that one cigarette after ten years, it was as if I had never stopped smoking. Never! I excused myself and walked over to the convenience store, bought a pack of cigarettes, and rejoined the guys. I smoked that entire pack by mid-morning the next day.

"The rest of it is history. I'm hooked all over again. And I can't stop the stupid things!"

"Sam, I am glad you shared that with me. I scheduled a vacation last week for the sole purpose of giving up cigarettes. So I stopped smoking for eight days. After Seven days, the nicotine was gone from my body. There have been many times I've thought I'll just have one cigarette, and it would be okay. The experience that you have just shared with me prevents me from ever believing that I can have just one cigarette and still continue as a nonsmoker."

"Man, I'm sorry to be out here smoking around you. That's terrible on my part!"

George replies, "No. It has been my first real test, and I withstood the urges. I'm glad we did it."

"George, don't ever bend to temptation and smoke even one cigarette or cigar. Don't do it!"

"Thanks for guiding me along the path and keeping me from the temptation of another smoke."

"Now back to business. I anticipate the need for one of your consultants to come in and spend some time with my general sales manager. He needs to be more organized, and your company may just be the answer. However, the timing is not good, so I'll have to let you know when the time is right."

"You know I will help your company anyway I can."

"I know that. I just saw my factory representative pull on the lot, so I need to spend some time with him. I'll put out this stupid cigarette and go back in my office to greet him. It's always great to see you. Let's do lunch soon, okay?"

"You bet. I'll look forward to it."

*Thinking about the visit and Sam smoking, I'm still startled,* George thinks. *I paid close attention because others tell me the stench from smokers is disgusting, but I didn't notice any odor. I guess it's too soon for me to pick up on smoker odor, as I've heard it called.*

Time flies by. George has been tobacco free for three weeks now. Not one cigarette! He pulls out the homemade calendar to show Carol. "Today is day twenty-one for me!" he tells her.

"You did it! You wonderful hunk of greatness! You really did it!"

"Well, I still have the urge from time to time, but today, it stands out to me that my habit of thinking about a cigarette and reaching for one is not as often. In fact, for the most part, it's non-existent."

"You should feel very special. Think of all the smokers out there that want to quit and can't. In reality, they can stop, but they don't have the drive that you have. You wanted to quit, and you did it.

"I can't imagine smoking. I tried a cigarette when I was about eighteen years of age and didn't like it. In fact, it almost made me sick. So I never took up smoking."

George reaches out to Carol, pulling her to him with an embrace. "You're my little angel, and I love you dearly."

"Oh, I love you too. More than you will ever know, you handsome, fabulous man."

"As a follow up from the recent meeting a few weeks ago, we have a pre–trade show meeting coming up, and then the company is participating in a trade show at Opryland Hotel in Nashville. Why don't we fly in there a few days before the meeting to enjoy ourselves and kinda celebrate my new life. I'm certain Leland's wife, Joann, will be there. You know her and would be comfortable hanging out with her while we are in the meeting. And during the trade show, the two of you can browse around, and come and go as you please. The actual show hours are between 10:00 and 5:00, daily."

"When is that?" asks Carol.

"Week after next."

"Our meeting is all day Tuesday, and the trade show begins on Thursday through Sunday. We can fly in on Monday and return the following Sunday night or Monday."

Carol responds, "I am scheduled to visit with seniors in an assisted living facility on one of those days, but I'll ask Martha to handle it for me. She is always asking when she can become more involved. And I believe the church has a special recognition luncheon scheduled for that Wednesday, but it's not essential that I be there. It would be nice to attend, but it's not a big deal. So a mini vacation in Nashville will be fun."

Carol continues, "I've never accompanied you to that annual trade show. What goes on? What do you do?"

"It's easy other than we're standing most of the Seven hours of the show. Owners and managers of many different business fields stroll throughout the floor, stopping by booths and displays to see if the product or service at that booth is of interest to them. If they react with an interest, we then go into details as to how we can benefit their company. Occasionally, a contract is written on site, but in most cases, we set it up for an agent like me to visit their business."

"So you are just being yourself, standing around smiling at everybody, running your mouth, and being your natural self, right?" Carol follows up with a hardy laugh.

"Well! I like you too!" he responds.

And the kidding continues, "Okay, if you'll behave yourself for a few days—I know that will be tough on you, but all I can do is ask you to try—then I'll go ahead and make the travel reservations."

# CHAPTER THREE

"I'd like to invite Pastor Jack and his wife Mandy over for dinner tomorrow evening. Is that okay with your schedule?" asks Carol.

"Sure, let's do it."

Carol looks at the church booklet for the pastor's home number. Instead, his cellular number is listed. She dials the number and Jack answers, "Hello."

"Jack, this is Carol Belten. Is Mandy available?"

"She sure is. She's standing nearby. Hold on."

"Hello."

"Mandy, this is Carol Belten. I apologize for the quick notice, but George and I would love to have you two over to our house for dinner tomorrow evening."

"Let me check with Jack. Hold on for a moment.

"Carol, we'd love to be there. What time and what can I bring?"

"Just bring yourselves, and will 7:00 p.m. be okay?"

"Seven will be perfect, and if you think of anything, salad, dessert, or whatever that I can bring, just let me know."

"Great. We'll see you tomorrow evening, Mandy."

The next morning, Carol reviews her meal preparations for the evening. A chicken and broccoli casserole can be the main course. Salad, side dish, and dessert will then be simple.

George cuts his day short and is home early and in time to be ready for their visitors. He greets Carol with a kiss and hello, then heads to the bathroom for a shower. After drying off, George puts on his favorite plaid shirt and dress slacks. While dressing, he notices the neatness of his closet as a result of Carol's daily attention to details in the home.

"Carol, tell me what I can do to help," says George

"You can watch the casserole, and if the oven timer goes off, just remove the dish and place it on top of the stove. If you will do that, I'll freshen up."

"Okay."

It's now a short few minutes after Seven, and the doorbell announces Jack and Mandy's arrival.

"Good evening, folks. Come right in," says George.

Mandy responds, "You are so gracious to invite us into your home."

Jack follows with a smile and laughter, "And beyond that, you're going to feed us."

Carol emerges from the kitchen. "We are so glad you could join us," she says as she reaches and hugs Mandy. "Come on in the family room and sit wherever you choose."

Mandy says, "Let me help you in the kitchen while the guys visit."

"Dinner is almost ready, and there's not much else we can do at this point. The china and tableware is on the table, so you and I can visit. I'll take out the casserole from the oven and put in the dessert."

In the family room, general conversations quickly go to a new direction.

"George, I recall your prayer requests to help you give up cigarettes. Tell me how you are enjoying your new life as a nonsmoker."

George paused for a couple of seconds and said, "I'm now in my twelfth week, and the urge is still there but it comes and goes, and less frequently. I can now say I'm a nonsmoker." Continuing, George adds, "I set a stop-smoking date five weeks in advance but had to change it to Seven weeks because of a business meeting and trade show. The first week was terrible, almost unbearable, but I got through it. The nicotine addiction was gone by then. For the next three weeks, my habit of reaching for a cigarette drove me nuts. Now that urge continues to fade away. I believe I will feel even lesser urge on my fourteenth week."

"Really? You're anticipating the urge will be even better in fourteen weeks. Why are you selecting the fourteenth week?

"I have come to believe that the number Seven played a part in my stopping the tobacco habit. Seven is in the Bible over four hundred times, and it plays a role in our life. The number Seven is sacred and signifies completeness and perfection. I noticed a difference in Seven days. After three more weeks, or twenty-one days, I noticed an improvement. Now I am twelve weeks into the new life, and the fourteenth week is a multiple of the number Seven and is going to complete another step of God's sacred number."

"Wow! That's very amazing. It seems that you did experience success along each sequence of Sevens." Jack follows up, "You're old enough to remember the movie, *The Seven Year Itch.* Do you remember it?"

"Vaguely. Yes, I do."

"As a pastor, I counsel with couples when their marriage heads in the wrong direction. Almost all are having marital problems at their seventh year of marriage. Most of the problem marriages are ending in their fourteenth year of marriage and actually divorced in their fifteenth year. Some relationships can't seem to get through the seventh and fourteenth year. Now, on the other hand, I seem to notice more permanency in marriages after twenty-one years together as husband and wife."

"That is amazing. A few years back, I recall reading that statistic about most marriages split up after fourteen years of marriage, and as I recall, the actual divorces are filed in the fifteenth year," says George

"George, it's biblical, and it began when God created everything in six days and rested on the Seventh, the day of completion. He denotes Seven as Spiritual Perfection. He blessed the Seventh day and sanctified it. When God created the heavens and earth, He had a plan for each of the six days. His well-planned-out six days led up to completion on the Seventh day, and God rested. You too designed a six-day plan and experienced success in eliminating nicotine from your body on your Seventh day. In your case, you then approached another Seven-day plan." says Jack.

George relates to his childhood on the farm. His dad would farm individual fields for six years and let it lay unattended on the seventh. He always said that the land must rest and rejuvenate itself on each Seven years.

"I believe I have hit on a topic of much deeper interest," says George

George continues, "You know I was married before I met Carol. My first wife and I were married fifteen years. That marriage ended with her desire to go in another direction. Seven years later, I met Carol and we got married. I have never considered the significance of Seven in my past until now.

"I believe Seven plays a significant role in our lives, in this world, and the universe. Recently, for some unexplained reason, I've been turning to the Bible with an interest in Seven. I could understand my interest in that number. Now I believe I have been influenced by the Lord. Oh wow! What a true blessing!"

"George, I believe you have hit on something worth your further study and pursuit."

Carol calls out, "Dinner is ready, guys."

George responds, "On our way, dear."


In the dining room, Mandy asks, "Where shall we sit?"

Carol tells Jack and Mandy, "You may sit wherever you desire. Seated in this area provides a nice view of the shrubs and flowers out back, if you would like. Just sit wherever you desire."

Jack pulls out the chair for Mandy. Then he selects a chair beside her. "Let's go to the Lord in prayer," says Jack

Their heads are bowed and Jack prays and thanks God for their health, the food, forgiveness of their sins, and continued help to George for his stop-smoking success.

As they begin eating, Carol opens the conversation with her admiration for George and his commitment to totally give up cigarettes. "He is my hero!"

There are nods and smiles around the table. Jack blends in with George that he has accomplished what many others have been unable to accomplish. In his case, it is apparent that he has God engaged and handling everything. "I believe that."

Throughout the evening, a variety of conversations ranged from growth at their church to yard work, automobiles, pets, and the Bible. Desert was a homemade apple pie with an appetizing crusty topping, served with a scoop of vanilla ice cream. Jack asked for a second serving, a genuine compliment to Carol.

*Time passed quickly* as Jack is now in his twenty-first week of being totally tobacco-free. He firmly acknowledges that he did not stop smoking alone. He knows with full certainty that God guided him through the entire process.

When he is in the area and his schedule allows, Jack meets his four friends for coffee at the Waffle House out on the main highway.

"Good morning," says George as he shakes hands with each of the four—Travis, Lewis, Fred, and John.

"Man, it's good to see you this morning. We understand that you are still not smoking," says Fred.

George turns to Fred. "I can now say that it has been the easiest, near-impossible thing I have ever accomplished."

Lewis then says, "I'm confused. That doesn't make much sense to me. Explain the easiest, near-impossible thing."

"I always saw stopping smoking as near impossible. With my plan in place and the help of our Lord through this, I now see it was easy."

Lewis then pleads, "Hmmm. I guess that makes sense. You saw it as impossible to stop tobacco, but now that you have stopped, you see it as easy. I would give anything if I could give up these awful cigars I'm addicted to!"

"It may appear as complex, but I'll be happy to share with you exactly how I conquered the addiction."

"Will you please do that?"

"Absolutely. I'll be more than happy to help you," responds George. "Let's hang out here for a while, and then we'll talk. Okay?"

"Are you sure it won't interfere with your other schedule?"

"Seriously not at all."

As usual, the discussions go almost straight to politics and world news as each of the group provides their opinion. Normally, Travis has opinions that do not seem to be factual. John and Fred ignore some of his viewpoints as one-sided, saying he only listens to one segment of news and never knows the complete story. Generally, George listens to all the discussions and converses only when he wants to make a point and believes his particular viewpoint has the integrity.

Changing the subject, John says he must now go meet his nephew to assist in a pickup truck purchase.

George asks, "Where will you be shopping?"

"I believe we're going to look around for whatever suits his needs."

"You may go by Paul's dealership. I like the way they do business, and Paul requires his sales force to be honest and helpful. That I know."

"I'll suggest that to my nephew."

"See you guys later. Have a good day," says John.

One by one, the coffee meeting trims down to only George and Lewis at the table, and George goes directly to Lewis's cigar habit.

George shares, "I absolutely love a good cigar! Of course, I no longer smoke cigarettes or cigars. I remember going to the emergency room a couple of years ago after I had given up cigars but still smoked cigarettes. I had a case of diverticulitis, but the intern mistakenly diagnosed it as colon cancer at the time. Later, the doctor diagnosed it as diverticulitis; and while in his office, I turned to Carol and told her, 'If I am ever told by a doctor that I'm terminally ill, I want you to take me to a good cigar shop. I'll spend the remainder of my life enjoying a cigar.' So, Lewis, I understand the depth of your habit and addiction."

George continues, "First of all, as strange as it may seem to you, giving up cigars has a lot to do with the number Seven. However, we'll see how that can benefit you later in this conversation. You are a Christian and familiar with praying, are you not?"

"Oh yes. My wife and I are members at the Ballard Falls Church. We love the Lord."

"Good. I assumed you were. I'm sure you'll agree that it's quite easy to pick out Christians in a crowd. First of all, don't do it now because you'll need to think everything through, but you must set a stop-smoking date well in advance of your commitment to give it up. That stop-smoking date must be in multiples of Seven from the day you determine it. In other words, you may firmly commit to give up cigars in Seven days from today, or fourteen days, twenty-one days, whenever. In my case, it was Seven weeks."

George stands, "We'll need a sheet of paper to make some notes. I'll be right back."

He walks out to his car and pulls a pad from his case. He always has at least one pen in his pocket, probably the trait of a business-and-sales person. He then walks back inside the restaurant and directly to the table where Lewis sits alone.

"Lewis, what is your current age?"

"Forty-one."

"How long have you smoked?"

"Twelve years on cigars and before that, about five years with cigarettes,"

"In your opinion, strictly as a guess, what is an age you believe you will reach in your lifetime?"

"How would I know that?"

"None of us know but just provide me with an age you may attain before your death."

"I hope to live to eighty-five."

"Good. Now on your paper, deduct your current age of forty-one from eighty-five. What is your answer?"

Laughing, Lewis asks, "Where are we heading with this?"

"Just go along with me. How many years remain?"

"It looks like I'll be around for another forty-four years."

"Now multiply that by fifty-two, and what do you have?"

"Looks like 2,288."

"Good. That's how many weeks you plan to live. Now, hang with me through this. What I'm going to share now is one of the most productive mindsets I used to stop all those many years of tobacco.

"The human brain will sometimes trick us. Here's how. If you were to put cigars aside right now and go about your normal day, you'll crave a cigar. Now your mind starts to bombard you with thoughts that you will be in this craving mode for the rest of your life. The mind goes on its job of convincing you that you'll crave cigars and be miserable for the rest of your life. If you have given up cigars in the past, you are now relating to the mind-twisting task I'm telling you; am I right?"

"You're right," says Lewis.

"So as we determine that we intend to stop smoking cigars, we must accept the fact that our mind will play this game and try to convince us we'll be miserable for our entire life. Now this is the smartest thing you'll ever do when you decide to stop cigar smoking: you determined that you will possibly live another 2,288 weeks, right?"

"Yes."

"First of all, remove the top sheet from your pad. Use this sheet to make thorough notes of our discussion. On the remaining pad, write 2,288 in the upper middle of that paper. You are going to crave nicotine for Seven days. On your paper, deduct Seven from the 2,288. So you'll never feel the need for nicotine for another 2,281 weeks. Pretty simple, isn't it?

"Next, we've got to deal with the habit, the habit of continually reaching for a cigar, the habit of tasting and feeling that cigar in your mouth. This will take a little longer, but it's like anything you want to kick as a habit. For example, Carol and I were eating ice cream every night, around 8:30. We kept telling each other that we must stop craving ice cream. Finally, we suffered through the initial few days and remained ice cream free for twenty-one nights. After twenty-one days, we no longer craved ice cream.

"That same twenty-one-day *kick the craving* applies in your case. You must establish the proper mindset to, if necessary, force yourself to avoid cigars for twenty-one days. Earlier, I mentioned the association of Sevens toward your smoke-free life. Three Sevens equal twenty-one. Now stay with me through this part.

"On your paper, first deduct Seven from the 2,281 balance. Next, deduct Seven from the 2,274 balance; and finally, deduct

Seven from the 2,260 balance. Each Seven-day period is addressed individually, and when one is accomplished, you then address the next Seven-day period, and the next. Here's why we'll do it individually. We want completion of each Seven-day term. You still have 2,260 weeks remaining without cigars. That's pretty neat, right?

"The number Seven is sacred. God created the world in six days. On the Seventh day, he rested and sanctified the Seventh day and the number Seven as perfection. You want to recognize each Seventh day of your task as completion and perfection. Each and every day of your stop-smoking endeavor, you must lean on the Lord and pray, pray, pray.

"You have, at this point, been cigar-free for a total of twenty-eight days. You will no longer have the craving. You will, however, occasionally find yourself reaching to your pocket and reaching to your mouth. So break down another twenty-eight days into four more Seven-day periods and plan to address those in Seven-day terms. You are now truly smoke free and still have 2,232 days remaining to enjoy your better life.

"Are you willing to follow exactly the notes you have made and give up smoking cigars?"

"I am."

"That is your commitment."

"Now you will set the "no fail" stop-smoking date at least Seven days ahead. You must change all of your normal activities for that entire week. Any questions so far?"

"This is how you quit?"

"It is. And there are other things you can do during that week in order to help with the urge. Things like taking multiple hot showers during the first three of days when the urge for nicotine bears down on you. Stay home. Do not leave home for any reason for those three days! Your main two concentrations must be to first focus on the few weeks as part of your 2,288 weeks, about 1 percent of your lifespan. Your commitment to stop tobacco now must be firmed up. This may seem elementary, but commitment is essential.

"I'm going to step away to the rest room, and I'll be right back. In the meantime, look over all the notes and make certain you are firmly committed and will not, cannot, fail."

George leaves as Lewis looks over the notes. Periodically, Lewis looks away toward the blank wall and back to the notes again. *This is a big commitment*, he thinks to himself. Initially, as he reviewed the notes, he wonders if he can really do this. He, like others, has "quit" many, many times, only to go right back to the old addiction and habit.

George returns and joins Lewis as they continue their discussion. George asks Lewis, "What do you think?"

"I think I'll try it."

"You'll do what? You think? You'll try it? You'll try it? You mean I have wasted my time sitting here, guiding you through exactly how to give up tobacco? Lewis! To go into this plan and 'think you will try' is not an option! I'll tell you what, my friend. We'll change the subject and no more discussion about smoking!"

"No. No. I'm sorry, George. That was wrong and does not represent my mindset. I promise you, I will quit smoking. In fact, I have already set a firm stop-smoking date for three weeks, or twenty-one days from now. See? I put the date on my phone already. I will quit on that date, period, paragraph."

"Okay. That's better. Now consider me as your support team. I am available to help you twenty-four seven. Starting today, you must tell everybody you know that you are stopping smoking on that exact date. Tell everybody."

"Whew. I really do look forward to being a nonsmoker and recognize it's going to be tough, but short term."

"You hit the nail on the head, my friend. It is short term, very short term. Remain focused on your initial few weeks as it relates to 2,288 weeks. That's the key. You may expect me to say, 'Good luck,' but it's not appropriate because it never ties in well to 'Congratulations!' So congratulations, Lewis!

"Do you have any questions, Lewis?"

"I have one. How did you come up with this program and the Seven days?"

"I can't specifically answer that for you. I've asked myself that same question many times. It has to be a divine inspiration from God. Giving up tobacco was not the inspiration. The recognition and acceptance of the sacred number Seven was the message to me and His further inspiration to use it. I have discovered Seven applies not only to becoming tobacco-free but in our finances, our relationships, and the list just goes on and on."

"I must say that I am finding all this very amazing! And I thank you for such a meaningful and iron-clad approach to my giving up cigars. George, I've got to go now because Jane wants me to meet her at Papa's Sandwich Shop for lunch. Would you like to join us?"

"Not this time. I appreciate the invitation, but I have a business appointment in Helton at 2:00 p.m."

George keeps in touch with Lewis, offering to be his support in his stopping cigars, but everything continued as planned throughout the next few months. Lewis is now sharing his stop-smoking history with other smokers.

George is happy to have discovered a way he could stop tobacco and that not only worked for himself but for a friend as well.

# Chapter Four

L ewis is in his doctor's office for his medical checkup and strikes up a conversation with an acquaintance, Brian.

"Time for my annual medical evaluation," says Lewis.

"Yeah, my wife Nancy is here for her checkup also."

"And Dr. Malloy is going to get on my case again," says Nancy. "Last visit, he told me to lose about fifteen pounds, and instead, I have gained five or six. After my last physical, I joined the exercise center; and within about five months, I was down seventeen pounds. I stopped working out and now weigh more than before. I'm disgusted with myself!"

"Oh, I know how that is. My wife Melanie went through the up and down weight like a yoyo six years ago. She did some extensive research and found that if she worked out and toned her body to lose weight, she would need to continue that extensive exercising for the rest of her life and that she would periodically need to increase the exertion and working out well into her senior years. Otherwise, she would probably be compared to an overweight blimp."

"But Melanie is so trim now. How has she kept the weight off?" asks Nancy. "How'd she do it?"

"She settled for walking about two miles, three days each week. She walks at a moderate pace to keep her heart rate up and burn calories. Most of all, she began eating properly. At first, she tried one of those food services that ships you a monthly supply of food and causes you to lose weight fast. She lost weight, a lot of weight, and looked great. However, once she stopped ordering her meals, she gained it all back about as fast as she lost it; and she gained back more than she had lost. She was actually considerably bigger than she was before the dieting.

"Please go on, I want to hear how she became the trim lady she is today."

"After some research, she found a website that tells the participant how much sugar, carbs, calories, etc. are needed on a daily basis to reach the goal they set and do it within a few weeks. She would go online, and select and input her three meals for the day. She could eat anything she wanted, and after scheduling a day's meals, the program would then give her options to modify the day's meals in order to meet that day's needs.

"Do you know what the program is?"

"It's MyFitnessPal.com. You eat whatever you want, enter it in the computer, and allow it to calculate and guide you through, easily maintaining certain levels of calories, carb, sugar, etc."

"And she hasn't regained any weight?"

"No. She now weighs about 125 pounds. That was her goal, and after attaining the desired weight, she simply adjusted the site to maintain her new weight. She may vary two or three pounds one way or the other, but she has been at her weight for just over two years now.

"Melanie loved, and actually craved, desserts and sweets each evening. However, she quickly saw that daily sweets were going against maintaining her new weight. But she was hooked. She had to have her sweets every evening.

"Do you know George Belten?" asks Lewis.

Nancy replies, "Not really. I have heard the name though."

"Well, George Belten is responsible for my giving up cigars, and he told me of other habits that can be conquered with prayer and the number Seven. So I helped Melanie eliminate desserts for twenty-one days, a multiple of Seven. After twenty-one days, she has no longer craved deserts."

"One of my problems is drinking sodas, and I'm not sure I can't seem to give it up. I've tried everything."

"Well, let me share my own findings with you, one that guided my wife to give up desert. She can and does eat deserts occasionally, but she no longer craves sweets. I'm telling you that if you pray often and employ Seven, you can kick the soda cravings."

"I'm listening," says Nancy.

"George shared a biblical finding that helped me give up smoking cigars. It has to do with the number Seven. Seven is mentioned in the Bible over four hundred times. So I used the same approach to guide Melanie through giving up desserts."

"Are you with me so far?"

"I'm listening."

"Okay, when you decide to give up sodas, you tend to see yourself as being miserable and crave just one more soda because you know it will conquer that craving. Also, your mind plays tricks on you by telling you that the cravings are not short term, that you will crave sodas for the rest of your life. Not true. You will need to condition your thinking to a short-term, twenty-one-day time frame.

"Now back to Sevens and its role in giving up sodas. Fact! If you give up sodas for three Seven-day periods, for twenty-one days, you will no longer crave a soda. You will be able to enjoy a soda occasionally without craving another."

"Are you serious? I have never heard of that."

"Neither had I. It works beautifully, but you must recognize the holiness of the sacred number Seven and pray to the Lord for success and completion of your habit forgiveness. And let me share this with you. I once thought I had to have a nice steak every Friday and Saturday night. I craved my steaks. I used the same principle and would not allow myself to eat a steak for twenty-one days. Now I eat steak whenever I want but no longer crave that food. I eat more fish and chicken along with other healthier foods."

"Lewis, I am going to take your advice and become acquainted with MyFitnessPal website. I'm also going to give up deserts for twenty-one days. Yes! Woohoo!"

Laughing, Lewis turns to Brian. "How's your golf game?"

"It would be better if my business would afford me the time to play. I'm on an expansion model in my company, and it's taking all my time."

The nurse calls out, "Mr. Hartier. Lewis Hartier."

"Here I am," responds Lewis.

"Follow me, Mr. Hartier. Go in room 4, and I'll check your vitals for Dr. Malloy."

Lewis sits comfortably while the nurse reads his blood pressure and temperature.

"How is my blood pressure this morning?" he asks.

"It's 122 over 66. Dr. Malloy will be in shortly."

"Thank you."

Lewis sees the AAA Travel magazine nearby. He picks it up and begins flipping through the pages. His ambition has always been to travel to Australia. As he goes from page to page, it seems to automatically stop on a featured story and illustrations about Australia. Such an unusual culture, unusual to our own here in America especially in the outback area of the country.

Dr. Malloy enters, "Good morning, Lewis. Are you having any issues we need to check today?"

"No. I probably couldn't be any better if I tried," responds Lewis with a slight laugh.

"I'll listen to your chest and heart rhythm." Dr. Malloy goes through normal medical checkpoints and turns back to Lewis. "Your lungs sound pretty good. It appears you're healthy and going strong as ever."

"That's what I wanted to hear, doc. I gave up smoking a while back."

"You just added a lot of years to your life. I'm sure it was tough, but certainly worthwhile."

"I know."

"The recent injury and infection on your right arm seems to have healed remarkably well. Are there any prescription needs? Anything we need to check or discuss at this time?"

"Not that I can think of."

"Give this to the front desk, and I'll see you next time."

"Great. Thank you."

At the receptionist's desk, he looks around in the lobby; and apparently, Nancy must be in an examination room awaiting Dr.

Malloy. Brian is in conversation with another guy. The receptionist swipes his card for the co-pay and slides the invoice before him for a signature.

He then walks toward the door and stops by, tapping Brian on the shoulder. "I apologize for interrupting your conversations, but if you will, keep me posted on how Nancy does as follow up with our discussion."

"I definitely will do that. Thank you, and it's good to see you again, Lewis."

"Have a good afternoon."

"You too."

Lewis walks toward his two-year-old sedan while fumbling in his trouser pocket for the keys. With the ignition key pointed toward the car, he presses the tab and unlocks the driver door. *That's pretty slick. Just press a button from a reasonable distance and the door unlocks. I can even open the trunk in the same manner*, Lewis thinks

Approaching the car, as usual, it's noticeable to him that his car's front-quarter pancl is misaligned. Week before last, in the early morning while driving on Wallace Road, he caught a glimpse of a deer crossing the road from his left. He swerved sharply to the right in an attempt to avoid the animal but caught it in its mid-air leap. Immediately, his left light beam was shining slightly downward, so he pulled over to check the damage. The deer was nowhere in sight, and the fender was not dented, that he could detect, but was knocked out of alignment with the hood area. It's not even noticeable unless you know to look for the slight damage. The headlight adjustment was necessary.

Seated in his car, he closes the door, starts the engine, backs out of the parking area, and drives to the street and traffic.

"Hey! There goes George. I thought he was traveling today. I need to talk to him," Lewis says to himself.

George observes a car approaching from behind with head-lamps blinking. At first, he thought it was an emergency, and then he identifies the car and driver.

"I wonder what Lewis wants," George says as he turns on his right-turn signal and enters a restaurant parking area. Lewis parks nearby and walks over as George gets out of his car and closes the door.

"George! My friend, how are you?"

"I'm doing great," responds George.

"I want to thank you from the bottom of my heart. Your guidance resulted in my completely stopping those nasty cigars. You're my hero!"

"Well, I'm not sure I deserve that. I'm just sharing my understandings of Sevens as in the Bible. In fact, I am now going through the Bible, highlighting many mentions of Seven and then going deeper to understand how it is used and why it was used in scripture. It's pretty amazing how much I see of the number Seven as it relates to our lives. I am beginning to understand there are six steps that lead up to the number Seven as a completion in our maturity, finances, marital relationships, and the list seems to go on and on."

Lewis shares, "My brother-in-law smokes cigars. When I am near him, the stench he reeks through his pores is horrible. To think that I had that same odor once is embarrassing." Lewis continues, "I need to share this with you; you know Brian and Nancy, right?"

"Oh yes. Two wonderful people."

"I saw them at Dr. Malloy's office and shared my stop-smoking success. That worked into Nancy's desire, actually a need, to lose weight. I really didn't have the knowledge but stumbled through the possible use of Seven as a weight-loss plan. And I probably didn't know if Seven applied to her need or not but felt that if it worked for me, it could work for her. I feel the need for you to follow up and help her."

"Tell me about the conversation. I may learn something from you."

"I shared my success in giving up tobacco, thanks to you, and its role with the number Seven. One of her problems is drinking sodas."

"I told her how my wife gave up her nightly ice cream cravings. Now she still eats ice cream occasionally, but she no longer craves it. She made herself go without ice cream for twenty-one days and no longer craved it afterwards. And I pointed her toward a website,

MyFitnessPal.com, that can help plan out her meals each day and help lose weight."

"Perfect! Why don't you follow up with Nancy often to give her encouragement as you continue emphasis on twenty-one days and the website use."

# CHAPTER FIVE

" I have been asked to hold a meeting at a Freedom Valley church and discuss the use of Seven in handling individual finances. That meeting will be Sunday afternoon at four in the afternoon in case you know somebody that is struggling with finances, especially credit card debt."

"How about me? I have credit card debt that is about to get out of hand. I never want to go into my investments to pay off cards."

"Come on. Do you know where that church is located?"

"I've heard of Warren Cove but don't believe I know the location."

"It's about fifteen miles down the Bradford highway. When you see the Wal-Mart store on your right, the church is about half a mile on the left. The church sits back off the highway but very visible from the road."

"Now I can go right to it."

"Very good. I'll see you Sunday, 4:00 p.m. I suggest that you arrive about fifteen or twenty minutes early."

On Sunday afternoon, George and Carol arrive at Freedom Valley church forty-five minutes in advance of the meeting. Pastor Jimmy says the deacons want an advance review of the meeting content. So the two of them go to a meeting room at the back of the sanctuary.

Jimmy introduces George, "Gentlemen, this is George Lewis. I invited George to discuss how our church members and guests can handle personal finances."

The deacons greet George with a hardy "good afternoon."

Deacon Sid asks, "George, what is your background that leads up to guiding people on how to manage their money? Are you a certified financial planner?"

"No, sir. I have no professional training or any formal education on the matter."

"Really? I guess I'm looking forward to what you have to say," responds Sid with a slight giggle.

Then Deacon Harold adds, "Sir, I'm curious about your program as you think it can be helpful for our church members."

"Not much to it. You know that the number Seven is throughout the Bible. Our financial matters tend to be most successful when we apply the number Seven to it. It's that simple."

Sid now calms down with, "Now you've got my attention. In quoting and referencing the Bible as your foundation, I believe you may be a true blessing to our church this afternoon."

"Gentlemen, do you have any questions or comments we can discuss at this time?"

The board of deacons looks at each other and all nod with indication of "no."

"Then, I will take a few minutes to set up the materials I will be covering."

A last minute decision is to not use the podium but to reflect total relaxation by sitting in a chair at times and standing, walking around the stage at times. As members and guests arrive and are being seated, George estimates about forty people are seated or being seated.

It's now four o'clock. George clips on the wireless microphone transmitter as pastor Jimmy makes the introduction. "I have the pleasure of introducing a gentleman that has helped others through some of life's challenges. This afternoon, we have asked George to come and talk to us about managing our personal finances. May I introduce Mr. George Belten."

"Thank you for those kind words, pastor. Let's take a moment to bow our heads and go to the Lord in prayer." He leads the prayer and at closing, thanks the Lord for all the many blessings.

Walking across the stage, he pauses and looks out across the group while making eye contact with many. He breaks fifteen seconds of silence with, "If you have a monthly budget, please raise your hand."

It appears that everybody in attendance held up their hand, indicating their pride in managing their monthly finances successfully.

"Now, I want to say something that may surprise and confuse you. Your monthly budget is worthless! It is very limited in its effectiveness for your financial needs."

Again, silence. All of a sudden, he has the audience's undivided attention. Nobody has ever heard of such a statement and is very eager to hear more.

"When you leave here today, you'll see why I say that your budgeting is a burden. You will go home and begin a new way of handling your finances. I wish all schools taught the art of handling money, I really do. But most don't find it that important.

"I grew up on a large farm, an only child, and my dad only completed the Seventh grade. As the oldest brother in his family, he had to take over when his father died at age fifty-six. So my interest in money was soon self-taught. One of my jobs when I was in the Seventh grade was to gather the eggs from the hen house. One day, as I delivered my gatherings to the kitchen, my mother commented that for the last couple of days, our chickens were not laying as many eggs as they should. Normally, she counted about twelve or fourteen eggs each day. Now the count was about half. She couldn't figure out why the hens were not laying their normal daily count.

"The school bus drove by our house, and I normally was on my way to school by seven o'clock. The bus would then turn left and make a thirty-minute tour through the countryside to pick up other students, and then it would re-enter the main highway about three miles south of our house. It then continued north by a community grocery located about one-mile south of my home. Next, the bus turned to the west and picked up more students on its way toward Eldridge Elementary School.

"I knew the store owner bought eggs from local farmers and would then resell them to non-farmers. Over the last two days, I had been skimming six eggs from the batch I gathered. Instead of catching the bus at home, I had the bright idea of walking about a mile to the community store and then get on the bus as it made its way north and then west toward school. That was my opportunity to sell the eggs that my mother expected to be in her basket. I took twelve eggs to the storeowner and sold them for 30 cents. That was a smart investment for the storeowner as he resells them for 45 cents per dozen.

"In those days, we could buy Wrigley's chewing gum at 5 cents per pack or could purchase three packs of the gum for 10 cents. All the financial intuition I could muster led me to invest my 30 cents to purchase nine packs of gum and try to sell it to other students at school for 5 cents each. By my calculations, I could go back home with 45 cents in my pocket. Few students had any change, but I attracted those with a nickel and the desire for chewing gum. On that day, I became a successful salesman and money manager, in my opinion. This business venture grew to the point that I was buying gum and candy for resale.

"Finally, Mr. Rayburn Stevenson, our school principal, confronted me to stop selling candy. But I continued. He then announced at a school meeting in the gymnasium, "Do not buy any candy from George Belten. You will get in trouble if you do!"

He shut down my enterprise, temporarily. Students no longer approached me to buy candy and gum. So I broke open small packages of candy and lined up a few students at the end of our gymnasium so I could throw the candy for them to run and pick it up. They had free candy. That attracted other students over to the gym, and I was back in business with lots of customers.

"So my streak for multiplying pennies at that point became a multiplication of dollars. You are probably thinking that is what guided me to be standing before you today, right? Not the case. I am proud to be here discussing finances before you today as a direct influence of the Bible. In fact, the number Seven is my financial message to you.

"The number Seven is in the King James Version of the Holy Bible several hundred times. Seven is a sacred number, a sign of completion, sanctified by God. Our God created our earth in six days. On the Seventh day, he rested and declared His creation complete. When we use the number Seven, we acknowledge to God that Seven is anointed. You must have a six-step plan that leads up to completion—Seven. God had a plan for the six days of creation that led up to the Seventh day and completion. Seven is a sacred number.

"I'm going to step outside finances and tell you that I believe when we use Seven combined with prayer in other areas of our life, we see positive results. I smoked for over thirty years. Use of the number Seven is a direct responsibility for my being nicotine-free today. I look back on my life and see Seven playing not only a role, but the solution in so many aspects of my life."

"Materials in support of our discussions today have been distributed. Is there anybody that does not have these materials? No? So everybody has a packet. That's good. Now let's get started.

"Now why in the world would I stand before you this afternoon and tell you to do away with your monthly budget? That is absurd; I'll bet you thought at the time. So let's see why a monthly budget should be replaced with a new method. Replacing your budget with a Cash Flow Plan and going forward always refer to our financial budgeting as Cash Flow Plan, or CFP, as we'll refer to it. Are you okay with that?

"But how does the number Seven fit into this CFP, you ask. Remember that Seven is biblical. Seven signifies completion, all is good, it is done. Your old budget has always been formatted on the first day of each month and went through to the end of that month. Then, it starts all over again for the next month, right?

"Here is the hiccup in that monthly budgeting. You start the month with a balance in your available cash. You plan out the bills for that entire month and all is good, right? But what happens when on the fifth day of next month, five weeks from your budgeting, you have an unscheduled bill for mower servicing, as an example. Now that month has become dysfunctional, so to speak.

"Let's look at CFP. Please refer to your materials. Regardless of when income is received, using excel spreadsheet or any means available, we'll start by setting up one column for categories, and then

Seven weekly columns, each week is to be dated as the next Saturday's date across the top. Saturday's income must apply for the next week's use toward expenses. Do not list expenses this week toward income realized on Saturday. Vertically listed along the first column, section A, list income sources and an area for totals.

Next column, in section B, list tithing, all loans and expenses, with an area for totals. In section C at the bottom, enter total expenses, then total income, then difference, and then balance forwarding. At the top of each column, beneath the dated Saturday, set up Balance Forwarded in the first line. Are there any questions thus far? No?

"Let's now enter your income in each of the appropriate weekly columns. If you are paid once each month, you will enter only one income. Then, if your spouse is paid weekly, enter that amount across the Seven columns. Do not total the incomes.

"Next, enter all your expenses beneath the week it is due. Next, we enter each expense within its due date column. Enter in all Seven columns, listing everything, Groceries, miscellaneous, everything that you may be paying out, especially money to your savings account. Do not total the expenses yet.

"Let me insert something here. I strongly recommend that you never allow your savings account or investment monies remain idle for any month. Make certain you have a category set up for savings. It is important that you add to your reserve money, or savings, if it's only a few dollars. You must be growing financially each month instead of remaining idle or on a decline in available cash. I can't over emphasize the importance of this statement.

"Once all your incomes and your expenses are entered, total each column expenses across the Seven weeks. Start with first column and deduct the expenses from the cash available.

Any remaining, Balance to Forward, cash is then added to the next column's top, Balance Forwarded section. If you are short on cash that week, then look at the expenses. Begin your juggling of expenses. You may need to pay one of the bills on the next week when allowed. A special alert must be given to the Balance to be Forwarded section in the Seventh column or week. If it is positive, little effort is necessary to meet all Seven weeks of cash needs. If it is negative, additional income or deferred expenses will be necessary.

"As each week ends, you then enter data in the new Seventh week. You will always know all your financials seven weeks in advance.

"Questions of anybody? None? You folks are good.

"Okay. I won't ask you to raise your hand if you have credit card debt. I will ask, but don't answer this, would you like to pay off your card balance in a make-sense way? Then would you like to pay off your card each month?

"Paying off a card can be easy and simple. It's not rocket science. Let's say the cardholder is maxed out with $3,000 at 18 percent rate. Paying $75 monthly, you will pay fifty-four months before the card is paid off. Pay $75 each month plus the interest reflected on your statement, you pay it off in forty months. Pay $100 each month plus interest pays the card off in thirty months. Paying $125 monthly calculates for twenty-four months. Each month, the interest you are paying above your base payment reduces. Each month, you give yourself a raise!

"Obtain a low-limit card for use and pay it in full every week, not every month. Never allow Card for Use build up a balance; treat it strictly as if it were cash.

"You do not want to use these cards, so you cut all cards up, right? Not necessarily. I recommend that you fill a plastic jug with water, suspend one card on a string in the center, and freeze it solid. You will then need to think about it for a couple of days before using the card. In fact, for anybody that has a tough time handling their spending and need to use cash only, that is an effective way to avoid card debt until absolutely necessary.

"Any questions?"

A question from the second row. "I have three cards, all at maximum debt. How do I determine which card to pay off first?"

"That's a good question. There is no pat answer that applies in every case. You may want to look at the lowest-balance card to attack first. However, another card may have a couple of hundred dollars more in it with a lower rate. More payment is going toward principle reduction, and it could pay out earlier than the lower balance card. I will be happy to look at it with you, one-on-one.

"There are other ways of paying off credit card debt, but I find this method to be very simple and easy. Taking the balance owed, divide it by the number of months until paid in full; and each month, add the interest amount showing on that monthly statement. That's all.

"You may have questions as you advance through today's presentation, and you have my contact information in the paperwork distributed earlier. Feel free to contact me. I will help and there is never a charge.

"Let's summarize the cash flow plan step-by-step:

1. list incomes, monthly bills, and expenses
2. enter Seven upcoming weeks across the top of each column
3. enter expenses beneath each due date/column
4. enter incomes
5. total all incomes and all expenses in each column. The balance, negative or positive, is carried forward to the top of the next column.
6. Adjust or juggle payments to reflect a positive balance at bottom of each column.

"If columns will not balance, you must plug in more income or reduce expenses.

"Now let's summarize paying off a credit card.

1. divide your statement balance by the amount of payment you can afford, "base payment."
   Example: $200 monthly base payment toward a current balance of $2,400 projects a twelve-month payoff.

2. add each month's interest/finance charge to that base payment

"Each month, the base payment remains the same. The interest amount added to that base payment reduces each month, so the amount you pay out decreases each month.

"Above all, build six phases, or steps, toward your success or completion of Seven and lean on the Lord with your prayers.

"Thank you and may God continue to bless you."

Pastor Jimmy steps up before the group. "At this time, the deacons will collect a love offering for George."

As the deacons pass collection trays through the aisles, the collection keeps building. As they turn the collection over their deacons for counting, George steps up to the podium again. "Folks, you are very gracious. I thank you from the bottom of my heart. You no doubt have a family in your community that will benefit from this love offering. Please show your Christian love by reaching out to help any such family. Will you please do that?"

Pastor Jimmy then steps back to the front, turns to the congregation, and begins to clap. In response, the entire church attendance stands and claps their hands in a show of thanks to George. Somebody in the middle section begins to sing Praise to the Lord, and everybody, including George, joins in.

Pastor Jimmy then quietly asks George, "Can you and Mrs. Belten join Barbara and me for dinner at the House of Eats?"

"That will be nice. I'm sure my wife Carol will enjoy the fellowship. I'm not acquainted with that restaurant, so why don't we follow you?"

Sid, the deacon chairman, approaches George at the back of the sanctuary. "Mr. Belten, I am not only impressed with your love for the Lord, but your extended Bible research in the number Seven. Today, you have performed a great service for our church and this small community. May God continue to bless you, sir."

George replies, "Well, thank you, Sid. You just made my day."

Sid then says, "One other thing. I told the director of music at Grove church that you were scheduled to speak about finances, and he wants us to tell him how this meeting went today. He will want to talk with you. Do you mind if I give him your number?"

"No. Please do."

"His name is Howard Smith."

"Very good."

George stood near the front door, shaking hands with those in attendance as they leave the building. He can sense the Spirit in this church. *These people love the Lord. What a blessing*, he thinks.

Then George and Carol walk to their car, hand in hand, and then while Jimmy and Barbara comes out the door and to their car, Carol leans over and hugs George. "You're amazing, George. I knew you always seemed to have a special talent for handling our budget. Oops, I'm sorry, our CFP. That is the first time I have heard your presentation about Seven as it structures financial matters, and I'm impressed."

"Well, Seven may not structure such things in our lives, but when acknowledging its fulfillment and combined with prayer, Seven certainly influences completion. It's up to us to accept and use Seven as we deal with life's opportunities and challenges."

Jimmy pulls out and motions for George to follow.

Carol continues, "I feel very fortunate that you manage our finances so well. Now I understand a small portion of why and how you do it."

"Thank you. I believe God influences those of us that accept His guidance; furthermore, directing attention to Seven is a plus. It's His number. His number of completion. We are recognizing it as His sacred number."

In the twelve-minute drive to the House of Eats, they pass several other restaurants. Many are nationally recognized eating establishments, so Carol is looking forward to this new restaurant she has yet to dine in.

Most parking spots are taken at the restaurant. Jimmy locates an opening, motions George to drive and take it while Jimmy then parks on the side of the street next to the restaurant.

Only four others are in front and being seated as they walk up to the hostess station.

"How many are in your party?" asks the hostess.

Jimmy replies, "Four."

"Will a table for four be okay? Or do you prefer a booth?" the hostess asks.

Jimmy affirms that a table will be good. Seated, they order one tea for Carol and three glasses of water for Jimmy, Barbara, and George. Discussions flow from the growth of this church to George's presentation.

"On behalf of the deacons, the entire attendance today, I can't thank you enough for your financial ministry and its place in our church. As we were leaving, the deacon came up and told me that our love offering intended for you was just over $4,900. George, that within itself shows the appreciation for your ministry."

"Wow. Jimmy, as I diverted those funds over for use in your community, I visualized a helpful hand out to somebody, hopefully about three to five hundred dollars." George then adds, "And I just recognized another thing. That $4,900 is a direct multiple of Seven. Just thought I would throw that in the mix of praise to the Lord."

Opening up the menu, Jimmy offers a couple of comments. "If you like seafood, their grouper is fresh, and I like it fried. The pork chops are tender and well-seasoned. With most anything you select, you can expect excellence in preparation and presentation."

"I normally eat a very light dinner," says George. "But this menu looks so inviting I will probably overdo it here," he laughs.

Jimmy says, "We always like eating here, both lunch and dinners."

Barbara then endorses Jimmy's comments. "I believe the food here, especially seafood, will stand tall against any other restaurant in this region of the state."

Carol then asks, "What do you recommend?"

"Oh my goodness. You're putting me on the spot. I tend to like the blackened mahi-mahi. It's just my favorite. However, I don't believe you will be disappointed with any entre you select."

George turns to Carol. "Honey, I believe I will order the shrimp creole and a side order of fries. Told you I was going to blow my normal of lite foods for dinner." Laughing again.

"I'll go for the Mahi," says Carol.

"Jimmy, what is your choice?" asks Barbara.

"Gotta go for the fried chicken, mashed potatoes, and slaw. Can't lose with their chicken," responds Jimmy enthusiastically.

George's phone rings. "Hello. This is George."

"Mr. Belten, my name is Howard Smith. I'm the music director and assistant pastor at Fair Life church. Am I interrupting anything?"

"No, sir, go right ahead."

"I've heard from other churches that you have a very good ministry helping others through financial issues and difficulties."

"Well, thank you. I try."

"Would you consider a meeting with the pastor and me to discuss some needs in our church that you may be able to help with, if your schedule and time allows?"

"Sure. When will be good timing?"

"Mr. Belten, as early as tomorrow afternoon at our church would be ideal. However, any other time you would like will probably work for us."

"I believe my late afternoon schedule tomorrow will work well. I travel about a 150-mile radius, and tomorrow is set for local appointments."

"Great. I'm looking at our pastor's schedule, and it looks like he will be available. Can we set 1:30 tomorrow?"

"Howard, later in the afternoon will be better for me, say around 3:30."

"Then 3:30 it is. Do you know where our church is located?"

"Yes, sir. I do. So I'll be there at 3:30 tomorrow."

"Thank you, Mr. Belten."

George looks at each and says, "I'm sorry for that interrupting call. But I'm glad I could take it when I did."

Everybody seems to thoroughly enjoy their meals. The dessert menu went unopened. They were full and dessert just did not seem a huge desire. George reaches for the check, and Jimmy is faster. He pays the check, and the four proceed toward their automobiles. Jimmy shakes the hand of George and thanks him again. George thanks him for the dinner.

Barbara reaches out and hugs Carol.

The next afternoon, George drives to Fair Life church and parks near the building side door, assumed to be the office entrance. He knocks on the locked door and then notices a speaker box with a button at the bottom and presses it.

"Hello," a voice comes out of the speaker.

"I'm George Belten, and I have an appointment with Mr. Smith," George tells the speaker.

The buzzer sounds off and the door clicks open as the voice says, "Come on in, Mr. Belten."

Inside, George is then greeted by the voice. "I'm June, the church secretary. If you'll come with me, I believe Howard Smith and Pastor Brent King are waiting to see you."

Entering the small conference room, Howard greets George and introduces Pastor Brent King. The three visit informally for about ten minutes, discussing various topics. Then Pastor King speaks up, "Howard tells me good things about what he has heard of your help to people in their financial matters. We have a few people in our church that are in need of some guidance and beyond what we feel we are qualified to provide."

"Mr. Belten, we wanted to meet you and ask if you would meet with a few of our church members."

"I would like that. We may need to play with actual dates, but we'll get it done."

"We have our Wednesday evening service at 6:00 p.m. Of course, Sunday afternoons are generally always available. You tell us. What would be a good time for you, Mr. Belten?"

"It sounds like Wednesday evenings would be good for your group, and I can make it work on my end. How many people are involved?"

"Howard, I have heard the needs of five individuals. Do you know of others?"

"No."

"We can schedule those five to be available immediately after the evening service. That will be about 6:30 when the service is over, maybe five minutes after 6:30."

"I'll be here. In fact, I'll plan to be here for the service as well."

"Very good. What we normally do is serve food at five o'clock. A prayer meeting begins at 5:45, and we are normally through by 6:30."

"Then I'll plan to be here for some good food at five."

George shakes hands with Brent and Howard, and then walks briskly to his car. Inside, Howard and pastor Brent King nod and comment their appreciation for George and his ministry.

Howard tells Brent, "Rather than set up their meeting in the conference room, can we have them gather in your old office? It has a small conference table and area within the office."

"Sure. No problem."

"Our choir practice is at 7:15, so I would like to listen in on George's meeting from my office located next to their meeting. I'm anxious to hear about his program."

"That's a good idea," Pastor King responds.

Wednesday afternoon, George is in a late afternoon meeting with Ernie, a client over in Huford. He estimates the drive to Fair Life church will take about forty-five minutes even in ideal traffic conditions. As the meeting continues, he starts to realize that he will probably be late for the church evening service, but he cannot cut this meeting short. He can always call the church to alert Howard and Brent that he may be a few minutes late.

George drives away from the client's office and turns left toward his new destination. It's now 4:16. He may be at the church on time after all. Traffic is sometimes backed up throughout the city at this time of the day. Taking the by-pass can cost an extra five minutes but places him there earlier than traveling through town. He decides to take the by-pass.

He looks at the time. It's now five o'clock, and he seems to be on schedule to be at the Grove with a couple of minutes to spare. At 5:10 p.m., George enters the church parking lot. Taking a long breath, he feels a relief. A church greeter welcomes George to Fair Life church and provides him with the program for the evening service.

They have a food bar set up, serving chicken, green beans, mashed potatoes, and salad. He selects a plastic glass with water and seats himself at a table with three others that he is not familiar with. The others in the room complete their meal before George due to his late arrival. Then Pastor Brent stands and solicits any praises experienced to share by members. Next, he reads the scripture for the day. At the end, he then asks for any special prayer requests around the room and prays.

George is then met by Howard. Howard is a taller man, very slim in stature. He has a great smile. That smile doesn't seem to be a natural smile, but it was nice and accommodating. "Come with me and we'll set you up in the pastor's old office. It's just down this hallway. The folks you will be working with should already be there and waiting."

Approaching those standing near the office, Howard says, "George Belten, I'd like for you to meet Billie, Alice, and Drew." George shakes hands individually with each of them there.

Howard then adds, "A fourth person was scheduled to be involved, but something come up that prevented him from attending."

The office appears fully functional in spite of being told it was Brent's old office. Apparently, the office is being used along with another. A small conference table is ideal for George's meeting.

George turns to Howard, "I will gather information at this meeting and distribute their assignment paperwork. It will be an overview for the materials to be covered, somewhat motivational. Above all, I will instruct the group on some critical information needed for our next meeting. They will have my contact information in case they have any questions whatsoever between now and the next meeting. Future meetings will always be one-on-one instead of a group session."

"I don't believe that is what's expected. Why don't you continue ongoing group sessions? Brent and I believe group counseling will be good for all."

"I understand. However, we'll be discussing personal finances that are not normally comfortable when shared in a group, and each person's financial needs are generally different. I should be able to meet with each for about fifteen minutes to review the accomplishments to that point and assign the next week's agenda."

"Well, okay. I guess."

"You folks have a seat anywhere you would like. As Howard said, my name is George Belten. I am not a normal financial planner as you may categorize as such. However, I am a financial planner outside the normal. I never charge anything for what I do. I do not try, nor intend, to sell you anything."

Continuing, "We're going to look at new ways of solving financial issues that may be causing concerns. Such things as simplicity in paying off debt and saving money regardless of income and outgo. We'll even discuss holding your monthly gasoline bill to the same amount regardless of the per gallon pricing. After a few weeks, Seven weeks in fact, you'll smoothly manage your personal finances with ease. You'll have plans ready for use to address any unforeseen money surprise that may appear. Much of what we do will involve the number Seven.

"'Why is Seven important?' you may ask. Seven is biblical and reflects, 'well done,' 'completed.' I can go deeper into how the number Seven plays its role in our lives. You would be amazed at how much direct accomplishments are associated with that number.

"So with that being said, let's turn to the Lord in prayer." George thanks God for His grace and asks for His guidance during this session.

"Now here's our first week's assignment. Does everybody have a computer or access to one? On your computer, design a spreadsheet. In my handout, you will find thorough instructions for setting up your Cash Flow Plan. Now let's review the materials. If you have any questions, feel free to ask them as we go through the plan.

"The first column will contain the due date for each income and outgo of money. The next column is labeled Description, as the source of income and list of all bills you must pay. In your next column, at the top, enter the next Saturday's date. Continue to write the dates across Seven sections of your spreadsheet and date each heading for the following Saturdays.

"The first horizontal line should be described as Bal Fwd, abbreviated for Balance Forwarded. Your next line will be titled as Income. You may have different sources of income and allow as many lines as needed to allow for entering that information. Next, the Description is Total Income. In this line, you will total your income for that week.

"You may have incomes weekly, biweekly, on the fifteenth and thirtieth of each month. You will still have weekly dated columns that you will be working with. Are there any questions at this point?

"Okay, moving forward. Next, we'll itemize each and every bill or payment we must pay out each month. Include childcare, auto expense, even periodical oil changes and maintenance. On periodic expenses, you will reserve money for that future expense. In other words, a one-hundred-dollar expense anticipated to be paid out several weeks from now will result in us setting up and allocating a weekly toward that expense. Example may be with $100 due in ten weeks, you will reserve $10 weekly so that future expense becomes no hurdle. That may seem elementary to you, but you will see the benefit through resetting your brain to deal with finances in a new manner. So plan to do it.

"After listing all expenses, a line is allocated and labeled as Total Exp. Next description is Total Income. We will simply enter the total income amount from the top of column. Then the last description is Forwarded. This means the amount of money remaining after paying your bills that will be entered in the next week's Forecast column as a starting balance for that column.

"As you enter data, all dollar amounts will be entered in the appropriate columns only across the spreadsheet's Seven columns. All weekly and monthly expenses will be listed for arrival at the bank or company on or before the due date. Continue listing expenses in each Forecast column across the spreadsheet.

"Do not total and calculate totals until all data are entered. Then total income and expenses.

"Shift payments around so that you meet your obligations that are due over the next Seven days and then add one new week that will become your new Seventh week of the spreadsheet. We'll meet here next Wednesday. At that time, hopefully, you will see some great stuff in your next Seven weeks of managing your money.

"If you do have questions during the week, please do call me at the number showing on your paperwork I have provided.

"Let's take a couple of minutes to review a gasoline management technique that works well. A gas credit card is needed for this technique. If you do not have a card specifically for fuel purchase, you'll want to order one. Your monthly fuel billings will always reflect the same dollar amount, regardless of whether gas prices are $2 or $4 per gallon. To avoid month-end surprises, establish the dollar amount you want to forecast and pay each month. Let's assume you forecast $100 monthly for gasoline. That is basically $25 weekly. Now if you drive more during a particular week, once you have purchased $25 on your card, you then must walk in the station, pre-pay the excess fuel with cash. You maintain your forecasted card payment, and it helps you to be more conservative in travels in order to avoid that awful and embarrassing trip inside the station to pre-pay your fuel purchase.

"Now we'll schedule fifteen minutes for your individual cash flow review at our next meeting. Who would like a 6:45 p.m. meeting?"

Alice raises her hand. "I'll do 6:45."

Good. "Drew, how about 7:00 will that work for you?"

"Sure."

"I'll be here at 7:15," says Billie

Everybody professes to understand the spreadsheet content needed before their next meeting as they walk to their cars. George looks around for Howard and Brent but sees neither. So he walks through the hallway and out to his vehicle.

Brent and Howard remain at the church and briefly discuss the evening worship and attendance. Howard then said, "I remained in my office with some paperwork while George met with the others. His discussion with the group was plainly audible to my office, so I wasn't attempting to overhear the meeting. I'm convinced the participants didn't understand a thing he said. It was complicated to me, and I know it was not at all understood by them. They expected more than they got, a lot more, in my opinion."

"In what way?"

"Well, the bottom line is that I believe it's a waste of time. George mentioned God and seemed to begin with a prayer, not a sincere prayer though. I believe he went through the motions of a very brief prayer. I just don't see God being involved in what he is doing. From what I heard and understood, these people are not going to gain any benefit from any meetings."

"Well, George comes to us as highly recommended. We probably should show our support and see how it all shakes out."

Howard does not agree. "But he's going to feed them a lot of stuff they don't understand, and very quickly, they are going to drop out of the meetings. They're going to recognize the lack of benefit to them. However, I'll continue to monitor any progress and may talk with the individuals attending for their feedback."

He changes the discussion to Sunday's service as he wants to make certain the songs from the choir tie directly to the sermon that will be preached by Brent.

After some brief discussion, Brent bids Howard good night and walks to his office and reviews tonight's prayer list before laying it on the secretary's desk for publication. After their discussion, Howard abruptly left the building. Brent then locks the door as he leaves the church.

At home, Carol asks, "Did you eat dinner at that church?"

"Yes. One of their church members volunteers and prepares the Wednesday-evening dinner. He is a terrific guy, and he definitely knows how to cook a good meal."

Carol says, "That's great. So how about coffee and dessert? I made a cherry pie earlier."

"Fantastic," responds George.

"And in addition to coffee, you want water to drink, I assume."

"Sure."

"George, I don't want to complain. But you are working too many hours since you've taken on several hats and helping others, don't you think?"

"I understand. It's just in my heart to do what I feel I'm being led by the Lord to do. I just don't want to stop, nor slow down. I can see accomplishments as I go about sharing information and guiding people to enjoy life more abundantly."

"Well, I want to encourage you to keep some time aside for family, okay?"

"That goes without any emphasis."

"Here's what I see as it relates to people's lives and the number Seven. Seven's role in people's lives is not scientific. In other words, it is not tied in any way to an idea that humans scientifically evolved from other organisms. God sanctified the number Seven, in the seventh day of creation, as a completion to the task. Personally, I have seen and still see Seven in my life. Whether Seven has the same result and completion on others remains to be seen. Following six phases, combined with prayer, it gives an individual a tool to use as their stepping-stone toward their own needed completion. Does that make sense?"

"Oh yes. It does. I am a witness to it in our lives, especially in yours."

At various times during the week, George receives calls and has opportunities to guide each of the three financial participants through completing their weekly assignment.

Drew was asking, "I am maxed out on two credit cards and paying minimum payments on each. I can't seem to see a way out of this mess."

"Don't worry about it. We'll cover that next Wednesday. Bring your last statement from each of the card banks. Getting out of credit card debt can be pretty simple. So just bring your information and I'll help you."

Wednesday-evening church service was uplifting to everybody. Afterwards, each of the meeting participants made their way toward the conference room and waiting for George's arrival. He approaches and said, "Let's go to the Lord in prayer to be with us through this forecasting meet." Afterwards, Alice seats herself at the conference table. The others remained seated outside the office.

George asks to see Alice's spreadsheet. "Okay, I see you have totaled your incomes. Your payday is on the fifteenth and thirtieth of each month, I see. You have totaled the expenses. Now we'll take the projected income and deduct expenses in the first column. That leaves you with $300 that can carry forward to the next week at the top of your column. There is no income that week. You have four expenses of $122, 18.18, $93, and $117 for a total due to be paid out of $350.18. You are short $50.18."

"So what can I do?" asks Alice.

"No problem. At first, I glanced at your Seventh week available balance that is to be forwarded, and it reflects $93. That tells me your balances between now and then are easily dealt with by adjusting some payments. In your next week, it appears you will be paid your salary and with money left over after paying that week's bills. So we're going to shuffle some money around to make everything balance for this week. Of the $117 and $122 payment due this next week, if you call that creditor and ask them to allow you to pay that bill next week and without charging you any late fee, which company will do that for you?"

"The $117 is my electric bill, and they will probably work with me."

"Okay, remove the $117 from this first column and put it in the next week's column. Now you have 66.82 left over that can be added to the top of next week's Balance Forwarded column. I notice that you do not have money allocated for groceries and gasoline."

"Yeah, it's all lumped in the miscellaneous expense," says Alice.

"Break it out and list it. You want to identify every anticipated expense you will incur."

"Okay."

"All right. You are doing great. You're heading in the right direction. I want you to now adjust and total every forecast column and shuffle bills around to allow for a positive cash flow through the Seventh week while meeting all your obligations. As you get further in your use of this system, you must add a new Seventh week as you end a week. Always keep Seven weeks active on your spreadsheet. Okay?"

"Yes, sir."

"Drew, Come on in. Let me see your spreadsheet. Wow! You're ahead of the class. You have totaled and balanced every week. I'm impressed."

"I saw where this was headed and anticipated the income and payment schedules for each weeks balancing. My biggest hiccup is my credit card debt. I owe $3,000 on one and $6,600 on the other."

"Let's look at your bank card statement. Your $3,000 balance has a high rate and looks like the minimum payment required is $75. This month's interest is right at $50. You're only reducing the balance by $25 and that will take several years to pay it in full. Drew, have you been paying your card payments on or before the monthly due date?"

"For the most part. I was about two weeks late back in December of last year."

"Okay. Are you in position to pay an extra amount on one of the cards? In other words, rather than pay $75, you pay $100 as your base payment, plus the interest reflected on the most recent statement. Your $3000 balance will now be paid off in thirty months at $100 per month plus interest."

"I can do that."

"I want you totally committed to pay what we agree upon here, now. So are you committed?"

"Yes."

"Good. I want you to call each of the card companies and ask them to help you by reducing the interest rate. They will either do so, or they won't. If they do not, call back next week and ask them again. Makes sense?"

"It does. And it is simple. I love it! George, thank you so much. You are a godsend."

"And I thank you. Thank you for being so receptive and proactive in managing your finances.

"Billie? Billie, come on in here. Let's see what we have to work with. Shall we review your spreadsheet?"

"George, I am so sorry. I have not had the time to complete mine this week, but I still wanted to come and let you know in person that I'm not giving up. I do want your help."

"I understand. Tell me what kept you from addressing your financial matters this week."

"I'm a single parent of two beautiful children and works from 8:00 to 5:30. Then I take care of my mother that lives in the other side of our duplex. She is ill. I prepare her meals and handle her washing along with other needs. Honestly, I did not have a spare thirty minutes since we met last Wednesday. That is unless I skipped church and that's just in my genes, I guess."

"Don't you worry one bit. We'll get through this together. I promise I'll help you organize your dollars."

"How?"

"If, one evening, we find somebody to watch your children, prepare, and serve their meal along with dinner for your mother, will you be able to devote an hour and work with me as we address your financial matters?"

"Oh yes. I sure can."

"Then I'll call you within the next twenty-four to thirty-six hours to set up a meeting. Enjoy the rest of your evening, and I'll get back to you, okay?"

"Okay. Mr. Lewis, I thank you so very much."

"You are certainly welcome."

George notices Howard at the desk in his office as he and Billie leave the meeting. George briefly halts and looks toward Howard. "Good night, Howard. Have a blessed evening."

"Okay," responds Howard in a non-enthusiastic tone.

George continues outside and notices Billie's car as she opens the driver door. "Billie, that's a nice car. But we may need to forecast the expense of a set of tires for the future."

"I know.

Howard then leaves his office and walks down the hall toward Brian's office. Brian is not at his desk.

Walking around and searching further, Howard sees Brian in the sanctuary.

"Brian, that was a nice service this evening, don't you agree?"

"I do. The Lord's Spirit was with us this evening."

"Speaking of the Spirit, I couldn't help but overhear George's discussions with the group. I'm very concerned, Brian. I am concerned about George and his program. I do not sense God's spirit involved in George's program. I believe he's in it for the money."

"But there's no money involved for him. Tell me where you're coming from in this assumption."

"I'm not sure I can explain. I listen to him talking with the group and there's not sufficient reference to the Lord. It's just him and him alone in there, along with those attending."

"Oh no! You mean he doesn't go to the Lord in prayer at any point during their meeting?"

"Well, he does. Briefly. But quickly and with not enough sincerity is detected."

"Hmm."

"And I had a call yesterday from The Landing Church's chairman of their deacons. He had heard about George's money ministry and wanted to know more. Unfortunately, I was not able to provide any encouragement."

"What did you tell him?"

"Only that from our perspective, George is acting on his own and without God's guidance. He meets with individuals and promotes his own program that he says will give them safe haven from their financial woes."

"I wish you had not indicated the conversation as ours. It was your viewpoint, not ours."

"We're both have the same impression of George's program, don't we?"

"Not at all, Howard. Apparently, he has a lot of support from other churches for his Sevens ministry. I want to provide him with our complete support. I believe he does have something worthwhile for these folks. My wife is waiting on me for dinner. I'll see you tomorrow, Howard."

"Right."

# CHAPTER SIX

G eorge arrives home and quickly goes to Carol for her assistance in finding somebody to help with serving food and providing family care at Billie's house while he counsels with her.

Carol questions, "When and how long?"

"I need about one hour of uninterrupted time with Billie. And either tomorrow evening or the day after is my preference."

"You know who immediately comes to my mind? You know Cindy and Lou from our church, don't you?"

"Sure. Why do you think she would help?"

"Call her. If she is not available, she may know of somebody else that can help."

"I'll call her now," he says as he reaches for the church directory and dials Cindy's home phone number. George is beginning to assume they are not at home after the phone rings five times.

Then Cindy's husband, Lou, answers, "Hello!"

"Lou, this is George Belten. I hope you folks are doing well this evening. Is Cindy available?"

"What do you want with her?" he asks and slams the phone down against the table.

After almost a minute, Lou returns to the phone. "She'll call you back!" and the phone connection goes dead.

"What did she say?" asks Carol

George quietly responds, "That was Lou. Cindy was apparently busy and she'll call me back.

He is assuming that Lou and Cindy may be having a family argument and that she may not call back. If not, he and Carol will come up with another helper. As last resort, he may need to approach Carol to fill in.

The following morning, Cindy calls. "George, this is Cindy. Lou says you wanted to talk with me."

"I do. I appreciate your response. Cindy, here's what I've got. A Christian friend needs my help in a one-on-one meeting at her home. A problem is that she has so many responsibilities after work and at home that she doesn't have time. As soon as she arrives home, she cooks dinner for her, the children, and her mother next door. She says she doesn't have any spare time between that schedule and bedtime. So I'm searching for somebody to entertain two children and serve them a meal that I intend to pick up on the way."

"When?"

"This evening or tomorrow evening from 5:30 to around 7:00."

"Today may be better for me. But I will need to discuss it with Lou."

"Today is perfect."

"Okay. I'm on our house phone. Let me use my cell phone and call Lou."

Cindy scrambles through her pocket book for her cell phone and dials Lou at work.

Lou promptly answers his phone, "Hello."

"Lou, George needs me to help by watching a lady's children this evening as he meets with their mother. Is that okay?"

"It doesn't matter to me. Do whatever you want to do! I've gotta' go now. Bye!"

"George, I can help you. What time will you pick me up?"

"How about 5:15. Her house is not far from your address."

"I'll be ready."

"Okay. I'll pick up the food to be served and then pick you up."

Later that afternoon, George purchases a large portion of chicken and side items on his way to Lou and Cindy's house. Cindy has been watching for the car to pull in her driveway, and now she walks to the car, opens the passenger door, and seats herself.

George greets Cindy, "I appreciate your help as we serve the Lord this evening by helping Billie."

In doing so, he notices that she is crying softly as she seems to hide it from him.

"Are you okay, Cindy?"

"I'm all right, thank you."

At Billie's address, George parks on the street in front of her duplex as there is no specific driveway. The front yard needs some attention to the tall grass, and children's toys are strewn all around the area. It's quite evident to George that she has nobody available to tend to yard work. He rings the doorbell, and Billie invites him inside.

He introduces Cindy to Billie. Billie then introduces them to her two boys that are busy playing computer games.

"Billie, I stopped by the Good and Fast Chicken restaurant, and here are some foods for you and your entire family. I also have a chicken dinner for your mother next door."

"Oh my goodness. Thank you, George. You didn't have to do that."

"I understand, but I wanted you to be free and concentrate on our forecasting."

"Billie, Cindy is a friend of Carol and mine. She and her husband are members at our church, and she will relieve you of your family responsibilities while you and I take a look at your finances."

Billie looks at Cindy, "Cindy, you are a blessing. I appreciate you taking off your time to help out. You may find little Roger, my four-year-old to be mischievous, but he is easily pulled back in line."

Cindy searches the kitchen cabinets for plates, tableware, and place settings for the children and their grandmother next door. She places some chicken, mashed potatoes, and a roll on each plate, along with a plate of food for Billie to eat later in the evening. She and the boys walk next door and ring the doorbell.

She hears a voice inside, "Who is it?"

"Ma'am, my name is Cindy, a visitor with Billie next door, and I have a plate of food for you."

The door opens, "Well, I sure do thank you, young lady."

"You are welcome. I hope you enjoy the food. If you need any-thing else, let us know."

"God bless you. Cindy, right?"

"Yes ma'am"

Back at Billie's side of the duplex, she sets the food and plates on the table for the children.

Roger jumps in the chair, crosses his arms, and refuses to eat.

The older boy turns to Cindy and whispers, "He's a mean little brat. Ignore him and he'll finally eat." In response to his comment, Cindy giggles lightly, and she seats herself to eat with the boys.

George asks Billie, "I see your computer over there. Can we set it up here on the table?"

As the computer goes through its startup, she realizes just how anxious she is to absorb George's training she has heard about from others.

"Okay. Set up a one-inch column on the left and Seven smaller columns across the page. Set the type style as Arial and the type size to eight points. Across the top of each column, type in each upcom-ing Monday's date which will be used to enter income and bills for the upcoming week.

"Now, at the top of each column, beneath the date, label it as Fwd'd for forwarded. Below that, list a name for each source of income you may experience and leave one extra line blank for miscellaneous.

"Beneath the miscellaneous line, label the next line as Total and then, skip a line. On the next lines, you will begin to list every expense and payment you may experience. On the very first line, you will want to type in Tithing. Include food, gasoline, etc. along with your normal scheduled expenses."

The room is quiet as Billie gives thought to expenses and lists tithing, rent, groceries, utilities, cable, car payment, bankcard, gaso-line, furniture payment.

"What about childcare?"

"My mother cares for the boys when I'm not here."

"That's right. I didn't think about that."

"However, I believe you did overlook a payment, Billie."

"What?"

"Actually, I see two that must be added. You must allocate some money each payday to Savings and another to Reserve. You'll see that reserved money is necessary to accumulate toward an upcoming quarterly or periodic future expense. That way, the expense does not surprise you a few weeks from now. For example, your automobile servicing costs of oil changes, belts, and etc. need to be anticipated, listed, and prepared for."

Billie adds Savings below Tithing and Reserve at the bottom.

"Allocate a line at the bottom and label it, Tot. Exp. for total expenses. Skip a line and add the label, Tot. Inc. for total income from the top. Beneath that, add Tot Exp.; and finally, enter Bal Fwd for balance forward.

"This may appear somewhat complicated to you at this point in time; however, the benefits will soon emerge, and you'll have a new perspective on successfully handling finances without any worry going forward."

"Whew! I'm always fighting dollars. I hope this helps me."

"This system can eliminate your worries. You'll always have a clear view of your future cash needs. Let's continue.

"In the first column, let's plug in all numbers that apply. In the second line, the Bal (Balance)."

| DESCRIPTION | Scheduled Payments | WEEKLY DATES | | | | | | |
|---|---|---|---|---|---|---|---|---|
| | | 14th | 21st | 28th | 4th | 11th | 18th | 25th |
| **BAL FWD'D** | 9 | | | | | | | |
| Mo. Income | 1704 | 1704 | | | | 1704 | | |
| Child Supp. | 500 | 125 | 125 | 125 | 125 | 125 | 125 | 125 |
| Other In | | | | | | | | |
| Misc. | | | | | | | | |
| **TOTAL INCOME** | 2213 | | | | | | | |
| | | | | | | | | |
| **EXPENSES** | | | | | | | | |
| Tithing | 222 | 56 | 56 | 56 | 56 | 56 | 56 | 56 |
| Savings | | 50 | | | | 50 | | |
| Rent | 800 | 800 | | | | 800 | | |
| Groceries | 400 | 100 | 100 | 100 | 100 | 100 | 100 | 100 |
| Utilities | 120 | 120 | | | | 120 | | |
| TV Cable | 109 | 109 | | | | 109 | | |

continued on next page

102

| | | | | | | | | | |
|---|---|---|---|---|---|---|---|---|---|
| Cellular | 38 | 38 | | | | | 38 | | |
| Automobile | 180 | 180 | | | | | 180 | | |
| Auto Ins. | 48 | 48 | | | | | 48 | | |
| Credit Card | 120 | 120 | | | | | 120 | | |
| Gasoline | 120 | 30 | 30 | 30 | | 30 | 30 | 30 | 30 |
| Furniture | 34 | 34 | | | | | 34 | | |
| Reserve | | | | | | | | | |
| Misc. | | | | | | | | | |
| Other | | | | | | | | | |
| **TOT. PAYMENTS** | | | | | | | | | |
| TOT. INCOME | | | | | | | | | |
| TOT. PAYMENTS | | | | | | | | | |
| **CASH BAL FWD** | | | | | | | | | |

*Note: Do not total. Enter all income and payments.*

What appears to your Scheduled payments section is all that most people see as their "Budget" without upcoming surprises that may be just ahead.

To a degree, we can see that, like most people, you're living on the financial edge. Fortunately, you have good health in your family and without sudden and unpredictable expenses hitting you. But unfortunately, those unforeseen expenses do occur into our lives, all of us. We're going to work toward being able to handle surprises when they come up.

"Now, let's date the Seven weekly columns, beginning with this upcoming Monday."

"But I'm paid on the tenth day of each month, not weekly."

"That's good. We still have weekly expenses that must be accounted for and paid."

Billie dates each column with Monday's date for the next Seven weeks.

"Now put in your incomes in their appropriate date. Do not total the entries. Next, take some time and enter each bill you must pay over the next Seven weeks and in the week they are due, allowing mail or transit time so no bill is even one day late. Do not add up and enter any totals at the bottom of any column. Take your time."

As Billie makes Seven weeks of entries, George turns to Cindy. "Cindy, would it be possible for me to have a glass of ice water?"

"I'll get it." She brings the oversized glass of water and locates a coaster to set it upon. In doing so, she observes the intensity in Billie's concentration on completing her assignment from George.

Billie completes the entries and alerts George.

"Now go back and total each column's income, each expense, and calculate the balance to be forwarded. Set your program to handle the totaling and forwarding for you.

"As we view the next Seven weeks of forecasting Cash Flow Plan, we'll see beyond this week, this plan so to speak. We'll also be able to make adjustments well in advance of a problem. Naturally, most people tend to recognize this week's money left over after paying bills as spending money, found dollars. Then two weeks from now, there is no money to meet all obligations."

| DESCRIPTION | Scheduled Payments | WEEKLY DATES | | | | | | |
|---|---|---|---|---|---|---|---|---|
| | | 14th | 21st | 28th | 4th | 11th | 18th | 25th |
| **BAL FWD'D** | | 0 | 144 | 83 | 22 | -39 | 189 | 128 |
| Mo. Income | 1704 | 1704 | | | | 1704 | | |
| Child Supp. | 500 | 125 | 125 | 125 | 125 | 125 | 125 | 125 |
| Other In. | | | | | | | | |
| Misc. | | | | | | | | |
| **Total Inc.** | 2204 | 1829 | 269 | 208 | 147 | 1790 | 314 | 253 |
| | | | | | | | | |
| **EXPENSES** | | | | | | | | |
| Tithing | 222 | 56 | 56 | 56 | 56 | 56 | 56 | 56 |
| Savings | | 50 | | | | 0 | | |
| Rent | 800 | 800 | | | | 800 | | |
| Groceries | 400 | 100 | 100 | 100 | 100 | 100 | 100 | 100 |
| Utilities | 120 | 120 | | | | 120 | | |

continued on next page

| | | | | | | | | |
|---|---|---|---|---|---|---|---|---|
| TV Cable | 109 | 109 | | | | 109 | | |
| Cellular | 38 | 38 | | | | 38 | | 35 |
| Automobile | 180 | 180 | | | | 180 | | |
| Auto Ins. | 48 | 48 | | | | 48 | | |
| Credit Card | 120 | 120 | | | | 120 | | |
| Gasoline | 120 | 30 | 30 | 30 | 30 | 30 | 30 | 30 |
| Furniture | 34 | 34 | | | | 34 | | |
| Misc. | | | | | | | | |
| Reserve | | | | | | | | |
| **TOT. PAYMENTS** | 2191 | 1685 | 186 | 186 | 186 | 1601 | 186 | 186 |
| | | | | | | | | |
| TOT. INCOME | 2204 | 1829 | 269 | 208 | 147 | 1790 | 314 | 253 |
| TOT. PAYMENTS | 2191 | 1685 | 186 | 186 | 186 | 1601 | 186 | 186 |
| **CASH BAL FWD** | **13** | **144** | **83** | **22** | **-39** | **189** | **128** | **67** |

*With all data entered, you may now total all columns.*

107

| DESCRIPTION | Scheduled Payments | WEEKLY DATES | | | | | | | |
|---|---|---|---|---|---|---|---|---|---|
| | | 14th | 21st | 28th | 4th | 11th | 18th | 25th | |
| **BAL FWD'D** | | 0 | 144 | 83 | 22 | 17 | 139 | 78 | |
| Mo. Income | 1704 | 1704 | | | | 1704 | | | |
| Child Supp. | 500 | 125 | 125 | 125 | 125 | 125 | 125 | 125 | |
| Other In. | | | | | | | | | |
| Misc. | | | | | | | | | |
| **Total Inc.** | 2204 | 1829 | 269 | 208 | 147 | 1846 | 264 | 203 | |
| | | | | | | | | | |
| **EXPENSES** | | | | | | | | | |
| Tithing | 222 | 56 | 56 | 56 | | 112 | 56 | 56 | |
| Savings | | 50 | | | | 50 | | | |
| Rent | 800 | 800 | | | | 800 | | | |
| Groceries | 400 | 100 | 100 | 100 | 100 | 100 | 100 | 100 | |

continued on next page

108

| | | | | | | | |
|---|---|---|---|---|---|---|---|
| Utilities | 120 | | | | 120 | | |
| TV Cable | 109 | | | | 109 | | |
| Cellular | 38 | | | | 38 | | 35 |
| Automobile | 180 | | | | 180 | | |
| Auto Ins. | 48 | | | | 48 | | |
| Credit Card | 120 | | | | 120 | | |
| Gasoline | 120 | 30 | 30 | 30 | 30 | 30 | 30 |
| Furniture | 34 | | | | | | |
| Misc. | | | | | | | |
| Reserve | | | | | | | |
| TOT. PAYMENTS | 2191 | 186 | 186 | 130 | 1707 | 186 | 186 |
| TOT. INCOME | 2204 | 269 | 208 | 147 | 1846 | 264 | 203 |
| TOT. PAYMENTS | 2191 | 186 | 186 | 130 | 1707 | 186 | 186 |
| CASH BAL FWD | 144 | 83 | 22 | 17 | 139 | 78 | 17 |

"We'll now go beyond a typical budget and make our cash flow available to pay the bills. When driving your car out on the open highway, do you observe the most distant point or just look out a short distance in front of your car?"

"I don't know, probably both."

"Your Cash Flow Plan is very similar. You want to look at the very last number posted in the Balance Forward line. That is your ultimate goal that you must prepare for. In this case, after a $50 savings account allocation, you have a  balance. That tells us that if you did have a shortage during your Seven weeks, you will be able to move some payments around slightly to offset any shortage. On the other hand, if you ever have a shortage in your Seventh week, it requires more juggling to handle that deficit.

"So let's search for a solution to any possible shortage. Where would the money come from? "Your bank card payment is $120 and cable bill is $109. Don't those creditors have a five-day grace period on payments?"

"I don't know."

"I'll bet they will work with you, without any penalty when you call in advance. Let me see your recent bank credit card statement.

"I see on the disclosure section and back side of the statement that a ten-day grace period is granted. That means you can pay within ten days of the due date shown on front and no late payment fee applies. So let's plan to pay the card so that it arrives within that grace period.

"How is your relationship with the cable company?"

"Okay, I guess. I haven't been late on a payment in a very long time."

"Good. You can always call the cable company and alert them that you will be paying a few days later than normal. Then ask them to waive any late payment fee for you. If you normally pay on time and need a few extra days, and you call them well in advance of the due date, they will work with you.

"In case you ever do need extra time on those payments, call them; and after they agree to work with you, then you can adjust your forecast to reflect the rescheduled dates for payment."

"Every weekend, you must update everything. As you are ending a week, you need to add a new week that becomes your new Seventh week. You absolutely must commit to tracking your money. Will you firmly commit?"

"I will."

"One other item for our discussion. I see that your credit card rate is 22.99% on a balance of around $3,000. Pay your next three payments on time, not one day late, certainly not beyond the grace period. After that, I'll guide you on how to call them to request a nice reduction in rate as you commit to a payment in excess of the minimum required payment. You will be asking them to work with you to pay off the card and relieve some debt."

"George, I am so grateful that you are willing to share your time and help people like me. I can see this to be my answer to less financial stress."

"Thank you, Billie. But you know what? I'm the grateful one, grateful to the good Lord that I have been rewarded with a talent that benefits others."

"Cindy? Are you ready to go?"

"Yes."

"Billie, you have two precious little guys. And your mother is adorable," says Cindy

Billie responds, "Thank you so much for coming over to help out this evening."

"It was my pleasure."

George intersects with, "Okay, we'll be on our way."

"Thanks again to you both."

It's only a few minutes' drive back to Cindy's home, and George assures her of how much he appreciates her help this evening.

"George, you're a deacon at our church, aren't you?"

"No. My travel schedule would make it near impossible to be available as needed and perform as the deacon I would expect myself to be."

"Well, I know you love the Lord and you seem to be active in counseling with others. May I ask you a question?"

"Sure. What's on your mind, Cindy?"

"Lou and I seem to be arguing at each other's throat an awful lot lately. I just don't know what to do. I can't seem to do or say anything right these days. We're no longer happy with each other. I need to turn to somebody that can help us, and you seem to have experience in helping people."

"I am truly sorry for the problems you and Lou are experiencing, but I am not a marriage counselor and certainly not qualified to become involved in other people's relationship issues. I'm sorry. I just can't help you."

"We met briefly with a marriage counselor, and Lou said he didn't feel like a counselor would help, so we never went back. We met twice with our pastor and that helped temporarily. But the problems remain and seem to grow. I hear from others in our church that you have been instrumental toward helping with their various problems. I observed your help to Billie tonight and felt you might be able to help me."

"There are a couple of areas that I seem to help people through and head them in a new direction, but I just don't feel qualified to intervene in any marriage issues. I wouldn't know where to start. So the best I can do is try to help you find a professional that you both feel comfortable with in a session."

"Have you and Carol had relationship problems over the years?" asks Cindy

"I believe most marriages face arguments and issues over time. Yes, we have. Nothing major but we've had our share of arguments."

"How did you get through the pain of arguments?"

"The course we took to eliminate relationship pain may be difficult for others to follow, but when we first married, Carol would get upset with me over something that I had said or done and I had no clue about what brought it on. She would stomp around the house for two or three days not speaking to me. I was lost for a solution because I didn't know what she was upset about.

"I knew our marriage could not sustain its happiness without communication between the two of us. We began working on discussing the problem at hand. And over time, I knew it was up to me to lead us through a solution that would get the irritation out of the way promptly. So when we had a quick blow up at each other, I began to make it a point to resume normal communications within a very few minutes. In other words, whether I was on her case about any issue or she was disgusted with me, within about fifteen minutes, I would have some normal remark or discussion with her as if we had never had the argument in the first place."

"I can relate to the multiple days of not communicating, and it hurts. It hurts deeply," says Cindy.

"It took some time for Carol to follow my method of communication because she was being led by my example, not my verbal solution to her, so to speak. These days, we may have a three-minute spat; and within a short time, life is back to normal between us. I love it."

"I wonder if mine and Lou's problems have grown beyond your way of correction."

"Do you really think so? Cindy, I doubt that. You two are too in love for it to be too late. How long have you and Lou been married?"

"We're in our eighth year of marriage."

"Aha! You'll be okay. You're beyond that Seven-year itch and heading for fourteen, then on to your twenty-first and beyond."

"What do you mean?"

"Statistics reveal that marriages have problems in their Seventh year. You've gotten through Seven years. I don't know how I can be of help to you. Would Lou be agreeable to third-party discussion?"

"I believe he would do that."

"Would you be okay to be a part of a meeting between Lou and a third-party person?"

"George, I'll do almost anything to save our marriage."

"As you consider your schedules, when would probably be an ideal time to meet for an hour or so?"

"Saturday or Sunday afternoon comes to me as a good time for both of us."

"Professional counselors probably don't normally work on weekends, but let me work on this and I'll call you. There is somebody out there with a solution for you two. You just need to be connected to the right one."

At home, Cindy notices Lou's car in the driveway. He is home from work and by now has probably eaten the food she had prepared for him earlier. She then opens the car door and then turns to George, "Thank you, George Belten, for all you do for others. You're a special, special man."

As George backs out of the driveway, he briefly prays for Lou and Cindy's happiness.

The next morning, as George sips his coffee, he looks over to Carol who was in obvious prayer with her eyes closed and lips slightly moving. George was also praying before she came to the dining room. After a few moments, Carol then made eye contact with George and offered a nice smile and said, "Good morning, dear."

"Good morning to you too, my beautiful, classy wife."

Both began eating, Carol with her dry cereal and milk with slices of banana and a few blue berries mixed in. George, as usual, has a bowl of oatmeal and throws in a spoon of roasted pumpkin seeds.

"Carol, why is our marriage as congenial and rewarding as it is, in your opinion?"

"Oh, that's easy, honey. It's all because of you." Carol responds with a giggle.

"No. I mean what is different with us? Why aren't others as happy in their relationships as we are?"

"You've got me on that. Maybe we try harder, but I tend to think it's a natural for us."

"When we first married, for a short time, we were not quite as content as we are now. That's normal as relationships need to adjust toward each other, and that doesn't happen overnight. I'm just trying to recognize some magic so I can share it with Lou and Cindy."

"I always thought they were happy," says Carol.

"Me too. But I'm finding out that problems, nothing of a serious nature, exist between the two of them."

Carol then offers, "One thing that stands out to me is when you sat with me before we married and told me that you will never do 100 percent of my expectations, and I will only do 90 percent of your expectations."

"Yeah, I remember. I'm always performing at 110 percent and getting back only 90 percent. Yet you're always doing more than your share at 110 percent and my share is only 90 percent. That may have been more of a remarkable relationship sustainer than we realized at the time."

"Yes, we seem to accept that as a way of life within our marriage."

"And what else?" asks George.

"Gosh, I don't know. It just happened I guess."

"We've been married nineteen years now. Long ago, I recall reading that most divorces are filed in fifteen years of marriage. And a movie is out named *Seven Year Itch*, originally filmed staring Marilyn Monroe and Tom Ewell. *Seven Year Itch* hits on the unhappiness after six years of marriage."

Carol is still looking intensely at George and wondering where this conversation is going.

George continues, "Back to the Bible, the number Seven is a number of completion, sometimes success and happiness, other times reflecting only a completion. You and I never had the Seven-year itch that I know of (laughing). However, at about that time, we did experience a boost and sense of solidifying our marriage. Do you agree?"

"We did indeed."

"Now four years ago, we survived statistical records of being part to the fifteen-year numbers. Actually, it seems that marital problems hit couples and seem to be no longer bearable for some. The fifteenth year then becomes the year of divorce. Do you see where this is leading us? I reference Seven in success with finances and addictions. I believe now that the number Seven, God's number for completion and rest from His accomplishments, is becoming more and more significant in human lives and our planet. For example, my dad would grow his crops on specific fields of the farm for six years. The Seventh year, he always allowed that field to remain untouched."

"But how does that apply to Lou and Cindy?"

"I believe it applies. How it applies is the question. I don't know. I do believe the answer is in the Bible and will point to the number Seven. It's a matter of any relationship going through growing pains and issues toward the Seventh stage and to recognize the rewards and accomplishments."

Friday afternoon and George calls Lou and Cindy at home.

Cindy answers the phone, "Hello."

"Cindy, this is George. I have yet to come up with a suitable counselor to diagnose and work with you and Lou. However, if you still want me to participate, I may have come up with something helpful to you and Lou. If you are available, I can visit with you and Lou for a few minutes tomorrow. Do you believe Lou is receptive?"

"He is. I have alerted him that you may call and provide us with somebody that will help us. "Who did you come up with to help us, or will you do it?"

"At the moment, I still have not been able to come up with a counselor. The first option would always be to go see the pastor, but you've done that. Let's sit down and talk, just the three of us, to see if we can set a plan of action. Will that work for you folks?"

"It will. When would you like to meet?"

"Can we meet at your home? About 10:00 a.m. tomorrow?"

"Ten o'clock it is."

"Good. I'll see you two at ten."

Precisely at 9:57, Saturday morning, George arrives at the home of Lou and Cindy. It appears that Lou has pride in their yard. The edger and lawn mower are outside, and it's quite evident that he cut the grass earlier.

He presses the doorbell and hears the bell tone sounding inside the house.

Lou opens the door. "Good morning, George. Come on in."

Cindy speeds from another room. "George! We're happy you're here. How about some coffee?"

"That will be great. My coffee is like my gasoline, leaded, not unleaded; so I'll have my coffee black please. No additives."

Lou then asks, "George, where would you like to sit? Here in the family room or would the dining room table be better?"

"Why don't we just sit and relax here in the family room?"

"Then have a seat where ever you would like."

Cindy comes in. "We use a single-cup coffee maker, and it's fast. Here's your coffee."

"Lou, would you like a cup?"

"Not now. Thanks."

Their family room is furnished very nicely, somewhat stylish, no clutter, as George looks around. One feature standing out to him was the two wooden rocking chairs with straight backs and nicely padded cushions; so naturally, he selected one to sit in.

"This is different, in a positive way. I like the idea of straight-back rocking chairs in a family room. It encourages comfort as you sit straight and adequately postured. This is a great idea."

"Thank you. The rockers were Lou's idea. He ordered them online and then assembled each one."

"You told me that you folks have been to a marriage counselor, and I assume you didn't see full benefits from the visit so you declined any future appointments. Am I correct in that assumption?"

Cindy glances over to Lou as he nodded and then said, "Yes."

"Let me emphasize to you that I am not qualified to say and do things that will make you happy. I'm just not qualified to be here with you now to discuss your needs. However, now that you have asked me to act in a position I'm not worthy of, we'll work together toward a goal. Do you understand my lack of authority in a relationship-healing capacity?"

"Oh yes. I can't explain it, but we seem to have been drawn to you for help," says Cindy.

"Okay. Let's start down a path toward some happiness. Let's bow our heads and go to the Lord in prayer, asking Him for guidance in everything we do here today."

"Now let me pick on you, Cindy. I want to talk with Lou for a couple of minutes. Will you step outside on the deck area while we talk?"

"Sure."

She struggles with the sliding-glass patio door in attempts to close it. Lou quickly goes over to the door and closes it from the inside. "That door has become so hard to slide open and close, and I need to call a door company for them to come out to repair this track."

"That's a good idea. Our patio door did the same thing, and I thought I could take it down, clean out the grit, and reinstall it myself. I quickly decided we needed somebody out there that knew what he was doing because I failed as a door repairman, quickly," says George with a light laugh. He then asks, "Lou, do you love Cindy?"

"Oh yes."

"Do you want to remain married to Cindy for the rest of your life?"

"Without any hesitation, my answer is yes."

"Tell me about Cindy's actions that cause you to become upset."

"Oh boy. She will get upset about something, anything, Lord knows what, and stomps around the house. She won't talk. She just slams doors, throws towels, and so forth."

"What else does she do that rubs you the wrong way?"

"That's the main issue I guess. She is very stubborn. I can suggest most anything to her that we can do around the house, or something she can do that may allow her to feel better when she has an ache or pain, and she is immediately against it regardless of how worthwhile the suggestion is."

"I understand. There are always multiple issues in a relationship that can cause arguments. Tell me more."

"She gives me a hard time about spending money especially on things like my four-wheeler and boat parts. And I don't know, over the last couple of years, it's like she looks for something, anything, that she can get mad at me about."

George then summarizes the points. "Okay now, she gets upset about unknowns and won't discuss it, she faults you over money matters, and she tries to look for negatives in you. Anything else of significance?"

"We often have little quick spats sometimes, but normally, they don't last long at all."

"Tell me this. Tell me what you see in Cindy that is outstanding and good in your relationship."

"Cindy is an absolute Christian lady. I see her love for the Lord in everything she does, every day. In fact, I too am a Christian, but admittedly, she is my ongoing Christian hero. She is a sweetheart with me at times, and I certainly enjoy those times."

"Great. Why don't you open the patio door for her to come back inside while you enjoy some fresh air for a few minutes while she and I talk."

Lou opens the door and cracks a silly remark at her, "Better get ready, you're in the hot seat now. This guy George is going to be tough on you."

"Yeah, right," she replies.

"Cindy, before we get started, may I have a bottle or glass of cold water?"

"You bet! How about a glass of filtered water from the refrigerator?"

She reaches for a larger than normal glass and the refrigerator door dispenser dumps about five pieces of ice into the glass, and then she fills it with water. Walking back to the family room, she hands the glass to George while placing a coaster on the table nearby.

Seated on the sofa, Cindy says, "You do like those rockers, don't you?"

"I do. In fact, if you come to my house at some point in the future, you may find a couple of rocking chairs inside and two others out on our deck.

"Alright, let's see what we can come up with that will help my two dear Christian friends."

First of all, George asks, "Cindy, do you love Lou?"

"I do."

"Do you want to remain married to Lou for the rest of your life?"

"George, I can't imagine ever being without him in my life."

"I want you to tell me what Lou does that drives you up the wall."

"He doesn't appreciate all that I do around here. It's like I'm his maid. He walks in the house with muddy shoes, takes of his clothes at night, and throws them on the floor for me to either hang up or put in the laundry basket. The list goes on and on. He just doesn't carry his load around here."

"Okay. What else?"

"We have separate incomes and bank accounts. He runs out of money all the time because he goes out and shops for crazy stuff we don't need. As a result, he pays late fees on his truck payment all the time. And I'll bet he pays almost a hundred dollars each month in those late fees when combined with bank overdraft fees. His money handling drives me nuts."

"What does Lou do that strikes you as good?"

"Lou is a great father to our son. Anybody that knows us will quickly identify him as a man that loves his family"

"I like hearing that. What you said strikes me that you recognize his love for you."

"Oh yes."

"All right. I believe we can have a terrific dialog between the three of us that may lead the two of you in a new direction. I'm going to invite Lou back inside."

George taps on the glass door. Lou looks toward him. "Lou, come on in. Cindy and I are going to gang up on you. Man, you're in for it." George says with his light laugh. "Let's form a triangle in the seating arrangement; is that okay with you, folks? Cindy seems comfortable on the sofa. Lou, will you have a seat across the room in that recliner?"

"Let me share a story with you two.

"I have coffee on occasion with Fred, a Christian friend. He told me about a motivational speaker that he knew. The speaker shared a story about a male fox that got his leg caught in a trap which had been set to catch a coyote, not a fox. The fox knew the farmer checked the trap each morning, which was disturbing to him. He realized he would be killed tomorrow just after the sun rises.

"The next morning, the farmer approached the trap and saw only a fox leg, a leg that had been chewed off. He reset the trap and just threw the leg aside.

"As time went on, the farmer would see the three-legged fox and kept a keen eye on him. Finally, he saw that fox running across the small field toward a creek and wooded area. So he followed the fox. He eased around in an area where he thought the fox would be, and then, he spotted him. The fox was with his family. He was joined by another fox and three puppies that were trailing after their daddy. The three-legged male fox had recovered and was able to do everything he wanted. He no longer missed the fourth leg. That fox avoided a bad situation he could identify as coming. He saw that he had a problem, and he got rid of that problem.

"We're going to lean on the Lord as we go forward: identify a problem and get rid of that problem. You probably have some scars from past arguments and spats. As we address and deal with a current problem in the relationship, you must not scratch that scar from the past. Let it heal. And it will if you leave it be. Don't look to past scars or issues you have experienced in the past. Allow any scar to heal.

"Once you have conquered a problem, and you will, you'll then do the same thing with the next problem. You're going to just plain get rid of some problems one by one, slowly and methodically. As you do so, you will acknowledge God's number Seven in your completion. Seven is the number of completion. It completes the hardships and laboring as we look forward to reaching Seven or its multiples. For some people, a Seven for them may be seven days, twenty-one days, seven weeks, seven years.

"We're going to talk openly here, but first, I want you to talk to me, not to each other, fair enough?

"Cindy, you have expressed issues over Lou's handling of money, spending too much on his toys, and that he does not do his share in the house, leaving clothes lying around.

"Lou, you have problems with Cindy in that she wants to control how you spend money, she gets upset and won't speak for days, she is stubborn, and she is always attempting to find something she can get upset with you about.

"Please! Lou, do not look over at Cindy as if you are going to comment on our topic at hand. Only look at me during this structuring of an upcoming commitment.

"Cindy, Lou celebrates and loves you for your Christianity. Lou, Cindy loves and admires you for being such a wonderful husband and father. I see a nice foundation to build your relationship with each other. It's obvious you love each other. It's obvious to me that your communications with each other are being taken for granted. Your marriage and your relationship with each other is not broken. It's not even bent. You are going through some relations that are normal for eight years of togetherness in marriage. Instead of allowing a buildup of issues, you're addressing the issues early.

"As you know, my biblical studies of God's use of Seven throughout the scripture has alerted me to pursue Seven as a goal in whatever we do. Seven does reflect completion. Now that completion can be of negative content leading up to the number, or it can contain positive actions until the seventh stage is reached. We always want to lean on God's Seven as our sought-after light at the end of six.

"I believe you, as a team, can emerge as a happy couple, happy every day of your life as you go forward. I know of no marriage relationship that is absolutely perfect, but with a little effort and love, it sure can be a fun ride through life.

"Cindy, will you get a couple of pens and two sheets of paper? We want a clear understanding as to exactly what we are resolving. Each of you take a sheet of paper and print what you are going to work on to correct your relationship handicap. In other words, the topics that are troublesome to your partner, not you, are what you are listing.

"Now exchange papers and of the items listed by your partner, write down briefly what you will commit to doing to help your partner reach a solution to their problem that bothers you. You can see here that instead of addressing your own handicaps, you are helping your partner to resolve their own issues that affect you and that each of you have identified."

After a few minutes of discussion between the two, they plan their approach to this new viewpoint of helping their spouse change instead of just dealing with their own issues. Finally, they look to George. "We've got it," says Lou.

"Now this may seem child-like, but let's take it a step further. Make copies of your plan, placing one on each bathroom mirror in your house, place a copy on the refrigerator, another near each television set, and a copy on your car dash. These will remain in place over the next Seven weeks. On your refrigerator, place two small monthly calendars. Lou, you may use a green highlighter on Cindy's calendar, and Cindy may use a yellow highlighter on Lou's calendar. Each day your partner has fulfilled their commitment, you highlight that day. On your calendars, identify the Seven weeks that begin now by underlining the dates.

"Now in case of a slip up and your partner does not live up to their commitment one day, you must continue with this Seven-week program. You don't give up. Jointly discuss the slip up in a moderate, constructive tone; and if that partner agrees they did fall short of both your expectations, simply place a smiley face on their calendar for that date and briefly note the lack of following the commitment.

"You have Seven weeks to completely eliminate each and all the problems you have listed. If we're using Seven as the completion stand, you may ask, 'Why don't we set it as Seven days?' Relationships can be very complex, more so than modifying eating habits and properly handling finances. That complexity involves changes in human behavior. Therefore, you will need Seven weeks as your completion date.

"You must pray individually and jointly on a daily basis as you ask God to help you change the way you handle your marriage, always praying for success by the forty-ninth day, your seventh week. I cannot over emphasize the need to keep the Lord in your focus with your day-to-day activities.

"One other thing, I will be your coach over this route to success. If you have an urge to be your old self one day, or if your partner is showing signs of not living up to their commitment, don't argue; just remind them that you're both on a written commitment to improve relations."

Cindy walks up to George, reaching out her arms as to hug him and says, "George, we have been to a couple of meetings intended to help our marriage, and none have set out to guide us the way you have done. I would never have dreamed of building our marriage around a number, number Seven."

Then Lou shakes George's hand firmly as he offered, "I don't know how you came up with this program, but I can see it being our answer. I feel in my heart that we'll emerge as a new husband and wife. We both thank you."

"Working with you two is going to be a pleasure. Lou, you asked how I came up with the Sevens program. I'm not certain exactly how or when. All I know is that I was led to begin a review of Sevens in my life and circumstances. That led me to the Bible and further studies. I now believe our lives incorporate the Seven and use of Sevens in everything we do. We seem to identify how it fits into any challenge we are facing."

"Do you want to know something? When I sat down in your house this morning, I had no idea as to how I could or would go about helping you two wonderful people. Now that I look back on what we have drawn out as a plan, I'm amazed. What you have seen here this morning is not my doings. God has led us all to a solution. Children of God, He intervened, and you will do well."

Lou and Cindy both have tears rolling down their cheeks. They say nothing as they stare at each other, holding hands.

"Thank you both. Pray and lean on the Lord through the next Seven weeks. Bye now."

"Goodbye" is the reply of both Cindy and Lou.

George opens his car door and seats himself, then goes to the Lord in prayer, a very connecting, loving prayer, thanking Him for His ongoing love and help for His children here on earth.

# CHAPTER SEVEN

Arriving at home, he finds the next-door neighbor's child had left their small wagon in George's driveway. He partially pulls from the road and in the driveway, then stops, gets out of the car, and walks over to remove the toy.

"George!" calls out Dave from next door. I am so sorry little Benjamin left his wagon in your way. Let me get it for you. Please."

"Oh, that's okay. I really don't mind. He enjoys playing over here, and we should honor his preference."

"I'll put it back in my yard. Benjamin seems to enjoy your property more than his own," he says laughing.

"Let him play here anytime he desires."

George gets back in the car and pulls it on up the driveway and into the garage. As he gets out, Carol peeks out the door into the garage, "You have a phone call, dear."

"Be right there," he responds briefly.

He walks from the garage, through the utility room, and into the family room. The landline phone is off the hook, and he picks it up.

"Hello, this is George."

"George, this is Howard at Fair Life Church. You have a follow-up meeting next week with the people in our church that you are helping in their finances, don't you?"

"Yes, next Wednesday."

"We've had a change since you were here, and Pastor Brent King is no longer at our church. We have a new pastor. His name is Carlton Grissom. We'll miss Brent but we do like Carlton a lot. Anyway, Carlton believes he is adequately educated in personal finance to fulfill the needs at our church, and he will take over at helping those with financial problems in our church."

"That's very good, Howard. His financial talent will certainly be a welcome in your church. I'm happy that Carlton is able to fulfill the need and wish more pastors possessed that expertise. I appreciate your call and please do tell Pastor Grissom that I'm available if needed."

"I'll relay your message. Thank you. I hope you have a nice afternoon."

"Thanks for the call."

"Bye."

Turning to Carol he says, "I've been told that the Old Dakota Steak House has good food, and they have a clean comedy show one Saturday night of each month and that's tonight. How about a date night out for some good food and entertainment?"

"Sounds good to me."

"Oh no! I can't smoke at that restaurant," George says with a humorous tone.

"You what? What did you say? You had better not be smoking again!"

"Just thought I'd create a reaction from you. No, tobacco use is a thing of the past for me."

George calls Old Dakota Steak House to confirm the show time and makes their seven-o'clock reservation for him and Carol. He was told the show begins at eight so they can enjoy the dinner in a leisure pace.

"Carol? Let's plan on leaving home at 6:15, and we'll eat then enjoy the entertainment that begins at eight."

Arriving at Old Dakota Steak House slightly early, George gets out of the car, walks around, and politely opens the door for Carol. They walk hand in hand to the Old Dakota entrance. He opens the door and allows her to enter in front of him.

They are greeted by the hostess. "Welcome to Old Dakota Steak House. Do you have reservations?"

"We do. The name is Belten, George Belten."

"Give us a couple of minutes to make your table ready. You may have a seat over there or in our lounge."

"We'll wait here near the entrance."

George leans over to Carol, pecks her on the cheek, and says, "I sure do love you, young lady."

"Oh, thank you. I love you too."

George looks around the restaurant, "Man, this place is packed. The aroma of grilled steaks fills the air and makes my mouth water."

The hostess walks over near them. "Come with me, please."

As they make their way to a table, George, being the people person that he is, glances at others seated to see if he recognizes any acquaintance. The hostess pulls out the chair for Carol to be seated, then hands her the menu, and another menu to George.

"Your server will be right with you."

"Thank you."

The rear section of the restaurant provides scenery through large windows. Their view of the small pond and landscape offers a pleasant view. George points out the ducks drifting around in the calm waters, and Carol cuts in. "George, quick! Look at the doves in that bird bath! They're kissing! I have never seen that before."

"Neither have I. They did appear to kiss. I wonder if it was a sign of affection or they were sharing food or drink. I believe they were showing affection for each other."

"So do I. Many birds are affectionate toward each other and mate for their entire life, devoted to each other. It's shameful that human beings do not follow that same commitment even under contract."

The server approaches the table. "Good evening, my name is Peter, and I will be taking care of you this evening. What can I bring you to drink?"

George looks at Peter and exhibits his natural smile. "Thank you, Peter. My wife and I will have water. And we'll need separate checks."

Carols mouth drops open in response as she looks toward George over the top of her menu. Then she quickly looks at Peter. "Yeah, right. Not in this lifetime," she pledges.

With a hardy laugh, George turns to Peter and says, "Peter, I'm kidding."

"I kinda thought so but didn't want to question it."

"May I interest you in a glass of wine from our wine list?"

"No, thank you."

"I'll be right back with your water and tell you about our specials for the evening."

George reviews the list of appetizers while Carol turns directly to the steaks.

"Carol, how about an appetizer? Let's order escargot. What do you think?"

"I never pass up on escargot."

George hears a voice, "Mr. Belten!"

He turns to see a couple walking toward their table. "My name is Travis, and this is my wife Lora. We were present at Fair Life Church on the day you talked to our group about finances."

George stands and reaches out to shake the hands of Travis and Lora. "Yes, I remember you as part of the meeting. How are you both this evening?"

"We're doing well, thank you. Your cash flow plan has been very productive and convenient for us. I just wanted to acknowledge that to you this evening. I'll let you get back to the menu now."

"I'm glad you came over and hope you enjoy your evening."

Peter returns and places two glasses of water on the table.

"Our special for the evening is our fresh prime rib. It is marvelous."

"Peter, we have made our choice. We'll start with escargot for each of us. My wife wants the nine-ounce filet mignon, grilled medium rare, baked potato with sour cream only, and salad with thousand island dressing."

"Very good selection, ma'am. And you, sir?"

"I was going to have a steak, but when you mentioned prime rib, I gotta have it. I want the twelve-ounce rib, medium rare, baked potato with sour cream only, and how about a wedge salad with blue cheese. Also, I prefer horseradish instead of horseradish sauce with my prime rib."

"Good choice. You'll enjoy our very fresh cut prime rib. I'll get your escargot and salads on the way shortly."

Travis and Lora are now seated in a distant section as they enjoy the light music in the restaurant. Lora stares away as she seems to go into deep thought. Then she turns back facing Travis. "Do you remember what our music director, Howard, said at our Wednesday-evening service last week?"

"What?"

"He told everybody that our new pastor has taken over the role of helping people address their money issues. He says the pastor is most qualified and anybody using the system presented by George Belten should immediately disregard its use and contact the pastor or himself."

"Yep. And he shared his opinion that George's program is not driven by God as he portrays. I heard him tell Cordie that the Lord is not going to show favor to anybody trying to use that number Seven as a reward for any human efforts. It's God's number for His use, not for man's use as a tool like how George uses it."

"I don't see it that way."

"Neither do I! I see that he believes in God's number Seven strong enough that it works in his life. As he shares it with others, he does so through prayer to God, and it seems to transfer to others knowing Seven is God's completion as well done. I know George says that any person depending on using Seven as value to their cause must believe in the Lord and pray. I'm sure a person must truly accept Seven as a blessing from God in order to be blessed with it."

Silence for a couple of minutes. Then Travis adds, "Regardless of Harvey or our new pastor wants to believe, I will continue to share George's successful ministry of Seven as a problem solver to others."

Peter delivers the escargot to George and Carol's table. They admire the dish and acknowledge that by appearance, it is as appetizing as they anticipated.

"Carol, let's thank God for our blessings."

Both bow their heads and hold hands across the table. "Dear Heavenly Father, we thank You for allowing us to be in a country where we can still openly worship You and pray. We ask that You forgive us of our sins and ask You to turn our country back to its founding ways and love for You. The United States was founded on Your Word, and we have grown away from that founding. We need Your guidance to do what is needed to once again worship You as a nation. We ask that You bless this food for the nourishment of our bodies. We pray this in the name of our Lord and Savior Jesus Christ that died on the cross for mankind's sins. Amen."

They observe their dish of the normal Seven-piece serving of light-crust-topped escargot. Carol is first to taste the delicacy and exclaims, "Oh wow. That has to be the best escargot I have ever eaten. The sauce is perfectly seasoned."

"I agree."

"Did I tell you that Brandon at our local radio station called me?"

"No. What did he want?"

"He said he was having coffee with a group of guys and the main topic had to do with my ministry with the number Seven. Brandon had a lot of questions for me and then asked me if I would consider being on his morning show for thirty minutes to discuss my inter-pretation of the number Seven and how it should be acknowledged and used by Christians."

"And what did you say?"

"I just told him I will think about it and let him know next week. He said he has an opening on Thursday and asked if I would consider that date if I do decide to participate. I want to think about it and plan to call him on Monday."

Peter delivers the food. "Please cut into the steaks and make sure it is cooked to your liking."

Carol is first to respond as she looks Peter eye to eye. "Perfect," she says.

George responds accordingly. "Looks great. May I have some horseradish?"

"I have it right here," says Peter.

As they begin to enjoy their food, a tall, well-dressed young man appears on a small stage in the corner of the room. He addresses the patrons with a stern look, "Are there any comedians here?"

Waiting less than three seconds for a response, he then smiles and says, "Good. I don't like competition."

Then a shorter man jumps on the stage and stands alongside the other man.

"My name is Ronnie," says the taller man as he ignores the shorter guy. Finally, he turns to the guy with frustration and says, "I don't know this other guy. He approached me outside the building. He asked me if he could join me in hopes of a free meal. I said, 'No!' But it not seems I am having difficulty getting rid of him. He follows me about two steps behind everywhere I go.

Ronnie turns toward the other guy. "What's your name anyway?"

"Anyway is not my name! My name is Rudy."

"Good evening, Rudy."

"Now there you go, just like everybody else! You're saying things that you don't have any clue as to what you're talking about. Good evening? *Evening* originated as Eve kept fussing, and it became known to all that Eve is *evening*. Somebody added an *n* and it became as *evening*. So you're telling me that I'm fussing all the time?"

"How in the world did you get the name Rudy?"

"Originally, my name was something else. My mother then began calling me Rudy. She said Rudy fits me better because I was always so rude. I don't understand why she said that."

"Why did your mother originally name you Something Else? I assume Something was your given name and Else was your surname."

"My name is Rudy. Don't you understand anything?"

"Your original name was Something Else, and I don't see how Anything fits into that conversation as your name. Is Anything a nickname? Are you known as Rudy, Something Anything Else? What is your mother's name?

"Maudene."

"Mau Deen? What is your father's name?"

"Benjamin!"

"Ben Jamin? Jamin is his surname? You have a dysfunctional family. Your mother's last name is Deen, your dad's last name is Jamin, and your last name is Else. So Deen and Jamin got together and along came Else. That's weird!"

"Rudy Something Anything Else. I must say that I have never heard such a confusing name. Do you have any brothers or sisters?"

"I have a sister. Her name is Claudette."

Ronnie quickly cuts in, "I don't want to know. Don't even go there!" Then Ronnie continues, "What's your favorite food, Rudy?"

"Steak and taters."

"You mean steak and potatoes?"

"That's what I said, steak and taters."

"Rudy, do you have a girlfriend? And does she have a messed up name also?"

"I had one. Her name was Judy, but she left me and took up with a younger feller named Jody. And she took my bulldog with her."

"Why did Judy leave you for Jody, Rudy?"

"I don't know, and I don't care! I didn't like her anyway. I just want Buster, my dog, back!"

"Do you know where your dog is?"

"Yep. He's living under their deck."

"Have you thought about going to her house and try to get Buster back?"

"I'd like to do that, but he's now in love with her boyfriend's German shepherd and refuses to leave her side."

"So, Rudy, what are you going to do?"

"I don't know. Somebody told me of an attorney that can file paperwork for me to have joint custody. But I don't have money for the fees."

Carol is laughing as she turns to George. "These guys are good. I'm glad you selected this restaurant and show as a date night out for us."

"They are very entertaining," says George.

"You don't work?"

"I had a job but was fired."

"Why were you fired?"

"I worked for Jody, Judy's new boyfriend. He fired me last week and for no reason whatsoever."

"What are you going to do, Rudy?"

"You seem to be a good fella and you probably have a few dollars to spare, so I'm going to become your assistant."

"Rudy! I don't believe that will work. I don't need an assistant, and if I did—"

George's cell phone interrupts. "Hello, this is George."

"George, this is Hank, next door. Somebody is spinning in circles with an automobile on your front yard. It's really a mess over there!"

"They're on our property now?"

"They are. I have already called the sheriff's department, and they are on their way out here."

"Thanks, Hank. I'll be right there as quickly as possible. If you don't mind, see if you can obtain a vehicle description and their license plate number."

"What was that all about?" asks Carol.

"Somebody is tearing up our front lawn with their vehicle. We've gotta go!"

George estimates the meal cost including tip and lays cash on the table. On the way out, he tells the hostess to let Peter know of an emergency and that he left cash on the table to cover their meal, and he can keep the rest as his tip.

The drive home is normally about fifteen minutes. George takes a different route and exceeds the posted speed limit by up to five miles per hour.

Turning down the road toward their house, he speeds up. As he approaches the house, he sees their lawn is all torn up. It looks like a plow had been used on the section near the driveway and public road. He detects no sign of a vehicle other than the deputy sheriff's car parked on the road. No individuals other than Hank from next door and a deputy sheriff are standing alongside his driveway. As he turns in the driveway, Carol notices something on the front of their house.

"Oh my! What is all that messy stuff on the front of our house?" ask Carol.

Hank approaches George as he exits the car. "George, they sure made a mess out here and even threw eggs on your house."

"I see that! What in the world would have brought this on? And by whom?"

The deputy on scene is Steve, a member of George's church. Steve asks George, "Do you have any idea who may have done all this damage?"

"I do not. I really can't think of anybody that would want to damage our property. This is quite upsetting."

Steve then turns to Hank, "What did you see?"

"Not much. I heard a lot of noise from a car. I could tell it was nearby, so I ran out the front door just in time to see the car spinning around and around real fast and then it sped off. I tried to catch a view of the license plate number but was unable to see it. I did see the car was a black Nissan sedan, probably about four or five years old."

Steve says, "I'll check with other neighbors. Somebody in the area may have seen the incident."

Hank leans over toward George. "I see my son Barry on his way over here with our long water hose. He'll connect it and start spraying water on the eggs, hopefully completely removing that mess from your house before it has a chance to dry."

George turns to Carol, "Do you know where that twelve-inch brush with the extension handle is?"

"I'll get it," responds Carol

"Thanks. And I'll get the ladder. I believe it will be a good idea to brush the areas where eggs were thrown. Just to make certain we completely clean off the egg residue."

It only required about twenty minutes of Barry's and George's effort to remove the eggs residue. Then their attention was directed to the torn-up lawn. The full moon was providing enough light for them to have a clear view of the damage.

"I'll need to hire somebody with the right equipment to come out and relevel the area and, probably re-sod it with centipede. I still can't believe this has taken place. I don't know of any enemies we have. Maybe it was some youngster just wanting to be mischievous. I wish I could track down the culprit and talk about it."

Hank turns to Barry, "Son, is this something you and your friend Gary can do for George?"

"Yes, sir."

George follows up, "Do you have access to equipment that will level the lawn again?"

"We can do it with our small disk behind our riding mower and then finish the leveling with a rake. And, if you will have a couple of pallets of sod delivered, I'll put it down."

George pauses for a few seconds and then reaches out to shake Barry's hand. "You've got a deal young man. Just let me know when to have the sod delivered. When it's all finished, give me an invoice or tell me how much I owe you and I'll pay you."

George thanks Hank and Barry for everything as Carol walks toward the front door. George views all the lawn damage one more time and then walks toward the car to pull it inside their garage.

Inside, George takes a long sigh and remarks to Carol, "Wow. This has been an eventful and unusual evening. Did you get enough to eat, or do we need to prepare something here?"

"No, I'm okay. Let's just sit and relax for a bit."

George's cell phone rings.

"Hello, this is George."

"George, this is Drew. Hope you're doing well. Do you have a couple of minutes to talk?"

"Sure."

Drew continues, "As you know, our new pastor and Howard have jointly taken over your finance solutions program and changed everything. We're now told to disregard everything from you that we've been advised up to this point and follow their advice.

"George, they told me to immediately stop everything you taught us and have given me the name and toll-free number to call for help with my credit card debt. That company charges a fee. And, quite simply, I do not trust them."

"What is the company name?"

"Something like Credit Card Essentials, I believe."

"Ah yes. What they do is communicate with the card company, telling them you can't and won't pay them, so they offer to help the card company save some of the debt if they will reduce the balance and rate, and in doing so, the Credit Card Essentials will pay for you. They connect to your checking account and for example, hit your bank for $150 on a given day each month, then pay the credit card company a portion, maybe $100 and they keep the remainder, $50 each month in this case.

"Drew, you need to make your decision at this point. I don't want to undermine Howard and your new pastor in their attempts to guide you, but I would stay clear of turning all your personal and card information over to that company. If you do resume our program, I of course, remain available to help you."

"You will continue to be help me?"

"Of course, Drew. Do you still have the program you and I set up for you to follow?"

"Yes, I do. I'm not going to have any further discussions with our church leaders and will, instead, revert back to you for guidance. I won't say anything one way or the other to our church."

"Okay. God bless you, Drew. You'll emerge out of your little financial dilemma. If you choose to do so, just stay on track with the program that you and I have established."

"Thank you, George. You are a blessing to me and my family. Take care now."

"I will."

"Bye, George."

"Take care, Drew."

George leans back in his recliner and says to Carol, "Steve wrote up a police report on the incident out front, but I'm not optimistic that we'll ever know who did it or why they damaged our front yard and house."

It's Monday morning, midmorning, and George's cell phone alerts him of an incoming call.

"Hello, this is George."

"Mr. Belten, my name is Bing Houser. I'm the associate pastor at Prospect Community Church. We've heard several endorsements of your program involving Seven. Would you have time in your schedule to speak at our church?"

"How many members are there in your church, Mr. Houser?"

"Our normal Sunday-morning attendance is about 140."

"What is their need?"

"Financials, for the most part. Some may be interested in dealing with being overweight, including me."

"Bing, if we can plan on the third Sunday of next month, it will serve my schedule well. I would like to visit with you and your pastor at some point next week."

"Wednesday, late afternoon, will be good for us. Will that work for you?"

"Yes. I'll see you about 4:45, Wednesday."

"Thank you, Mr. Belten."

"Have a blessed day, Bing."

George then calls the local radio station and talks with Brandon. "I would be honored to be on your talk show Thursday as a guest."

"That's great, George. If you will plan to be here thirty minutes before the show starts, I'll be able to get you all set up. We'll go over everything at that time."

"What should I do in preparation?" asks George.

"Nothing, really. Just be here a few minutes early and we'll take it from there."

"Okay. I'll see you Thursday, Brandon."

"Carol, I just talked with Brandon, and I have decided to appear on his morning talk show."

"Aren't you nervous? How long is the show?"

"He says he will allocate thirty minutes for our session. I may be worn out by then. I'm kidding, of course."

"Do you know what, George? I could call a couple of church friends to solicit specific questions that you can easily answer and that should reduce your nervous tensions."

"No, Carol! I would never want to stage an interview. It must be meaningful, and for it to be meaningful, it must contain authentic questions and discussions."

Thursday morning, George parks and walks to the radio station's back door. The door is locked so he knocks. After three attempts, he looks up Brandon's cell number on his phone and dials the number. Brandon whispers his hello. "Brandon, this is George. I'm at the back door now."

"Oh. I'm sorry, George. Please come to the front door at this station. I left it unlocked for your entry."

Inside, George is intrigued with all the station's electronics equipment in each room. Brandon greets him and they go back to the broadcast room. "This is where we'll be conducting the discussions," says Brandon.

The station is currently on pre-recorded news and weather as Brandon goes through the process of getting George ready. The microphone is installed around George's head and Brandon tests the volume and clarity. In a few minutes, they are ready.

It's 8:00 a.m., and Brandon opens his talk show. "Good morning, everybody, and welcome to the Brandon's Talk Show. This morning, we have George Belten as our guest. George has developed a ministry in helping others through prayer and use of the sacred number Seven."

"George, tell us about how the number Seven has played its role in your own life and when you first identified something special about that number Seven."

"I cannot tell you an exact date. It just happened within the last year. I felt prompted to become focused on Seven which developed into a strong desire to study about Sevens and how it plays its role in people's lives and actually, everything we do.

"Years ago, I remember a statistic resulting from research that marriages have problems in Seven years and many end in fourteen years, an extension of Sevens, with divorce finalized in the fifteenth year. At some point in time—why, I do not know—I began to look at my life and the life of others as I determined that our lives develop a new phase, mentally and physically, every Seven years. As we focus on Seven as a solution in our lives, prayer from the heart to God, and through our Lord and Savior Jesus Christ, is the problem solver; and Seven is a phase of completion."

"How's that, George?"

"Look at the first Seven years of a child. Then between eight and age fourteen, they develop into a new phase. Age fourteen to twenty-one is what we may call the terror years, ha. After age twenty-one, children develop to a phase of settling down. This continues. and many workers become restless in their jobs around the age of twenty-eight. Now you may say that Seven has nothing to do with it. Refreshments in life happen at five years in some and ten years in others. I beg to differ. I do understand studies that substantiate Sevens. Personally, it became significant to me as I identified my integrity and character at the age of forty-nine and as it went through changes along the years, specifically in Seven-year increments.

"I have interviewed numerous individuals, and we determined that their lives seemed to update every seven years."

"That is very, very interesting, George."

I know you have worked through church groups and individuals toward bettering their lives with their use of Seven."

"I have seen Seven used toward a specific successful completion of a need. However, please understand that sincere prayer is the essential ingredient. Depending on Seven alone is limited in the hopeful purpose."

"Tell us your most unusual case."

"When working with somebody on managing their finances, we develop and use the Sevens Cash Flow Plan. I worked with a young man that was far beyond being frugal. He hoarded his money and hid cash from entry on his cash flow plan. His cash flow would never balance. He hid money from himself. He would go so far as open other bank accounts, deposit money in it over time, but never allow himself to know his accrued balance. He filed statements away, still in envelopes, without ever looking at them. Sometimes, he burned the statements. He did the same thing with stock purchases. He always paid his bills on time but would actually go hungry because he didn't have cash for food. He has no idea as to how much cash and investment value he has, and he has done it so long that he may not know where some of his assets are and has no idea how much or exactly where it was."

"You're kidding! He was broke? Yet he had lots of money?"

"Yes. That's correct. But you know what? You and I don't understand living like that, but he is happy. I believe he thrives on the misery of having lots of cash and liquid assets yet very little money for daily essentials."

"How long does it take to solve a problem using Seven?"

"That depends on depth, magnitude, and pace. It may be complete within Seven days, or it may take Seven weeks, Seven months, even years to enjoy the result of the six increments that lead up to completion. I'll emphasize that prayer, from the heart, is the most important part of any solution, and Seven only acts as the phase of the completion of a well-structured plan.

"When you depend on the number Seven as a stand-alone number, I believe it has little to no value without prayer. You must do your part. Seven represents fulfillment of six phases or steps, each surrounded with prayer of a well–laid out plan. A plan and prayer. I cannot over emphasize praying for plan guidance and prayer along each way. God had a plan consisting of six phases or days in the creation of our universe. His plan was structured day by day until it reached day Seven."

"Okay, George. The phone lines are lit up. So how about taking some calls?"

"Sure."

"Mr. Belten, my name is Becky. I've heard about your program through friends at our church, and I must say, I'm intrigued. I would like to know how you came up with the number Seven as a solution for people."

"Well, God introduced Seven to us through His Word. How I began to focus on how important Seven is and how we can benefit from it, I cannot tell you. I really don't know. It just came to my mind as a number that is important to God's people, and I, like you, was intrigued. I went to the Bible and read about God's creation and His admiration for His accomplishments in the creation of our universe in six days, then rested. God declared it as completed, well done. He sanctified Seven as sacred and Holy.

"I studied the applications and use of Seven in the Bible and began looking over my background, seeing that the number Seven was remarkably significant in my life. That led me to further studying the Bible and Seven. I found that Seven is important for Christians that support it with prayer. I can tell you absolutely that our Lord God influenced me to turn to Sevens. "Does that answer your inquiry?"

"It does. Thank you so much for all that you do, George. God bless you, sir."

"And I thank you, Becky."

"George, my name is Jamie. You guided a fellow worker toward becoming a nonsmoker. He gave up tobacco. My brother has an alcohol problem. Can you help him?"

"Jamie, it always gives me a lump in my throat to hear that God's Seven and prayer continue to be helpful to others. I have never seen Seven used by an alcoholic. However, in my opinion, a lot of prayer and use of six well-formatted steps are necessary in leading a person toward their Seven and completion. If you will have your brother contact me, I would like to talk with him. I'll put you on hold and ask the radio station operator to provide you with my personal contact information.

"God's Seven is my guide to solutions, to fulfillment, or completion. My belief is that anybody that does not know and love the Lord and tries to have expectations from Seven may never see any benefit from it. In my own life, I have experienced Seven and seen it work in others. It's up to others to pursue."

Answering the next call, "Mr. Belten, in what profession is your PhD?"

"I have no doctorate in any field, and I sincerely hope I do not come across as such. I merely feel as though the Lord allowed me to stumble upon something that has a worthwhile meaning for others that capitalize on prayers and the number of Seven as fulfillment and completion."

"And you believe Seven has a special function in your life?"

"I do. Not only do I believe that Seven is special, I have experienced it in my life and have seen successful use of Seven in other people."

"I can see your point. Sometimes, the human brain will accomplish the wishes of people when they believe it strong enough. Thank you, Mr. Belten."


"Good morning, welcome to the Brandon talk show."

"Good morning. My name is Sarah, and I can't seem to stay on top of my monthly budget. I have heard that you do seminars on finances. What can I do?"

"I have an upcoming Seven financial meeting at the Christian Focus Church. I believe that presentation is scheduled for 3:00 p.m., Sunday afternoon. Would it be possible for you to participate?"

"Yes. I'll be there."

"Okay, I do not have the church telephone number handy but will you call their office and register for that meeting?"

"Oh yes. I'll call this morning. Thank you."


"Good morning, welcome to the Brandon Talk Show."

"Hey. You are trying to tell us you have magic power with Seven. I don't believe you! I don't believe you have the power to do what you say you can do! And that God you talk about doesn't even exist!"

"Tell me your name, please"

"Jake."

"Thank you, Jake. You are right. First of all, I do not believe in magic. I do not have any power, nor do I say that I do. It's God's power, and it's His will to use His power as He sees fit. I only direct others through their own level of love and prayers toward God and His Seven as completion of their needs. They must pray to God through Jesus Christ, and Seven becomes the phase of completion. Are you a Christian, Jake?"

"Nope. I remember going to a church a few times when I was a kid. All the preacher did was ask for money. I got nothing from it."

"I'm sorry you were not fulfilled and to the point of feeling a connection to God while in church. Preachers are to be ministers and deliver God's message to the people. Now let me say this. Our financials of income, investments, etc. are God's and the result of His will. He guides us in financial matters and allows us to keep the money but share 10 percent for use in sharing His word across the planet."

"Now you're saying I need to give my money to a church! You're doing all this Seven stuff just for money, just like all those preachers out there; you want people to give you money. I knew it from the start! You're a stinking rip-off. Goodbye!"

"Good morning, welcome to the Brandon Talk Show."

"Hi. My name is Takkeia. And my five-year-old son is wild and unmanageable. I'm in tears most of the time just trying to make him straighten up. What can I do?"

"Are you and your son well connected and attending church on a regular basis?"

"Not every Sunday."

"How often do you and your son go to church?"

"About once a month. I'm a single mom, and Sunday is my day to sleep in and get some rest."

"I know it's tough, and you should see your rest as precious. I agree. However, attending church and having your five-year-old son in church every Sunday is important toward solving the management of your son's behavior. Now I am not able to provide you with a direct and specific Seven solution for your child's behavior. Generally speaking, his behavior is typically a result of the parent's behavior. Have you been to any counseling as it pertains to parenting a child?"

"No."

"There are counseling services available that may help you and your son. Now back to the purpose of the call to question if the use of Seven is beneficial in your son's behavior. Minus of my exposure and experience in such matters, I believe the combination of deep, sincere prayer combined with focus on six planned phases of progress will lead up to your Seventh phase as satisfying for you and your son. You, as the parent, must set up the six steps that lead you toward Seven. In other words, you may see phase one as showing even extra love as you expect a show of love in return. Phase two, may be calm instructions and expectation of your son. In other words, all orders to the child in a low tone, no screaming at him. Each of these phases would normally be in one-year periods. In your case, the periods may be like one Seventh of the months between now, his age five, and his Seventh birthday."

"Are you with me on this?"

"I believe so."

"Each Seven-year period in our lives introduces a refreshed time period toward the next Seven years. The first Seven years deal with learning and test what a child can and cannot do. At age fourteen, we begin to think and act independently. Age twenty-one is the Seven-year period of becoming independent; they know it all. At age twenty-eight, our mind and body begin their term of achievement. These Seven-year mind-and-body periods continue throughout our lives. Between each Seven-year completion, each year of the six years is a growth period toward that next Seven-year accomplishment. Above all, exposing your child to church every Sunday is essential."

"Our next caller is Nancy. She wants to know more about the use of Sevens toward losing weight."

"Good morning, Nancy."

"Good morning, George. I recently saw Lewis, whom you had helped kick the cigar addiction. He said you helped his wife get away from eating sweets and she is maintaining her slim figure. I joined the local workout center and it helped, but when I stopped, I gained weight and became more overweight than before."

"I'm glad you are serious about losing weight, and I'll be happy to share my viewpoint. First of all, walk at least one mile and work up to two miles daily at least three days weekly. I see people that work out, and unless they maintain and even increase the exercise throughout their entire life, they can regain and even increase their weight. So I believe daily walking exercise is sufficient when combined with a lower calorie change in eating habits; it is the real key to weight loss. I believe that some exercise salons rightfully promote their workout programs when actually, they do not believe their service will result in the extended-term hopes and expectations of the customer."

"But I eat a lot of foods and snacks as a result of actually craving them, especially soft drinks and potato chips."

"You must exert discipline and follow a specific Seven's routine. Here is what will work for you. Gather up all the snacks and soft drinks in your home or surroundings. Donate them to your church or to a worthwhile cause. In place of sodas, drink water instead. Now without these fattening foods, you are going to experience near misery for Seven days. After Seven days, you will tend to ease off on your cravings. On your twenty-first day, you will no longer have the urge for those drinks and snacks. You will be able to periodically enjoy a soft drink or chips without the craving or becoming addicted. Next, do the same thing with foods that are unhealthy, especially breads. You may want to modify your breakfast with oatmeal or a low-calorie breakfast. For lunch, eat a grilled chicken salad. If daily, it sounds as though you will become bored with chicken, but after twenty-one days, it becomes second nature. You enjoy the better foods. I do recommend organic foods, of course."

"Wow. That's quite a change for me."

"And are you willing to invest twenty-one days toward a healthier, slimmer life? I assure you that you will feel and look healthier."

"George, *our* next caller is Juan."

"Good morning, Juan. What's on your mind?"

"I'm not familiar with your Seven's program. Just happened to tune in this station and overheard some of the conversations. How can a Seven help if you don't really have any problems? My life is good; I have no health, work, or financial problems. I'm married to a wonderful wife, and we have two beautiful children."

"Juan, you are a Christian, aren't you?"

"Yes, sir."

"What you just told me causes my heart to swell with love for you and your family. That's wonderful."

"Thank you, sir."

"Juan, the number Seven is mentioned in the Bible hundreds of times. It began, as you know, with God's creation of our universe. He created everything we see and know in six days. On the Seventh day, God rested as He looked at His creation, admiring everything while acknowledging it as complete, accomplished, done. The same six phases or steps, combined with prayer, apply to our lives today, all toward the step Seven as we admire it as complete.

"So Seven can be extended to fourteen, twenty-one, and so forth as you mentioned to the previous caller. We have chickens. You know what? Chicken eggs hatch out in twenty-one days and baby chicks come out."

"But what about childbirth? It takes nine months for a child to be born."

"We may need to ask God when we get to heaven. You can be assured that He has the absolute answer."

Laughing, Juan says, "Mr. George, thank you for your study and the apparent help you are providing many people out there. God loves you."

"Thank you, Juan. Have a great day. God loves you too."

Brandon takes over with, "Have you ever given thought to writing a book about God's Sevens?"

George laughs. "If I do consider writing, I have already learned that you don't tell anybody, friend, or relative of your intent to become an author. They may either laugh at your lack of qualifications or go into total silence and change the subject. Nobody offers encouragement. It's as if I walked up to a close friend and said, 'Guess what? I'm going to fly a 737 out of town tomorrow morning. I'll be seated in the captain's seat in the cockpit.'

"The friend would not believe me to be qualified to sit in the captain's seat and fly a 737. Many potential authors do not see themselves as qualified and do not believe they can write an article."

"George, we have just a few minutes remaining. Will you give the listeners a review of the number Seven?"

"I believe, in one way or another, Sevens is involved in everything we do. We're actually surrounded by Sevens. It's part of God's plan. God created the universe and all its living things in six days. On the seventh day, He declared it as complete and He rested. As one example, farmers toil the land for six years and allow it to rejuvenate in the Seventh year, and you'll find that done back in biblical days. Our lives enter into a refreshed phase every Seven years throughout our lives here on earth.

"Many uses of Seven, I have not yet experienced or seen. I can attest to its successful use to completion in stopping the tobacco addiction, handling of finances, weight loss, and addictions to foods and marital relations. We must start out with prayer as we plan out the six phases that will lead up to Seven, and then we must remain focused on Seven as we pray throughout the process."

"George, I can't believe it, but all the phone lines are still lit up. However, we're out of time. Can we talk you into coming back on our show at a future date?"

"We'll work that in. Sure."

"Thank you, George."

"Everybody out there, thank you for tuning in to the Brandon Talk Show this morning and your participation in George Belten's discussions."

George hangs out in the studio for a while, talking with the station manager, Joe Carroll.

Joe said, "George, I guess I'm blind and deaf. I had never heard of your use of the number Seven until this morning. I am normally real busy at this time of the morning but not today. I stopped what I was doing, leaned back in a chair, and listened. I now find myself scanning for how Seven can help in my life. Above all else, I see everything you have done and are doing as spiritual. Like others, I'm sure this use of Seven has to be inspired to you from heaven. There is no way you could have initially uncovered the use of Seven on your own and deliver it to others. I don't see the human mind as being that creative."

"Mr. Carroll. I am beside myself with your sudden response to hearing about Seven for the first time. You have made my day, sir."

"George, you have impacted my life. My mind is on fire, whirling and thinking of different situations out in the communities and how your ministry can change their life. I heard Brandon asking if you will come back and be on his show again. I hope you will."

"If I find that being on your station is helpful to the community, I will be here."

"Thank you, George. I hope you have a blessed day."

"And you too, Mr. Carroll."

George feels an overall comforting effect on his way home, thinking, *I can sense that my show may have favorably led callers to use Seven as they address issues in their lives. That gentleman, Jake, disappointed me though. I wish I could meet with him one-on-one. He is a harsh, troubled man. If anybody needs to lean on the Lord and the number Seven, he does.*

George arrives back home to find Barry and his friend working on his front lawn.

"Barry. I didn't expect you to level the dirt and lay new sod so quickly. I'm impressed. Who is your helper?"

"Mr. Bolten, this is my best friend, Joe. We do a lot of things together. Joe always tries to work faster and better than me, but he never can quite do it," he laughs.

"Hi, Joe. It's a pleasure to meet you. I'll bet Barry is stretching it a bit. I'm sure you probably show him up much of the time."

"Yes, sir. But he won't admit it."

"Okay, guys, I'm going to let you get back to your project, and I'll go in the house now. How about I ask Carol to deliver you an iced beverage of your choice out here. Joe what would you like to drink?"

"Mr. Belten, water will be great."

"And I'll have water also, if you don't mind," says Barry.

"Okay."

George drives on into the garage and enters the house through the utility room door.

"George! I listened to you on the radio show and you were great. You dealt with each caller in such a rewarding way for their needs."

"Well, thank you, dear. But you probably heard that one caller. I believe his name was Jake. I would really like to spend some quality time with Jake. He is such a sour person. He needs the Lord in his life. I'm really bothered and feel deeply for his soul."

"I heard him."

"Hey. Will you provide Barry and Joe out front with a couple of bottles of water and a glass of ice for each? I'll take it out to them."

"I can only imagine how thirsty they are out there. They have been working for hours. Here you are, two waters and two large glasses of ice."

"Okay. I'll be right back."

Phone rings. Carol answers the call. "Hello."

"Mrs. Belten. This is Steve with the sheriff's office. Is George there?"

"He is. He's outside with the young men working on our front lawn. Hold on and I'll get him."

"Thank you."

"George, you have a phone call."

"Who is it?"

"Steve."

"Okay, I'll be right there."

"Hello, Steve. You've got a suspect already?"

"Not yet. But I have a backup lead. Your neighbor to your right was walking their dog when the vehicle used at your lawn sped by. She said the guy seemed very upset and was purposefully swerving on the road. He darted his vehicle toward her and then turned away at the last moment. The car was a black Nissan, probably three years old. She did have part of the license plate number, specifically the letters of NJJ as part of the entire number. Nothing in the license plate bureau provides enough information to associate part of the license to that particular vehicle. So I'm asking you to note that information, and if you see such a vehicle, call me. Do not pursue the vehicle yourself. Just call me and follow the car from a distance if you feel safe doing so. Okay?"

"I'll watch out for it."

As the evening goes on, neither Carol nor George are paying attention to their favorite TV show. Their thoughts develop into brief discussions about their property damage. Nothing like this has ever happened to them. They have tried to think of any person they know, even slightly, that would want to act up like this person, who-ever it is, has done. It may just be some younger person out wanting to joy ride and show himself up to a friend riding along with them. Or if not, whoever wanted to damage their yard may come back later with the intention of doing even more.

After an evening of thoughts, they have no conclusions at the end of the evening and as they make ready for bed.

The next morning, George and Carol are up early and actively beginning their day. George plans to go across state today and make some unscheduled business visits. He has a good client base in his business, but he's always focused on expanding that base. Specifically, he wants to visit the regional office of a national distributorship that recently relocated about an hour east of George's home and office.

Steve from the sheriff's office drives up to George and Carol's home. He walks to the front door and presses the doorbell. *Ding dong, ding dong,* inside the house sounds.

"I'll get it," says Carol.

She opens the door and Steven is standing there. "Come on in, Steve."

"Is George here?"

"He sure is. George, Steve is here from the sheriff's office and wants to see you." Carol escorts Steve to the family room where George is watching the morning news.

"Hello, Steve. You're fast! You've already got more information about the damage to our property?"

"Not yet."

"George, I'm here on another matter of concern. Last evening, I responded to a call from the New Brand Hotel. The hotel management has filed a complaint against you."

"A what? From where?"

"A misdemeanor charge with some possibility of criminal charges has been filed with the sheriff's office by New Brand Hotel, saying that you, George Belten, with a home address matching this street address and the telephone number that matches your home phone number, were unruly, combative, and disruptive during your check-in at that hotel yesterday."

"Steve! I have not been near New Brand Hotel in almost two years. That is absurd. What caused them to name me? What the heck is going on here?"

Carol stands nearby, observing while her mouth had dropped open in response to her alarm. George is pacing the floor, looking to the floor at times yet looking out the windows occasionally. It's evident to Carol and Steve that he is very upset. Steve stands by and allows George to collect his thoughts in hopes that he will quickly calm down. After almost a full minute of silence, George then turns to Steve and says, "And they think I was in that hotel yesterday?"

"George, I believe you. As a police procedural formality, I want to ask you a couple of questions. Where were you yesterday in the late afternoon, between five and six o'clock? And do you have any knowledge whatsoever as it pertains to the complaint filed against you?"

"I was right here with Carol. We sat out on the deck having tea, as usual. And no, I have no knowledge of anything taking place anywhere yesterday between five and six o'clock other than enjoying my wife's company on our deck!"

"Knowing you as I do, I couldn't visualize the George Belten that I know causing such a ruckus, but I had to pursue the case. I'm like you. I'm confused. If somebody has the same name as you, why would they come after you specifically. When I was there in response to their complaint, they had your home address on their registration and your home telephone number as the contact information."

"You mean they used my credit card to make the reservation also?"

"Apparently not. They always expect a credit card on file with every reservation made. However, they do not require advanced payment for a reservation when the individual making the call assures the hotel they will check in before 6:00 p.m. on the day of their stay."

"What in the world is going on all of a sudden? First, somebody tears up my yard. They threw eggs all over the front of our house. Now I'm about to be arrested for something that I had absolutely nothing to do with."

Steve responds, "George, of course, I'm not going to arrest you and take you downtown. I believe you. Something strange is going on in this case, and I'm going to do some further investigating. Just remain calm and allow me to do my job. You should carry on your life normally. I'll get to the bottom of this, and I'll get back with you. Okay?"

"But what should I do? I can't just sit back and hope for the best through this? I'm seeing jail time here if convicted. And false convictions happen all the time. I have never been arrested for anything and have never even seen inside a jail cell."

"George, my friend, I know this is upsetting for you. I would probably be just as upset as you are if something of this nature happened to me. I'm asking you to remain calm. Don't worry about this case. Just carry on as normal. Let me do the leg work in this complaint."

"Okay. I'll stay out of it. But I can't assure that I'll carry on as normal."

"All right, I'll get out of here and go to work on this unusual, mind-boggling case. The case you have created. Ha! Ha!"

"Then get outta here and get to work, Steve," jokes George.

"Well, you could have at least offered me a cup of coffee or something while I was here and working so hard to make you appear innocent of everything," laughs Steve in a joking tone. "Sincerely, George and Carol, you folks have a great day and don't worry about this hotel case. I'll handle it."

152

Carol thanks Steve. "Steve, we're so blessed to have you as the investigator in this case. Our faith in your ability and friendship is our hope."

It's now 10:15 a.m., and George had intended on being on the interstate and in fact, near his first business call for the day. All planning was delayed by the discussions with Steve earlier. He has already placed the files and paperwork in the passenger seat of his car for use in his business calls today. Before walking out the door, as he does occasionally, he places four bottles of water in his small travel ice chest for today.

The house phone rings and Carol answers.

"Carol, this is Steve again. Sorry to bother you, but is George still around home?"

"He is. He was just about to leave. I'll get him for you. George, you have a call."

"Who is it?"

"Steve, again."

"I'll be right there."

George picks up the phone. "Brother Steve, how are you? Long time no see. And I hope you have some good news for me."

"Doing great. Staying busy, real busy these days, but that's good. George, I would like the hotel employees that were involved in the incident to meet you. Here's where I'm going with this angle. The employees that were involved will expect to see the George Belten that was in their lobby and causing all the problems. However, as they see you, it should clear up your involvement in the incident. Are you available to meet me at the hotel in about an hour?"

George collects his thoughts, switching to his schedule for the day. "I'll meet you there, Steve. I have a question for you. Doesn't that hotel have videos of the hotel inside and outside? I would think they can see the identity of the man in question."

"They do have adequate video coverage. However, he was purposefully hiding his face from the cameras while wearing a hat with a full brim. The employees could see his eyes and face. Yet the cameras did not capture the eyes and upper portion of his face. His shirt was a size larger and not tucked in his trousers. So identifying him without full face exposure and clothing that altered his weight and size appearance makes it more challenging."

"Okay. I'll meet you there."

"I'm hoping we can put this to rest and settle their assumption that you were involved in that turmoil. I believe your appearance today will take you out of the deal. I have a strong lead toward the culprit that did the dirty work, and I'll tell you about it later."

"I'll see you at 11:30."

"I'll see you in a while, George," says Steve.

Walking over to Carol, George says, "I'm going to the hotel so the management and employees can compare my appearance with the individual claiming to be George Belten during the big episode over there. Steve indicates he is near an arrest in the case."

Carol says, "George, I'm still puzzled about how somebody knew your full name, your address, and telephone number, and then used that information toward reserving a room at a hotel.

"Do you want me to go with you?"

"Oh no. I won't be gone very long. I'll walk out front and talk to the young men that are working for a few minutes, and then drive over to the New Brand Hotel."

"Okay, hon. Please drive carefully out there. I love you."

"I love you too," says George.

Outside the house, George walks over to Barry and Joe as they worked at restoring his lawn. "Guys, I only had one pallet of sod delivered. Is that going to be enough?"

"I believe so," says Barry. "In fact, we may have three or four pieces left over, and I thought I would place them around the edge of that flower bed."

"That's good. I'm going to drive over in town. Is there anything, anything at all, I can get for you while I'm out?"

"No, sir. We should be through within a couple of hours, and we'll be out of your way."

"No. No. You're not in our way. You're a blessing to us. I'll be back later. Don't work too hard and take breaks as you need. If you need more water or anything, just tell Carol."

George waves to the two workers as he drives down the driveway. The drive to New Brand Hotel is less than forty-five minutes and that should put him there in advance of the meeting. He is very anxious to put this disturbing accusation to rest. He still can't imagine how he became involved.

At the hotel, George pulls his car over to the right side of the overhang, in a normal visitor parking area. He quickly notices evidence of a fresh remodeling of the front area as he walks toward the revolving main entrance. Inside, he admires the décor as he enters the lobby and actually stops for a few moments, just looking around in his continued admiration. As he makes way to the check in counter, with his normal smile freely displayed, he speaks to several members of the hotel staff and looks around for Steve. Looking at his watch, he is still some ten minutes early, so he decides to have a seat and wait.

An attendant approaches George. "Sir? Would you like a fresh cup of coffee?"

"You know. That would be great. Where can I find it?"

"I'll get it for you. Would you like anything in it?"

"Just as it comes out of the coffee maker."

Hotel employees are walking about the lobby and nearby area; they are all very friendly as they go about their tasks. It is his nature to observe management and employees of any business he is visiting. In this case, his observation guides him to see outstanding customer service training in the employees, apparently from their upper management and policies in place.

"Here is your coffee, sir."

"Thank you. Thank you very much."

From a door near the hotel check-in area, he spots Steve walking toward him accompanied by a well- dressed lady. He stands and reaches out his hand to greet Steve.

"George, thank you for agreeing to drive down here and participate in this review. This is Marsha. Marsha is the hotel general manager."

"A pleasure to meet you, Marsha."

"Likewise," responds Marsha.

"Okay, let's have a seat over here and review the case. First of all, George, you may have noticed busy hotel employees scurrying about. Most of these employees that you saw were involved in the disruption caused by a person identifying himself as George Belten, you. As a result of the employee feedback, you have been ruled out from having anything to do with the disruption. We have viewed camera footage of the event and combined with employee observations, your appearance in no way fits that of the other person claiming to be George Belten. In fact, we have also determined that the other person is considerably younger than you."

"Does that make you feel better, George?"

"It does. I knew I was not involved, but I remained very concerned."

"We have also viewed outside camera footage and saw the person in question leaving the hotel through the side door over there. He walked at a fast pace through some shrubs and onto the convenience store property next door. My next step is to find a business, hopefully the convenience store, that can supply footage that trails him further. So far, none of the footage we have studied provides us with any means of identification. He, we assume he was male, had a hat, shades, and oversized clothing that altered his appearance and prevented conclusive identity.

"So as expected, you are now out of the process except we may ask you to come back and participate in the arrest follow-up if we see fraudulent compromise by any intentional identity theft claim. Do you have any questions?"

"No. I feel relieved now."

Marsha speaks up, "I'm sure you do, Mr. Belten. I'm so sorry our hotel had to put you through this anxiety and frustration. We apologize to you, sir'"

"Oh no. You and your hotel did exactly what was expected of you. At no fault of your hotel, a third party, for God knows whatever reason he had, selected my name and information to reserve a room here. Did the individual use a credit card for the reservation?"

"No, sir. We normally ask for credit card information during our check-in process. However, in some cases, a person calling in to reserve a room may not have their credit card handy at the moment and assures us they will check in before 6:00 p.m., which was the case here. I believe the person was here around 5:30, and well before our 6:00 p.m. reservation cutoff.

"I'm curious. What the heck did the guy do?"

"Oh boy. His rate for a single was quoted at $125. At check-in, he wanted to argue that he reserved a suite at that rate and he expected a suite at that price. Our suites are much more expensive, and the front desk explained that to him. He became angry, began slamming his hand on the counter, demanding a suite. He grabbed some brochures and slung them across the floor. Our attendant called security, and they were there in less than one minute. He continued to scream and holler, stomping around the lobby, throwing items, and refused to co-corporate with security even after they told him that law enforcement was en route. Finally, just before the sheriff's department arrived, he hurried toward the side door and was out of site quickly. Steve here was one of the officers that responded, and we were able to provide reservation information that included your specific details."

"I don't know exactly why, but I feel I should apologize to the hotel for all that took place. Yet, I'm innocent, but I'll go ahead and apologize to you for such a bad experience by somebody pretending to be me."

"Oh no. We sincerely apologize to you, Mr. Belten, for putting you through all this."

Steve speaks up, "Do either of you have anything else to add at this point? If not, I'm going to interview some nearby businesses."

"Mr. Belten. Again, thank you for driving down here to help us. I sincerely appreciate it.," says Marsha

"And I appreciate the kindness that you and your staff extended to me through this ordeal. Bye now," responds George.

"George, I'll keep you in the loop as the case develops. Have a good afternoon and tell Ms. Carol hello for me."

"Thanks for all your work in this case, Steve."

George drives slowly away from the hotel as he looks at the different businesses nearby while assuming in his own mind the ones that probably have cameras and may still have footage of the event. Steve is good at what he does, and he'll uncover any, and all, details as they lead up to an arrest.

From his cell phone, George dials Carol at home. "Carol, I'm on my way home. Is there anything you need from the grocery store or elsewhere?"

"No. I don't think so. What did you find out at the hotel?"

"I'll tell you when I get home. Did Barry and Joe finish the yard work?"

"Yes. They just left. I had to pay them. I thought it was a lot, but Barry said it is what you all agreed upon. I wrote him a check for $1,000."

"You what? You did what?"

"I paid Barry and Joe $1,000. That's what you agreed to, right?"

"Carol! I had no agreement for any amount to those boys, and that's at least twice what we should pay them. Why didn't you call me? That is upsetting. I can't believe that you took it upon yourself to pay them whatever they asked you to pay!"

"George, my sweetheart that I love so much, I'm only kidding you. I decided I'd get your mind off the hotel. I didn't pay them at all. They didn't mention payment, and I knew an agreement existed between you and Barry and you'll handle it."

"You certainly grabbed my attention with that $1,000 statement. You do know that you shouldn't lie like that. Lies are sinful, you know."

"You do know I was kidding you."

"Okay. I'll let you get away with that little white lie this time," George says with a hardy laugh.

George thinks, *I'll get even with that little gal when I get to the house. Pay back is going to be tough on her.*

He slows down before turning into the driveway at home, observing the finished yard work and determined it is a well-done job by Barry and his friend Joe. While in the driveway, he notices that their shrubs alongside the house had been freshly trimmed, apparently by those two young guys. They went beyond expectations in their work today.

With his car in place, George engages the electric garage door open and close panel as he opens the door and walks in the house. He faces Carol with a solid look on his face.

Carol asks, "How was the meeting? How'd it go at the hotel?"

George looks out the kitchen window and pauses before answering Carol. "I don't understand it, Carol. I have never been charged with anything in my entire life and now I'm facing a felony and jail time."

Carol reaches her arms out to hug, George. "Oh my gosh, George. You can't be serious! That's impossible! You were with me at that time."

"I know. But they identified me. Steve was gracious enough to allow me to come home, and he'll be here in a few minutes. He's going to take me downtown and book me. A judge will set bail, and you'll have to bail me out."

Carol breaks loose from her hug and strolls over to a nearby chair, places her head in her hands in disbelief.

"Carol, you recall that $1,000 check you said you wrote? You recall the little white lie about it? Remember wanting to get my mind off the hotel incident?"

"Pay back is tough. I guess we'll both need to pray about lying to each other today."

"George Belten! You are a rascal, a bad, bad rascal. I was about to begin bawling!"

Taking a long breath to clear the emotions, Carol asks, "Now tell me about your hotel visit. Tell me the real story this time."

Both George and Carol laughed as he reached out to hug her. "They did determine that I was not involved. Steve is investigating further as he visits area businesses for any camera footage they may have."

"Dear, I know you've had a tough morning. Why don't we break away from all the mind-boggling stuff you've gone through and go to Harbor Furnishings to shop for a sofa and replace the old one in our family room. Want to do that?"

"Now let me get this straight. I've had a tough morning. Almost been accused for a misdemeanor and you tell me I should break away and go buy a new sofa that we'll seldom use? I'm one henpecked boy. I ask how high when my little wife says jump."

"Ah, shut up and do as I tell you."

Both break out in a hardy laugh as they go about their day, kidding and giving each other a hard time.

"Okay. Let me see if that expense is in my cash flow plan," he jokingly responds with a smile and adds, "We can at least look, I guess."

She adds, "I do believe stepping outside your normal crazy stuff you've gone through in the last couple of days and go out leisurely shopping will be good for you, dear."

"I'm curious. As punctuate as you are about following your cash flow chart, how will you juggle the sofa cost into your numbers?"

"Aha. I'll use magic. I have a magic credit card that I'll use to float the purchase and then fit it in the chart and pay it out when due with some reserve funds that is set up for miscellaneous purchases."

"You're amazing. I shouldn't have even asked. I knew you had it handled in advance."

"Have a coffee or water while I put on a new face with makeup. It will only take five minutes."

George nods and says to himself, "Five minutes? More like twenty minutes, I'll bet."

Turning the television to the news channel, he seats himself in his favorite rocker to review what's going on across the nation. Crime is raging across the country. The news commentators are discussing guns in the hands of young people. A law enforcement officer is being interviewed and says, "These youngsters steal, or buy a pistol that was stolen, and it becomes overwhelming power for them. They must use it to exert that power they now feel they have over any victim. With no real reason, they point the gun at some innocent person and squeeze the trigger. They feel a rush as they flee the scene, not realizing they just ruined their chance to lead a productive life. They'll end up behind bars for much of their life."

Continuing the interview, a commentator asks the officer for a solution. "Law enforcement enters the scene after a crime has been committed. It's a parental function to maintain family unity, discipline, and love in the home. We identify the majority of troubled youngsters come from single-parent homes, a home where they are not supervised, even as young as seven or eight years of age. They roam the streets, in many cases at that age, already learning about how crimes are committed. They learn to look to these teenage criminals. If we, as a society, could expect ourselves as married couples to put more effort in marriages and effectively encourage these families to be active in church, as a family unit, we could see a change out on the streets of America."

"Okay, George. I'm ready," says Carol as she walks through the house.

As they leave home and toward the store, there is no conversation, only the Christian radio station and "The Old Rugged Cross" is being played. "That's a good southern gospel version of that song," says George.

It seems George is stopping at every traffic light on their way to the store, that's annoying, but they're in no hurry, he thinks.

"George! You missed the turn. Harbor Furniture is on Mart Street, and you just passed it."

"Not really. I'll turn at the next street and go in behind the store to park on the side and near the entrance."

"This store's current sale price for a top quality sofa is far better than I've seen on other advertisements in the area. I went online, saw the exact sofa at two other stores, and called for a price. We're saving money by going to Harbor."

"How much savings? And how much are we planning to spend?"

"Just wait until we look at all the varieties. You may not like the one I have selected."

Walking in the store, George comments, "Man, this place is huge!"

"Good afternoon, welcome to Harbor Furniture. My name is Butch Reed, and I'll be helping you today. And what is your name, ma'am?"

"I'm Carol and this is my husband, George."

"What can I show you folks today?"

"We want to look at your sofas and especially the multi-shade beige one advertised."

"That particular sofa is on display near the back of our store, so just follow me, please."

Carol spots the advertised sofa as they approach the area. "It's even nicer than I expected, George."

"How much is that piece?" asks George.

Butch picks up the oversized sales tag and shows it to George. "The regular price for that sofa is $1,995, and we made a special purchase from the manufacturer, so we are selling the sofa for $1,197. That's 40 percent off."

Carol tells George that a competitor has the same sofa on sale for $1,695. "So I don't believe we can beat the price."

"Let me ask you a question, Butch. Should we decide to purchase a sofa from your store, will you deliver it free? We live about nine or ten miles from here," asks George.

"I wish we could, but at that great price, we just can't deliver it free. However, if you're within fifteen miles, we will have it delivered and set up in your home for only $40. And you may or may not be interested, but we'll also remove and dispose of your old sofa for $40. I understand there is a disposal fee charged at the disposal site."

George studies for a few seconds and says, "If we do replace the existing sofa, which in my opinion does not need replacing, we'll donate it to the Children's Lighthouse Home."

"If you folks will walk over to the check-out area with me, I'll see what the delivery schedule is for your area."

"But—" as George intends to tell Butch that he hasn't decided to make a purchase to be delivered yet, George's cell phone rings. "Hello, this is George."

"George, this Steve. Have you got a minute?"

"Sure."

"We were able to obtain video of the suspect's vehicle and license plate number. His name is Jake T. Pinklier. Do you know that name?"

"I don't believe so."

"He was driving a four-year-old dark-gray four-door Nissan sedan. Does anything stand out to you about that vehicle?"

"Not that I can think of, Steve."

"We picked him up and transferred him to the station where we questioned him thoroughly and learned that not only did he represent himself specifically as you in all that turmoil at the New Brand Hotel, but he is the person, and he admits, tearing up your yard. He claims he does not like you because he does not buy in to a lot of your religious beliefs and specifically in your Sevens program. Apparently, he gave you a tough time during a recent radio talk show."

"Oh wow! Now it all comes together. I did have a discussion with a guy named Jake on Brandon's Talk Show the other morning. He didn't disclose his last name, but I recall the name Jake. I don't understand his frustration toward me. I have never met the guy, and I'm quite certain he has never seen me. I guess he knows me but has probably never seen me. However, as I think about it, I'm just not sure. He may have made it a point to see me somewhere."

"Is he under arrest, Steve?"

"Oh yes. He will probably have at least two charges against him. One could be criminal, but the assistant district attorney will probably determine it as a misdemeanor in both cases. He is not a happy person. He does not have a prior record, and that's a good thing. He's out on bail now and you never know what's on somebody's mind after they have been caught committing a crime. The guy could come after you now, so be very observant in all that you do."

"Okay. What happens next?"

"He'll go before a judge to answer for his disruptions at the hotel and his destruction of your property."

"May I talk to this guy Jake?"

"That will not be a good idea especially at this time. He needs to remain clear of the hotel and of you through this process. Any contact with the suspect can alter the outcome of this case and we do not want to interfere. The assistant attorney will take over from here and proceed to the courts and judgment. Why would you want to have anything to do with the guy anyway?"

"I'm not real sure. Just call it a gut feeling on my part. I don't know this Jake Pinklier fellow, but for some strange reason, I have a feeling that there is something deep inside the guy that is crying out for help, help from a friend, maybe. Something that could make him a happier man. Does he have a family?"

"He says he and his wife are separated but not divorced. He called his wife briefly and asked where his son is, and then I believe he talked with the child."

"George, man, I've got to go. All of a sudden, I'm having incoming calls from all over. I'll see you at church Sunday, if not before.

"Steve, very quickly. I almost insist that I meet the guy face-to-face. I just want to see the root of his problem, if possible. We may have something to work with toward softening his frustrations. Please?"

"Let me think about it and talk to the district attorney. I'll discuss it with you in a day or so. Thanks for your help in solving the case."

"And I thank you, Steve."

Click. The phone call has ended and he walks back over to Carol and Butch.

"Well, what do you think?" asks Carol.

"If you want the sofa, let's buy it. Was Butch able to determine when they will deliver it?"

"Late Friday afternoon, around four o'clock, he believes."

"Okay, let's put the deal together and we'll head back home, okay?"

Butch completes an invoice for the purchase price, sales tax, and delivery, then gives it to George for his approval. George signs the invoice and provides a credit card for the purchase. He signs the card voucher, attaches it to his copy of the invoice, and they make their way to the front door. Butch accompanies them to the front, opens the door, and then walks outside a short distance as he thanks them again for their purchase today. That makes a nice impression on George.

"Carol, I like that young man. He was never pushy throughout during our product consideration, he was respectful and sincere in every aspect of the transaction, and after everything was complete, he still walked to the front door and opened it for us as he shook our hands with his sincere smile."

"And you know me. I write letters and emails to companies for the purpose of letting them know how a local store is doing, good or bad. This young man may very well hear from their corporate office after I share our experience in dealing with Butch. "What was his last name again?"

"Reed. Butch Reed."

"Okay."

Carol asks, "Who was that long-winded call from earlier?"

"Steve."

"Again? Anything new in that case?"

"They arrested the guy that was involved in the hotel incident."

"Really? I know you're glad that's over."

"You're not going to believe the entire picture here. His name is Jake, Jake Pinklier. The name Jake may ring a bell with you as he was the disgruntled caller on The Brandon Talk Show. He is the same person that damaged our yard and egged our house."

"Oh my gosh! What is wrong with that man? He's sick, sick, sick. Why in the world would somebody want to do all those terrible things to any human being? Yes, I remember him. Why do you think he is so ill against you?"

"That's the big question. I'm curious to find out, hopefully from him directly."

Turning in the driveway at home, George first checks the mailbox for mail, and it's apparently late today, so he presses the garage door opener and pulls inside the garage.

"I seldom drink anything beyond water, coffee, or tea; but I sure would like a soda over a glass of ice. Can I talk you, pretty wife, into serving me a soft drink?"

Carol goes to the pantry, pulls out a soda, and walks back to the kitchen for a glass. She knows that George does not like more than three cubes of ice when drinking from a glass. She deposits the ice and finishes it off with the soda.

"Here you are, George."

"Thanks."

"So what have you got in mind for that guy Jake?"

"I'm not certain. It is all in the hands of the court system, I guess. I do have it in mind to meet with Jake, or at least spend some time observing, maybe talking with him."

"Are you crazy? Why do you want to have anything to do with him? He's a criminal and definitely mean hearted!"

"Again, I'm not certain of that either. Maybe I just want to see if he's a troublemaker or just mischievous. And does he really not believe in God, or is it his distorted front he puts on? There may be something deep in his soul that is worth working with toward salvaging."

"George, that's what I admire about you. You always look for the good in others," says Carol.

"I have a terrific supporter with you by my side, Carol."

George yawns. "Know what? This old boy is going to take a late-afternoon nap. Wake me in time for dinner, okay?"

"Okay. Then I'll go to your office and will be on the computer for a while."

Next day . . .

George is on his way to the distant business contacts he had intended on making yesterday. Steve calls. "George, are you sure you want to get involved deeper in this Jake Pinklier case?"

"I do. From a Christian standpoint, I feel a need to interact with the man. I don't know exactly why, but maybe I can redirect his life or something. I just feel a deep, deep urge, like I'm being led to meet him."

Steve is still puzzled. "I don't understand why, but here's what I have in mind to do just for you. I'll talk with Julius Barr, the assistant district attorney assigned to the case and see if he will meet with you, Jake, and me. This is abnormal in our system, and Julius may not allow the meeting; and in fact, he probably will not allow the three of us to meet, but I'll ask."

"I'll appreciate it, Steve."

"I'll call Julius and get back to you."

"Sounds good to me. I appreciate your effort and help."

George looks at his schedule and realizes he has an 11:00 a.m. meeting scheduled with the CEO and marketing vice-president of GCRC Corp. He made this appointment yesterday while he was going to be in the general area, cold calling on other businesses.

The drive to GCRC takes about an hour, and he turns the car radio to a Christian station with southern gospel music playing. He knows he should be thinking about the upcoming meeting and his presentation, but he keeps thinking about Jake and hoping that meeting will take place.

Arriving just before 11:00 a.m., he approaches the receptionist, and she recognizes George. "Good morning, Mr. Belten. Are you here to see Mr. Townsend?"

"Yes."

She calls Mr. Townsend's secretary and then directs George to the executive conference room.

George takes the elevator to the fourth floor, turns right, and finds the conference room at the end of the hall. Opening the door and stepping inside, he is greeted by Lee Parks who then introduced him to Sid Townsend.

"Lee tells me you have a program that may benefit our bottom line. Therefore, I am interested in hearing what you have to say. Let's all have a seat at this end of the conference table, shall we?" suggests Sid.

"You do know we have met with another company that offers a similar plan to yours. I believe we have a follow-up meeting scheduled for that company, don't we, Lee?"

"Yes, sir."

"So we've scheduled about thirty minutes for your presentation. Do you think that will be sufficient?"

"May I ask who the other consulting company is?"

"It's East Coast."

George follows up, "I'm familiar with that group. I believe they are a good company."

The meeting went on for forty minutes. Sid and Lee kept asking questions that extended the conference ten minutes longer than scheduled. George is happy for the extended meeting as it is due to their interest in his presentation and program. Finally, Lee and Sid look at each other and Sid tells George, "I believe we have covered everything."

Sid looks to Lee. Lee indicates no further discussion needed, so Sid responds that George's program is very clear to them.

George then looks to Sid directly in the eyes and says, "Here is our agreement, and I would like to earn your business starting today, sir." He slides the contract across for Sid's review and signing.

"I'm sure you do, George. But we still have an open appointment with another consultant. And our attorney must review the content of any agreement presented to us for signing. I hope you understand."

"If you will tell me the time and date of the competitor's appointment, I would like to follow up with you immediately thereafter. I don't want to come across as pushy, but I have found our service to be a little more productive for our clients than any competition. I believe it hinges on not only our team's knowledge but it's the natural upbeat attitude that surrounds everything they will be doing for your company. And Mr. Townsend, you will find your valuable time to be respected. We work with your mid-management and meet with you and Lee to review progress one time monthly."

"We'll call you. I like your style, George. Drive safely out there."

George is disappointed as he leaves the meeting. He had met with Lee twice and assumed this meeting was scheduled for finalizing the contract. Now he finds that he has a competitor involved. But he still believes the contract is his.

He's about six miles from home and his cell phone rings. "Hello, this is George."

"George, this is Steve. I talked with Julius and as I anticipated, he says a meeting among all of us is not a good idea."

"I understand. Okay, I'm sure Julius is open for suggestions of penalty and if so, shares his ideas with the judge. So I want to talk with Marsha at the hotel, and if she agrees, then I would like to discuss my idea with you and Julius before the hearing. You see no objection to that, do you?"

"No, of course not."

"This may be a helpful idea for everybody. We'll keep in touch. Thanks."

George wastes no time in making his call to the New Brand Hotel. "This is George Belten, and is Marsha available?"

"May I tell her who is calling?"

"George Belten."

"Hold on please, I'll check."

After a brief hold, "Hello."

"Marsha, this is George, the guy that didn't cause any disruption at your hotel." George laughingly said.

"Yes, sir. Mr. Belten, how can I help you today?"

"I have an idea that may play out well for everybody in that case. May I come by and talk about it?"

"Yes, sir. When do you want to come?"

"If you are available, I would like to visit in about an hour from now."

"Sure. Come on in."

"Thank you, Marsha."

George has a plan in mind. As he drives to the hotel for a meeting with Marsha, the general manager, he is reviewing his plan so it makes sense to everybody involved in the Jake Pinklier case. His thoughts drift about, and it comes to him how great it is to be a non-smoker, finally with no urge to smoke. He gives credit to God for answering his prayers and use of a formula that concentrated on the result, the completion, the number Seven.

Arriving at the hotel, George asks the front desk if he can visit with Marsha.

"Yes, sir. I believe she is expecting you. Do you know where her office is?"

"I believe I do. Her door is down this corridor, second door on the left?"

"That's it. I'll alert her that you are on your way, so just tap on the door when you arrive."

The walk back to her office is short. He taps on the door, and Marsha responds, "Come on in."

"Good afternoon, George."

"Likewise, Marsha."

George wastes no time getting to the point. "Marsha, I don't know if you have any Christian conviction, but I am very much a Christian and that seems to be inspiring me toward changing the future for a person I've never met, namely Jake Pinklier, the man that went on a rampage at your hotel in my name."

Marsha cuts in, "I do have a home church, and I'm active as allowed by my demanding schedule at this hotel."

"I want to persuade you, the district attorney, and the courts to postpone Jake's final judgment in these misdemeanors as long as he absolutely does everything he is ordered to do and fulfills everything he is ordered to do for your hotel and for me on my property. I am proposing that he work here on a prescribed Saturday and Sunday, performing whatever chores you have him do. At the end of his work, you will sign off and grade him on his performance.

"You may not know about this but while my wife and I were dining out recently, he tore up my front lawn and egged my house. The day before, he called in on a talk show that I was on and became very controversial with me on the air. So my intention is for him to spend Seven weekends working on my property alongside me and go to church with Carol and me on Sunday mornings. Sunday afternoons, he is subject to listening to more about the Lord. Now if his performance is near perfect at the end of our expectations, his record could be wiped clean of any charges, but he must comply with every detail in his assigned services."

Marsha quietly listens as George continues.

"Here is what I'm asking. Jake must perform free services for your hotel, clean-up tasks as an example, for the predetermined period of time. He will then be assigned to me on weekends only for Seven weeks. I understand that Jake's father was a Christian. Jake is not. He claims that he does not believe there is a God. I want the opportunity to have him work, alongside me in most cases, on my property. I understand the district attorney and the judge in this case are Christians and that may make my plea fall upon receptive ears. Every Sunday morning and afternoon for seven weeks, Jake must attend church with my wife and me, and spend the afternoon with Christian friends and us.

"My hope is that Jake will be exposed to the Lord and actually experience God's love to the point he becomes a changed, happier man. It may take time beyond his time spent working with me and attending church, but I feel I can lay the groundwork that may change his life.

"Now if Jake fails to fulfill any part of the court's order, his arrest record remains, and he is subject to the normal punishment of the court, probably community service and possible probation.

"As you can see, the burden of changing Jake's current struggles will fall on my shoulders. And I'm willing to accept that role. I believe he can be redirected to a happier life."

"Mr. Belten, I am at awe over your devotion to this man that set out to destroy you. With your outlined punishment, I have no choice but give you full authority to go forward with your proposal. We'll certainly find something worthwhile for Jake to do around here during his assignment to the hotel."

"Marsha, you just made my day! If you'll allow me, I will write daily scheduled expectations of Jake and will share a copy with you along with the court system. I'll be on my way now and will share your decision with the district attorney's office."

"You'll get it accomplished; I'm certain," says Marsha.

In his car, George looks up. "Thank you, Lord," he says.

Back at home, he uses his home phone and calls Steve's cell number. The call goes in to voice mail and George leaves a message to return the call.

Carol walks in from an adjoining room. "You are a busy, busy boy these days. How about an update?"

George laughs. "I'm on a mission to work closely with Jake on weekends for a while. I believe I can work with him out here on Saturdays and then have him in church on Sundays, and with God's help, focus him in a new direction in his life. That's my story, and I'm sticking to it," he says with a hardy laugh.

Carol follows up, "That's a major undertaking. It sounds like a tough project, but you're a pretty amazing man, and I believe you'll get it done. But I have a question. What are you expecting to accomplish in the long run with him? Apparently, he despises you. Do you think you can change that hatred and make him like you?"

"Quite honestly, I don't know where this is going. That won't make sense to you, Carol, but I'm experiencing an inspiration to reach out and connect with Jake Pinklier. In fact, I feel that I'm being driven."

"Well, you already know this, but you have my absolute support all the way through."

He turns toward the front door. "I'm going to step out front and see how the fresh sod is doing. I don't want to over water it. If Steve calls me back, call me back inside."

George walks around outside as he views the areas of sod. "It looks good," he mumbles to himself. "There is some sign of armadillos and moles in one area and that can be addressed. The grass near their driveway and the main road is going to need edging again soon. Flower beds in the island area seem healthy, but that falls under Carol's green-thumb attention."

He walks back inside the house and shares his findings with Carol. "Basically, everything out front looks good except the edging, and you may want to check the shrubs and other plants in the island area. But that's your deal and may not need any attention."

"You had a call while you were outside, somebody by the name of Kenneth at Enlighten Church. Here's the number."

"Okay. I'll call him now."

He dials the number and listens as it rings four times. "Hello. Enlighten Church. This is Barbie. How may I help you today?"

"My name is George Belten. I'm returning a call to Kenneth."

"Hold please."

"Mr. Belten. Thanks for returning my call. We've heard about your use of Sevens in the field of finances, and I heard you on Brandon's Talk radio show. You have quite a useful ministry going on there, Mr. Belten. Our church is bombarded with members seeking help with their money, mostly credit card debt. Would you be interested in becoming involved?"

"Absolutely. We can work it into our schedules. Right now, my time seems to be prime. However, we can schedule a meeting after two weeks from now. What day of the week will be best for your church?"

"Mr. Belten, Sunday afternoons are probably best."

"Hold for a moment. I want to review my schedules. Will the second Sunday of next month work for your church?"

"We'll make sure it does work for our group."

"Then let's plan on 2:00 p.m. That gives everybody time to enjoy lunch and meet back there. Is that doable?"

"We'll be ready and looking forward to it. We really appreciate your scheduling our church, Mr. Belten."

"You're welcome. I will call you a couple of days in advance and to sit down with you before the meeting. We'll go through some preliminaries. Have a blessed afternoon, sir, and I have another call coming in so I need to go for now."


"Hello, this is George."

"George. Steve here, returning your call."

"Thank you, Steve. It almost seems as though my interests in the Jake Pinklier case is your only case load. But I know you probably have a mountain of cases you're juggling, so you don't know how much I appreciate your help."

"It's no problem, George."

"Here's where things stand from my perspective. I met with Marsha, the manager at New Brand Hotel. She agrees to allow the postponing of the hotel incident on Jake's record if he completely complies in every way with the orders of the judge and to her satisfaction. Jake must spend one weekend at the hotel performing whatever tasks assigned to him by Marsha and perform to the satisfaction of the hotel.

"Next, we want Jake to spend Seven weekends at my property working on Saturdays alongside me at whatever labor task I direct him to perform. On Sunday, he will be required to attend church with Carol and me. Sunday afternoons, he will be exposed to the Lord while we hang out at home or have guests visiting. The week-

173

end work may or may not be consecutive but must total Seven week-ends. Carol and I may travel and unavailable on a weekend or two during the session. He will be required to fulfill Seven weekends."

"Okay. I see where you're headed in this unusual penalty. I'm trying to visualize normal community service that he may be ordered by the judge and compare that to working on your property," says Steve.

"My real intent is to introduce him to the value of God's number Seven and how he can expect results when he follows the new path. He currently views Sevens as a hoax, apparently. As he works for and alongside me on Saturdays, he will be well exposed to Seven and the Lord. And I want to introduce him to God through our church services.

"Steve, I'm back to leaning on you to help this all become reality. I have done some research and found that Julius is a Christian, and the judge that may be overseeing the case attends Forest Church out east of town at Craven Road and Kellogg. I'm hoping this can be an easy sell to the decision makers in our court system. If Jake fails to produce for the hotel or me, he is then subject to the court's wrath and punishment. If he performs, there will be no record of the incidents. I, of course, am hoping that his exposure to Christianity at my home and in church services will at least introduce him to a new path."

Steve pauses for a moment and then says, "Okay. Here's what I need from you. I need all this in writing from you along with Marsha's signature as it represents the hotel. If you'll do that, I'll talk to Julius and ask him to run it by the judge being assigned to the case. We'll see what happens. That's all I can do."

"I'll email Marsha her portion of the mutual agreement, her expectations, and her signature in response. Once I have that agreement in hand, I'll combine it with my written requests and send it on to you."

"We'll see what happens, George."

"Again, my sincere thanks and appreciation to you, Steve."

"Glad to be of help to you, my Christian brother."

George reviews his goals for Jake as he considers, "I must first get to know Jake to know how he thinks, why he believes as he believes. That may take some time working with him. I can't rush Jake through the process or he'll balk. Oh well, I'll figure out how to handle it when the time comes."

George is backing his car out of the garage when his cell phone rings.

"Hello, this is George."

"Mr. Belten, my name is Julius Barr, assistant district attorney assigned to the Jake Pinklier case. I understand you have a plan you want us to consider. Tell me about it."

"First of all, I have never met Mr. Pinklier face-to-face. My only encounter with him was during the Brandon Talk Show and Jake called in to dispute the Sevens interview and Christianity in general. He admitted doing harm to my property and then causing chaos at the hotel while doing so in my name. I see Jake as a young man without a mission and heading down the wrong path in life."

"And you believe you can fix that?"

"I guess you could say that I'm on a mission. I believe I can work with him, side by side, and at least lead him toward the Lord. He may not get there, but he may see goodness in this world as he begins to understand there is an alternative to his way of life."

"What you're proposing is very unusual in the way our laws and courts address his type of crimes and punishment. Tell me more."

"I have the agreement of New Brand Hotel management for him to be assigned there on work detail for Saturday and Sunday, Seven hours each day. I then propose that he spend Seven Saturdays working on my property and alongside me. During those times, he will experience nice people being nice as he begins to develop a reason to turn to God. Sundays, he must show up at 8:00 a.m. and go with Carol and me to church. Sunday afternoons, he is stuck with us at our home until about 3:00 p.m. Some Sunday afternoons, we'll entertain other Christians from our church and again, expose him to nice, caring, people. In each assignment, he must comply totally to the hotel's instructions and my instructions. The hotel's general manager will sign off on his compliance there, and I will sign off on his fulfillment with me. If he does not fulfill every one of his assignments, he then defaults back to you, the courts, and normal judgment and penalty."

"Mr. Belten, this is so abnormal as a penalty that I want to discuss your proposal with somebody else in my office. You need to realize the presiding judge has final authority over your idea, and he's a tough judge."

"Yes, sir. I will appreciate your consideration in the case. I strongly believe he can and will react to the proposed guidance. Under normal court penalties, he remains the mean and confused person he has illustrated in this case. In my proposed penalty, he just may emerge to be productive in society without the anger he now apparently hosts. So please push it through for me and more importantly, for Jake Pinklier."

"I must say, you are strongly committed in the case. I admire you for wanting to pursue your viewpoint. One thing in your favor. You have become a household name within this community to a degree, and that may work well for you.

"I will get back to you. Have a good day, Mr. Belten."

"Thank you, Mr. Barr."

Now back to business, he has never called on Kimpersal Manufacturing Company. Today is the day. After the conversation with Julius, George is on cloud nine. He is up for any obstacle that may come up in a sales pitch. So this cold call is in order. Before going to Kimpersal, he needs some information about the company and its management. He flips through his business cards and sees a card for Vince Matt. "I feel certain that Kimpersal is a client of Vince's and his software program. I'll call him now."

Calling the number, a voice answers, "Good morning, this is Vince Matt."

"Vince, this is George Belten. How in the world are you doing these days?"

"Man, I'm great! And you?"

"Couldn't be better if I tried. You got a minute?"

"Sure. What's up?"

"I want to call on Kimpersal, but I don't know anybody there. I was hoping you could provide some decision-maker names that I can ask for at the receptionist's desk."

"Of course. Let's see now. Jerry Hamperson is in charge of corporate sales. Monty. Monty. I can't think of his last name, but you can ask for Monty and they'll know who you are asking for. But Monty is in charge of all purchases. The president is Billy Cambridge"

"I appreciate all this information. I owe you a lunch."

"George, you are a quality guy, and the Kimpersal group will recognize that in you. You'll like them and they'll like you. So go get 'em tiger."

"Thank you, Vince. I owe you."

George continues down the driveway and turns right at the road. He rehashes the Jake Pinklier conversations in his mind. *I now believe this will all come together. Steve is for it. Julius is now on board. I'm sure he will discuss the proposal with his boss, the district attorney, and they will go to the judge on the matter. All parties involved here are Christians. That is fantastic!*

Pulling in to Kimpersal Corporation, *The parking lot is full of employee vehicles*, thinks George. He always recognizes that employees driving newer vehicles indicates the better pay scale of the company and profitability overall. Furthermore, nice profits are generally more receptive to advancing ideas from account executives. The initial visit to Kimpersal results in a brief introduction of his program to Jerry Hamperson, vice president of marketing, and was just that, an introduction; but he was able to schedule a presentation for the fifth of next month. He accepts a future-scheduled presentation as a step in the right direction.

George continues making contacts with his clients as he works his way toward home. He has been in this business for a lot of years, and everything is like on "automatic pilot." Generally, he visits the clients with a few donuts for the ladies and just dusts off any little problems that exist between the client and his corporate staff. It's a beautiful setting.

He returns home early, just after 4:30 p.m.

As usual, he is greeted at the door by Barney, their Maltese dog. Daily, Barney watches for George to turn in the driveway; and he reacts by running through the house, whining, jumping at the door with his excitement. George picks up Barney as he wiggles around in his arms, showing his excitement for his master to be home. "Carol, Barney loves you too!" in a laughing comment.

Carol reacts, "He's our precious little boy. It's amazing to me how smart he is. Very few conversations around here take place without him knowing what the heck we're talking about. He's amazing!"

"I know. He knows the word 'go,' but a couple of weeks ago, I got out of my chair and told you, 'I think I'll check the mail.' Barney jumps up, runs to the door, and when I opened the door, he ran out to the mailbox and waited for me. I wonder how in this world did he pick up on and know what I said."

Barney jumps down from George's arms and captures his favorite toy. Barney wants George to act like he is taking the squeaker toy away, so he can playfully growl and keep it from being taken.

"George, you seem to be in a great mood. What did you do, close the biggest deal ever?"

"I guess you could say that. I believe my proposal for Jake is going to take place. The judge could turn it down, but I just have a feeling he will go along with us."

"You realize that's a huge undertaking on your part, our part."

"I do. But look at Jake Pinklier. If it all takes place as I pray it will, think of the accomplishment for Jake."

Tuesday morning and George answers his cell phone.

"Mr. Belten, this is Julius Barr."

"Yes, sir."

"I can't believe this is happening, but Judge Hawking will see Jake Pinklier, you, and me in his office at 6:45 a.m. tomorrow. I have already gotten a confirmation from Pinklier to be there and, of course, with the assumption that you will be available."

"You had better believe it. I'll be there."

"His office address is downtown, 1336 Miracle Answer Drive; it's a house that has been converted to his office."

"I know approximately where that address is. I'll see you then and again, thank you."

"See you at 6:45."

George is anxious and arrives at Judge Hawking's office at 6:25, earlier than scheduled time. There are two vehicles in the parking area. George has no idea who the cars belong to, but in case the judge is already in his office, he walks up to the door and cautiously turns the door knob. The door opens and he walks inside. A voice from another room calls out, "Can I help you?"

"My name is George Belten. I have an appointment with Judge Hawking."

"I'm Judge Hawking. Come on in."

George walks to the adjoining room, face-to-face with a well-groomed, white-haired man in his mid-sixties.

"Judge Hawking here. A pleasure meeting you Mr. Belten. You're early. I like that. Have a seat." Judge Hawking continues," Julius told me of your plan. I'd like to hear it from you."

"Your honor, I have become very involved with the biblical number Seven, God's sanctified number for completion, and rest. On the Brandon Talk Show, Jake Pinklier called in, portrayed himself as a nonbeliever in God, and became disruptive in my discussions about the number Seven. He then damaged my front lawn and egged my house. Next, using my name, he caused a problem at the New Brand Hotel, allowing them to assume me as the culprit. I have never met Jake. However, I feel I am being led to take him under my wing and change his future in the eyes of our Lord.

"I propose that he will work for one weekend at the hotel, answering to the general manager, Marsha, Seven hours Saturday, Seven hours on Sunday. Then for Seven weekends, I want him at my home by 8:00 a.m. on Saturday and on Sunday to work or do as I direct him for Seven hours each day. It is possible that Carol and I may travel, and I may contact him to not show up while we are gone and that open weekend would not count toward his required Seven.

In other words, it may require eight or more weeks for him to fulfill his required Seven.

"If he fails to perform and fulfill his obligation to the hotel or to me, he would then be turned back to the court system to deal with him as it sees appropriate."

"Mr. Belten. I have heard about your Sevens ministry. It seems to have a following that is growing. I have never performed as a judge in making such a ruling as you are asking. Just relax until the others arrive. I believe there is fresh coffee in the kitchen area. Feel free to help yourself."

"I'm okay, your honor."

At precisely 6:41 a.m., in walks Julius, accompanied by a man is his mid- to late-twenties. Judge Hawking maintains his position at his desk while Julius introduces me to the guy accompanying him, Jake Pinklier. As I shake hands with Julius and then with Jake, he does not make eye contact with me. He is looking down which reflects emotions are in play.

Judge Hawking tells the group, "Have a seat, gentlemen."

He looks at Jake, "Are you Jake Pinklier, and do you reside at 100-2 Philmore Terrace?"

"Yes, your honor."

"Mr. Pinklier, you are charged with malice and disorderly conduct at the New Brand Hotel while using another person's identity. You are also charged with destruction of property at 1078 Frontier Road. How do you plead?"

"I'm guilty, your honor."

"Mr. Pinklier, before I rule on this case, I would like to hear why you did all these disruptive things."

"Your honor, I'm not exactly sure. I certainly look back on it and wish it had never happened. I kept hearing about Mr. Belten's stuff about Sevens and about God, and I just became a little upset. I guess I wanted to get even or to make him give up all he was doing and saying about Sevens and God. Now I'm sorry."

"You are subject to some severe punishments here. Assuming another person's identity can be an extension of identity theft, a felony, and carries significant jail or prison time penalty. At the very least, misdemeanor charges apply to disruptions at New Brand Hotel and to Mr. Belten's property.

"I've listened to Mr. Belten's suggestion, and I'm going to tell you right now. George Belten is probably one of the absolute best friends you will ever have throughout your life. I want to repeat, George Belten is a friend like you have never seen before.

"My order to you, Jake Pinklier, is that you contact Marsha Bagley, the general manager of New Brand Hotel within the next thirty-six hours and be available to work at that hotel this next weekend, Seven hours on Saturday, Seven hours on Sunday. Do you understand what is required of you over the next weekend?"

"Yes, your honor."

"Next, after you have satisfactorily completed your work at New Brand hotel, and I will emphasize satisfactory completion of your work, you are to spend Seven weekends reporting to George Belten at his home, 9078 Frontier Road, beginning at 8:00 a.m. on Saturday of next week or as directed by Mr. Belten. Some days or weekends Mr. Bolten may tell you to skip working at his home until another weekend. In any case, you must fulfill Seven weekends of work, beginning at 8:00 a.m. on Saturday and 8:00 a.m. on Sunday. You are required to work or do as Mr. Belten directs you for Seven hours each Saturday and each Sunday.

"Do you understand what is required of you over the Seven Saturdays and Sundays?

"Yes, your honor."

"If at any point in time, either the New Brand Hotel or George Belten report to me that you are not or did not fulfill any and all of their expectations and instructions to you, you will be subjected to this court and your normal penalties, up to the fullest extent of the law.

"Mr. Pinklier, if you do perform as expected and both New Brand Hotel and Mr. Belten sign off that you have performed services at or beyond their expectations, your record will not reflect any of your misgivings hereof.

"One last thing. Mr. Pinklier, you may notice that you are required to work Seven hours a day for Seven weekends for Mr.

Belten. I hope you see a message here and hope you find it in your heart to learn about Sevens and join others, including me, in regards for Mr. Belten's Sevens ministry.

"I now release you back to Mr. Barr. He will instruct you further."

"Thank you, Mr. Barr, and especially you, Mr. Belten. Have a nice day. This session is officially over."

Julius, Jake, and George walk outside toward the parking area. Jake turns to George, "Mr. Belten, I sure am sorry for everything. It has been a terrible action on my part. I ask for your forgiveness, sir."

"I certainly forgive you, Jake. We both have an obligation to this court ruling today. You must perform and do as I ask you to do, and I must help you perform well. Is that fair?"

"Yes, sir.

"Julius, thank you, sir, for all you have done in this case. Jake, my contact information will be in the paperwork Mr. Barr will provide, but here are all my phone numbers and address; of course you know the address printed on this card. Call me on Friday of next week before you come out, and I'll see you at 8:00 a.m. Saturday. Till then, goodbye."

Back home, it's 8:05 as George walks in the house. "Hooray!" he screams out.

"Oh my gosh! What is it, George?"

"My prayers have been answered. The judge went along with everything I asked for. Wow! What a delight!"

"George Belten, you did not expect less. I know you. You set out to accomplish something, and you find a way to get it done."

"My dear, let's celebrate. How about winding down this week early and head out for a weekend down at San Destin, Friday and return on Monday. Want to do that?"

"Well! Do I really have to?" with a hardy laugh from Carol.

"We talked to Jim and Joan about playing the new game of Seven we now have. But I can put it off until Saturday of next week."

"Why don't we invite them to go to San Destin also? We can play the game and just hang out together and enjoy the weekend."

"I'll do that. And I know Joan. She will definitely persuade Jim to drop what all he has scheduled and join us."

The following week, George called Marsha at New Brand hotel. Marsha reported that Jake was absolutely outstanding as he worked at the hotel. She is in the process of completing a report and provide the work history of Jake to George, Steve, the state attorney's office, and the judge. George smiles as he hears the report and anticipates total success during the upcoming Seven weekends.

Today is Friday, and Jake called earlier, just touching base, and assures George that he will be at work by eight o'clock tomorrow morning.

On Saturday morning, George is out of bed before Carol wakes. He showers, shaves, and brushes his teeth, and is in the kitchen brewing fresh coffee at 6:15 a.m. The first cup of coffee is decaffeinated and is for Carol. His usual oatmeal breakfast is in the making while he reaches for a bowl and puts a spoonful of pumpkin seeds in it. Pumpkin seeds are considered healthy. It's just preventive health maintenance in his opinion. His coffee is regular. Neither his nor Carol's coffee contains sugar or cream.

"Here's your morning cup, dear."

"Oh thank you, dear. I'm getting up. You're already fully dressed. What time did you get up?"

"Just after 5:30. I guess I'm anxious to begin working with Jake. Actually, it's working on Jake, ha!"

"My oatmeal is ready, so I'll go back to the kitchen and set out your dry cereal, milk, and bowl for you."

"You're a sweetheart."

It's 7:25 a.m. and the doorbell rings. George opens the door. "Jake, come right in. How are you this morning?"

"I'm okay, I guess."

"How about a cup of coffee?"

"Nah."

"Do you drink coffee?"

"Yeah."

"Have you had a cup this morning?"

"No."

"Then I insist. Let me brew you a quick cup of coffee. Do you like sugar? Cream?"

"Just black."

"I heard a good report on your work out at New Brand Hotel. They were very happy."

"Yeah."

"Here is your coffee, Jake. Have you had breakfast?"

"I don't eat breakfast."

"Okay. Let's finish our coffee and we'll get started working."

The sun is not yet bearing down, so working outside is going to be comfortable. The early hours are spent out back cutting back some of the tall weeds and bushes that have grown up since last season. Let's take our time out here, Jake. We're not up against a time schedule with needing to cut out all these weeds and bushes by a certain time today. We need to just be thorough in the project."

George works alongside Jake, primarily allowing Jake to become comfortable around him. They work forty-five minutes and rest for fifteen throughout the morning. Carol walked out with a gallon of iced water in thermos type holder and two glasses. "I knew it's about time you gentlemen would be getting thirsty." She reaches out her hand to Jake, "Good morning, my name is Carol. I'm George's boss, ha!"

"I'm Jake."

Throughout the morning, George does almost all the talking, mostly questions.

"Jake, do you have a family?"

"Yeah. My wife and I are separated right now."

"I'm sorry to hear that. Any children?"

"Our son is five."

"What kind of work do you do during the week?"

"I work at Lamar's Auto as an apprentice mechanic."

"What type work does your dad do?"

"He died two years ago

Nearing lunchtime, Carol goes to the pantry and pulls out a quart of home-canned vegetable and chicken soup. While it heats up on the range, she is busy putting together a ham and cheese sandwich for the guys and herself. Lettuce and tomato are available at the table. Pickles and sweet potato fries are the sides.

She calls out to George and Jake, "Lunch is served. Come and get it."

Jake then says, "I brought lunch. It's in the truck. I'll eat out there."

"No way, Jake! You're eating with us in the house where it's cool. Carol has already prepared our meal, so come on."

Inside the house, George directs Jake toward the bathroom to wash his hands and get ready to eat. He then walks over to Carol, "Thank you, dear. You're the greatest. Most wives would not even consider inviting a worker into the home for a meal.

"You're all for it, so I'm all in too. You see value in that young man, so I'm your support team. We're in it together."

George walks over and puts his arms around Carol in a comforting, loving hug.

Jake emerges from the guest bathroom, sees George clinching Carol in his arms, and says, "Oh. I'm sorry!"

"Don't be, Jake. We're just having a moment of showing our care for each other. Come on. The dining room is this way." Carol directs Jake to have a seat. "We're having a ham-and-cheese sandwich, and the soup is from our storage of canned goods that George canned with the use of a pressure cooker. I believe you may like it. Salt and pepper is over here. Just build your sandwich as you desire with lettuce and tomato, or whatever else you want."

George then tells Jake, "Jake, we always bow our heads, close our eyes, and pray to the Lord, thanking Him for our food and everything in our lives. I'll do that now."

He pays no attention and makes no effort to see if Jake reacted and bowed his head toward prayer.

"Heavenly Father, we are so grateful that we're in a country where we can still openly pray and worship you. We love You and thank You for this food for the nourishment of our bodies. We pray that You will guide us through the day as we pray this in the name of our Lord and Savior Jesus Christ who died on the cross for our sins. Amen."

It's quite obvious that Jake is awkward to be in this setting after all the condemning of George that he did. George recognizes the air but believes he can get Jake to open up and become comfortable around him.

"Never had soup like that before," says Jake

"Do you like it?"

"Yeah. Could I have some more?"

"You sure can.," replies Carol.

"Thank you, ma'am."

"Jake, my name is Carol. I prefer that over 'ma'am.' 'Ma'am' is so formal."

"Okay."

"Where'd you get this soup?" asks Jake.

"Every year, we go to a produce farm about fifty miles from here and buy corn, green beans, peas, and other vegetables from the farmer. George then sometimes spends a day cutting corn from the cob, blanching everything, and seals the jars in his pressure cooker. Of course, I like the convenience of sealing some vegetables and lay them up in our deep freezer. We very seldom buy anything in a can at the grocery store. The flavor, the purity, the convenience of walking to our pantry outweighs any attempts to eat processed foods from the store."

George tells Carol, "Jake has a five-year-old son. I'll bet he is a precious little guy." He then tells Jake, "Carol and I have three sons, and we love them dearly."

They finish the meal and return to their work outside. It's a slow process, clearing out the tall weeds and bushes. But when they are finished, it will look a lot better. The afternoon goes along at a normal pace, work for forty-five minutes and rest for fifteen. Jake is to work here seven hours, not a normal eight hours. They began at 8:00 a.m., had thirty minutes for lunch, so they'll now stop. It's 3:30.

George invites Jake to wash up in the guest bathroom before leaving. He accepts.

Jake approaches George. "What are we gonna do tomorrow?"

"Well, after you shower and shave at home tomorrow morning, I want you to put on clean clothes and be here by eight o'clock, no later than eight o'clock. You'll be going to church with Carol and me."

"I don't go to church."

"Tomorrow, you are going to church with Carol and me. Sunday is part of the judge's order, and you're assigned to me; so we go to church. If you decide not to comply, you'll go back before the judge immediately and put on a work force, fined, and ordered to pay for all damages."

"I didn't know the judge wanted me to go to church. I thought I was going to work both days each weekend."

"Jake, let's clear this up right now. Will you be going to church tomorrow morning with me or revert back to your normal sentencing and with a record for the rest of your life?"

Jake looks up in the sky with a slight disgust in his expression. "I'll be here. I guess I'll be here at eight. I don't like it, but I'll be here!"

George opens the door for Jake. "Jake, you've been a tremendous help out here today, and I appreciate it."

"Okay. See you tomorrow."

George stands outside as Jake turns his sedan around and drives away.

"I've got my work cut out for me," says George to himself.

He then glances across the driveway and sees Hank walking over from next door.

"George. How's it going?"

"Very well, and you?"

"Good. Hey, that car that was in your driveway and just pulled out. I've gotta ask, was that the guy that tore up your lawn recently?"

"Yep. It sure was. The court system has assigned him to work weekends at my property, and he started that work assignment today."

"I can imagine how he feels around you after destroying this area of the front yard. I'll bet he has a tough time facing you."

"I can detect some personality withdrawals on his part, but he'll be okay. He'll open up, I believe."

"So did my son Barry and his friend Joe do okay working and repairing the torn up yard area?"

"They did. They really did better than I anticipated, and they worked fast. Those are two good young men. I paid them $50 extra for the good job.

"Thank you. We often wonder how Barry conducts himself when he's out in other settings. But he's probably okay. Anyway, I need to get back next door. I saw you outside and thought I'd walk over and say hi. We'll see you later."

"Okay, Hank. Have a fantastic weekend."

George walks back in the house and heads for the shower. Working outside all day requires a nice hot shower. After that, it's relaxation time, maybe even a nap.

Sunday morning and as usual, George is awake near 5:30 a.m. *Oh boy!* he thinks. *It sure is nice to wake up, sit on the side of the bed, and no longer have the slightest urge for a cigarette. How nice it is!*

Up and at 'em, George heads for the bathroom and reaches for the toothpaste and toothbrush. Next, he'll shower, shave, and brush his hair, what remains of it. He's in a jolly mood this morning and quietly goes back to the bed, leans over, and kisses Carol on the forehead.

Carol is startled for a moment until she realizes who it is. "Good morning, dear." Jokingly, she adds, "Where's my coffee?"

"I'll have it in your hands in three minutes."

They take their time with breakfast and getting dressed for church. George goes through his Bible study notes one last time before leaving for church.

Carol walks in, as beautiful as ever. "Okay, I'm ready."

"Just waiting on Jake to drive up."

"In fact, it's eight, and he should have been here before eight so we can leave on time."

George is thinking, *Don't do this! Don't you dare do this, Jake Pinklier.*

He walks over and peeks out the front window. No sign of Jake. Then the doorbell rings. George makes his way to the front door and opens it. "Jake. How'd you get here? Where's your car? I didn't see you drive up."

"I turned right instead of left up the road, so I just made a circle and came to your house from the other direction. I pulled up my car to the end of your driveway so I would be out of your way.

"Okay. Let's go to church."

"I'll back my car out of the garage so Carol and you can get in out at the end of our sidewalk, okay?"

"Yes, sir."

Their drive to the Hill Top Baptist church is an approximately twenty-minute drive time. Bible study does not start until nine o'clock, but arriving early is always good for a cup of coffee in the kitchen area while mingling with others before church begins.

"Jake, did you have breakfast already?"

"I had a piece of toast."

"The church will provide coffee before Bible study begins, and I'll bet we can find a couple of donuts in the kitchen."

Arriving at Hill Top Baptist church, George parks a slight distance from the building, allowing seniors and guests to park closer. He and Carol walk along the path, holding hands. Jake follows. George makes it a point to keep conversations going and with Jake involved, hopefully to make him feel comfortable during his exposure to church.

Carol breaks away and head toward her class. In the kitchen area, the usual six to eight men are standing with their coffee in hand, and all turn to George as he enters. "Gentlemen, I would like for you to meet a good friend of mine, Jake Pinklier. Jake is a first-time visitor here at Hill Top."

Each of the regulars walk up to Jake, shakes his hand, and welcomes him.

George reaches to the assortment of donuts and hands one to Jake, and then makes his way to the coffee urn and pours two coffees, one for Jake and one for himself.

Jake now has coffee, and he makes his way over and helps himself to another donut.

The guys reach out and pull him in to their conversations as they discuss some fishing experiences, among other topics. Jake thinks, *I thought these men would bombard me right away with some religious stuff. I guess that comes next.*

Ten minutes before Bible study, the group, one by one, makes their way toward the class. Some new faces are in this class and again, Jake is introduced to the class of all men. Ladies are in the classroom next door. The study is opened with a prayer, and at the end of their class, George was asked to offer prayer before they adjourn.

Jake had assumed the Bible study session would become an embarrassment to him. He sighs in relief as they leave for the sanctuary.

The church members and guests make their way to the sanctuary, more introductions, more handshakes, and a lot of smiles. Before the service begins, the pastor walks around greeting many of the congregation. He walks over to where George, Carol, and Jake are seated, reaches out his hand to Jake. "Good morning, my name is Ray Brinkly, the pastor."

George cuts in, "Pastor, this is a friend of ours, Jake Pinklier. He's a first-time visitor here."

"We are delighted to have you join us this morning, Jake." Jake nods.

The choir sings three beautiful hymns, and then Pastor Brinkly prays. The deacons go through the aisles as they pass out a tray for tithes. *Here they go, wanting money. I knew it! If that judge hadn't obligated me to be in church with Belten, I'd be outta here!* thinks Jake.

Pastor Brinkly opens the sermon with a prayer and welcomes everybody to the Lord's house today. His sermon begins in Genesis 1:1–3, and then to Matthew 1:18–25. Jake's mind wondered about, his son, his work, his obligation to work, and be here every weekend. He absorbed very little of the pastor's message. He did pickup on

God's creation taking six days and He rested the on the Seventh day. He wonders how earth, stars, sun, animals, people, and everything being created in six days; and with His limited Bible knowledge, he brushed it off as being impossible. It seemed that none of the message made any sense to him.

After the church service, he walked with George and Carol through the church and through the main door where he again shook the hand of Pastor Brinkly, who assured him how nice it was to have him in church and invited him to please come back again.

In the line of traffic emerging from the church, George turns to Jake. "Jake, we always go out for lunch after the church service. What would you like as a meal? It's on me."

"Doesn't matter," replies Jake.

"Would you prefer BBQ or Chinese food?"

"I like both. BBQ sounds okay."

"Then BBQ it is."

After several hours of association with George, Jake remains reserved, as if he is holding resentments.

Seated at Bobby's BBQ, George avoids jumping straight into the church and the service. "Jake, tell me about your work. Do you enjoy what you do.?"

"It's a way to earn a buck; that's about it. I almost get by."

"How long have you been working at the auto tire and repair center?"

"Just over two years."

"If you had your preference, what would you be doing as a career? I'm just curious, Jake."

"I enjoy working on cars. But most of all, I would like to manage our repair garage."

"In your opinion, what's keeping you from managing a center?"

"We have had two assistant manager's openings since I've been there, and everybody tells me I should be a manager at the shop, but they won't even consider me. The outgoing manager told me that I'm good at what I do; I'm good with customers. But he said the owner indicated he doesn't want me out front dealing with customers because of the tattoos on my arms. He's afraid it will offend customers and hurt his business.

"Unfortunately, that stigma exists out in the business community. I know a young man that would make a terrific sales representative, and nobody will hire him because he has a tattoo on his hands and arms from when he was in his late teens."

"Jake, you ordered the salad bar with a side of a half of a chicken. How do you like it? Is your lunch okay?"

"Yes, sir."

After lunch, driving back to George and Carol's house, Jake asks, "What will we be working on today? Continue the cleanup out back?"

"Jake, we don't work on Sundays. I really just want to enjoy the afternoon. You and I probably have a lot in common, and I'd like to spend the afternoon relaxing. Do you like to fish?"

"Oh yes!"

"Why don't we go fishing and see who can catch the most fish? I've got plenty of equipment and tackle, and I noticed people fishing at the lake just up the highway."

"That will be good," replies Jake.

At the lake, they stand side by side, casting and hoping for a nibble.

"You think the fish are biting today?" asks Jake

"Maybe, maybe not. It's fun anyway. The challenge before us as we try to outsmart the brim is what makes us tick when fishing. I always think the next time I throw out the hook, I'll catch a fish, so I always look forward to the next time I cast."

Silence for a short time, then Jake comes out with, "George, I still believe we all exist until we die, and then it all ends. But I notice something a little different about you people that believe there is a God out there. I can't describe what I picked up this morning when we were at the church. You people are a little different."

*Aha!* thinks George. *Finally! He is beginning to open up and converse with me. That's a milestone. Thank you, Lord!*

"Jake, I'm going to say this. There is a definite difference in Christians. Christians have no lingering problems in their lives. They experience problems just like everybody else, but big problems become simple problems, and are handled quickly and more easily. Christians love each other. They may not see eye-to-eye with another person and agree with the way they do things, but that Christian love for each other is in place. My neighbor's brother, whom I know well, committed a major crime. In my heart, I love the guy. I would do anything practical for him. But I do not associate with him because of his temper and his attitude toward some people, but the love is there. Does that make sense?"

"You Christians seem to be different. But you're worshiping a bunch of words written by man that are designed to make you think you're better than other people. I don't see why you all buy into those words by some man long ago."

"Jake, there was a time in my life when I, unlike you, felt there was a Greater Being out there but felt no connection to it. Let me put it in terms that may make sense to you. You're right. The words in the Bible were placed there physically by man. However, they were inspired by God. Sometimes, I like to view things as a 'what if.' So what if you are in Atlanta and see an old building collapse. For no known reason, the empty building just began to crumble to the ground. Quickly, police, fire trucks, and ambulances are on the scene. Fortunately, only one person was slightly injured from the falling materials. You are interviewed by the local television studio and you share with them the exact details you saw.

"Now another man from Boston was present and saw the exact same thing you did. You did not and still do not know the other gentleman. He returned home later that day and was interviewed by the Boston media, and he reported the exact same thing you reported in Atlanta.

"In the Bible, there are writings by different people in those days that did not know each other at the time, but they describe the same event. You find that to be the case in different books in the Bible, same basic story, or event, written by two different people. In my Bible studies at first, that added credibility to the actual occurrence.

"Jake, as you progress in teachings and studies, you will quickly learn to appreciate, without any questions whatsoever, the contents of the Bible in its entirety."

"Okay. It still does not make any sense to me."

"At one time, it didn't make sense to me either. Today, I find the Bible understandable for me, maybe not all the verses and words I read, but most.

"I don't believe we're going home with any fish today. Let's call it a day and go back to my house. You are done for today, unless you want to stay longer, and you're welcome to do so."

"I guess just I'll head home."

The week is normal as George goes about his sales and consulting activity. He recaps days with Jake and detect very little progress as he reached out to him, but not pushing him. He is pleased thus far.

Friday evening, George and Carol are relaxing and the phone rings. "Hello, this is George."

"Mr. Belten. This is Jake."

He has been addressing George as "George," not "Mr. Belten," and that let's George know a problem is about to be shared.

"Mr. Belten, my car is in the shop. I have no way to get there tomorrow."

"Jake, you're under court orders to be here at 8:00 a.m. on Saturdays and Sundays. You must be here on time."

"I don't know what to do. I've already called my wife, and she has to be at her work as they close out their month at the office. Two of my buddies are tied up and can't take me. The cab fare is $20, and I have no money. Tell me, Mr. Belten, what can I do? I'm desperate to get there!"

"Okay, Jake. Tell me your address, and I'll have somebody pick you up at 7:30 tomorrow morning."

"Thank you, sir."

"Okay. Just be ready at 7:30."

George could drive over there and pick Jake up, but he wants some Christian response to this situation. So rather than him picking

194

Jake up, he'll see if he can call somebody that Jake met in Bible study class for them to transport Jake.

"Buford, George here. Are you busy tomorrow morning?"

"No. Around noon, my wife and I are joining Bruce and Marion for lunch, but I'm free until then. What's up?"

"I need a favor. I'll explain later why I want another Bible-study Christian to handle this instead of me. You remember Jake, the guest in our class? His car is down and he must be at my house by 8:00 a.m. tomorrow. I can do it, but the impact on him of experiencing Christian love is part of our leading him to Christ."

"Oh boy! You bet! I'll do that and happy to do so."

"I'll text you with his address and phone number. He needs to be picked up from his home at 7:30 and brought to my house. I really appreciate your help."

"Glad to do it, my brother."

Buford arrives in front of Jake's mobile home. Jake has been watching for his transportation; and he comes out, locks the door behind him, and walks to the car. Seated in the passenger seat, he recognizes the face as Buford reaches out to shake hands and introduce himself again. "Jake, my name is Buford Penningdon. It's good to see you again this morning."

"Thank you, sir."

Making their way toward George's home, Buford engages Jake in regular chat. "Did you enjoy our Bible study last Sunday, Jake?"

"I did."

"We have an outstanding group of what we call 'prayer warriors' in that class. They are a mixture of all ages and outstanding Christians that love everybody."

"I've never been to a Bible study before now. And I don't understand a lot of what is covered in there. I probably need to mention that to the class, don't you think?"

"I wouldn't do that, Jake. Most of us, including myself, have been in that same situation within fairly recent years. I was in your exact position eleven years ago when I walked in a church, this church, for the very first time in my entire life. I had never been in church before that. So if I may offer some input, just approach it in your own natural way and plan to grow in your own style, growing in your love and understanding for the Lord God."

"Thank you, Mr. Penningdon."

"It's Buford."

"I know. Thank you, Buford"

Saturday morning, at 7:55 a.m., Buford drives up and Jake gets out of the car. George saw them pull in and walks out to shake Buford's hand and thank him.

Buford places his hand on Jake's shoulder. "Glad to be of help for this young man. I got to spend a few minutes with him on the way here, and I really like him."

Jake turns around and says, "Thank you, sir."

George winks at Buford. "Hey guys, let's have a cup of coffee and visit. I'm not ready to begin work yet anyway." He winks at Buford again.

Buford gets the message. George wants the three of them to sit down and visit. "I'd sure like a cup before I head back to the house," says Buford.

In the house, Carol offers breakfast. "I just made egg sandwiches for everybody, and it just so happens I made an extra one. I normally have cereal, yet like a dummy, I made one for myself, and I had already set up my bowl of cereal. So, gentlemen, as you have your coffee, you can enjoy a sausage and egg sandwich, and add tomato and mayonnaise if you like."

"Are you sure, Carol? I was planning on eating when I get to my house."

"Have a seat and enjoy," responds Carol.

Buford, Jake, and George go about enjoying their breakfast while talking. Buford and George make it a point to continually make Jake a part of their conversations and with subjects that Jake is probably familiar with.

Buford leaves as George and Jake return to their land clearing. Conversations between the two have become more jointly engaged, some about Christianity, some about other topics as they come to mind. George recognizes that Jake is opening up and becoming friendlier. It is now apparent the reservations Jake had in being around George are beginning to fade away.

"What's wrong with your car, Jake?"

"Transmission locked up on me. We can repair it at my job site, but it's still going to cost $1000. I have $300 tucked away, but I'm short $700. I asked my boss to help and take $25 weekly from my check. He said it's company policy to not loan employees money. He says he would like to help me, but if he strayed from policy for me, he would have to do the same for the next employee. He says he just can't do it. But I'll figure out something."

"How will you get to and from work?"

"Rooster, that's not his real name, but it's what we call him, lives out my way; and he says he'll pick me up every morning."

"George, that gentleman that drove me here, I believe his name is Buford, why did he do that?"

"What do you mean? He was available and volunteered to be of help to you, I guess."

"What does Buford do? What kind of work?"

"I believe he is a carpenter, or a handyman. Something like that."

"You're kidding. I assumed he owned a big business. He was so considerate, kind, and easy going."

"He seemed different."

As the day winds down, George volunteers to take Jake to his home. He lives in a clean neighborhood, in a mobile home park, and the outside appearance reveals his home is probably clean and well kept. "Carol and I will come out and pick you up tomorrow morning on the way to church, say about 7:45?"

"I'll be ready."

Sunday morning, Carol and George make certain they are ready to leave the house a few minutes early to allow for the extra out-of-the-way trip to pick up Jake and be at the church by about 8:20.

George pulls in the small driveway at Jake's house to see him standing out front and ready.

"Hmm. That's a good sign. He seems anxious to go to church, or maybe he's anxious to get these Seven weeks over with," he smiles and jokes to Carol.

"Good morning, Carol. Good morning, George."

Carol responds, "Great to see you this morning, Jake."

"I noticed a lot of the men in your church are wearing white shirts. I pulled out one, washed, and ironed it so I could wear it this morning."

Carol and George glance at each other, both with the same thought, *Wow. Thank you, Lord.*

"You know how to use an iron? You did a good job ironing it."

"My mother died when I was a youngster. She taught me how to cook and to wash and iron clothes. So it has come in handy since then."

"So you're a good cook?"

"I do okay. I seem to have an intuition for cooking and do many things without the normal measuring, or I may modify a recipe because I tend to predetermine how a certain variation will affect the taste."

"I'm impressed," says Carol.

At church, in the Bible study and in the sanctuary, it becomes evident that Jake is not as uptight as he was last Sunday. George is careful not to be pushy but allows Jake to ease into this new environment with comfort on his part. Basically, George is beginning to feel good with the progress.

After church, instead of going out for lunch, Carol prefers a meal at their home. They run it by Jake, and he is okay with the suggestion. Carol thought about today's feast and prepared much of the food in advance.

At home, George placed three large pork chops on the hot gas grill while Jake looks on and says, "I haven't had a pork chop in quite a while. My mouth is watering just thinking about lunch."

Carol continued preparing the food inside.

As time goes on, Jake is becoming more and more comfortable around them. The property damage and identity damage attempts are no longer a front-runner in his mind. He has no brothers or sisters, and he begins to recognize George's efforts as what a close family could be like for him.

Lunch is served with those beautiful grilled pork chops, mashed potatoes, fried okra, and fresh corn. George prays and thanks the Lord for everything, and they begin eating. He is hoping Jake will begin to develop and turn away from being a nonbeliever and accept Christ to the point that he can ask him to bless the food when dining with them.

After the hearty meal, George and Jake relax in general conversation. "Jake, what are you going to do about your car and transportation?"

"I don't have a solution. I guess I'll have to save up the money. In the meantime, I'll have to rely on my friends. My wife lives about three miles from me and she will bring my son over to visit. In fact, I would like to bring him with me to your church soon, if he is able. He is sick now and under doctor's care for an infection.

"George, I still have five more weekends to work out here for you. I will try to find a way here on Saturday and Sunday, but if I cannot, will you help me? I do not want to go back before that judge again."

"You will be in Carol and my prayers for a solution."

After lunch, Jake joins George on the back deck. In conversations back and forth between just the two of them, George guides much of their conversations toward their church and Christians, how a true Christian lives, how they approach and solve problems in their lives, and why they believe in and love the Lord. Later in the afternoon, he drives Jake back to his house and says, "I'll see you again Saturday morning at eight o'clock, Jake."

"Yes, sir."

The next three weekends pass quickly. Each weekend, George can see changes in Jake that is pleasing to him. Jake has become more outgoing in church. Almost every day when he is around George, he is continually asking questions about Church, God, and Christianity along with offering some very worthwhile feedback of his own. With the sixth weekend coming up. Jake still has no transportation of his own.

George wants to do something toward Jake's transportation needs but just loaning him the $700 he needs to repair the transmission is not the best thing to do. Helping Jake needs to have a Christian impact on Jake. He needs to recognize God's involvement.

He decides to reach out to Herman, a member of their Bible study class. "Herman, this is George. How are you this afternoon?"

"Me? I'm just mean as ever," Herman says with a coarse laugh.

"Herman, you don't have a mean bone in your body."

"Anyway, let me run something by you. Jake is not making very much progress toward the repairs on his car's transmission, and I'm trying to come up with some ways to help him. I could loan him $700, but I don't believe that's the best thing to do. I want him to recognize the Lord's involvement. Give me some ideas. How can I help him?"

After a brief silence, Herman addresses the question. "I've got an idea. Without looking, I believe we have about $900 or so in class fund from our weekly donations. That fund was set up and used to help those in need out in our community. Helping somebody like Jake is why we have the fund. And in this case, he is new to our church and our class. We should, as a class, help this young man."

"I knew we had that fund, and from time to time, we learn of a need in some person and family, and we vote, as a class, on the need. If the class can accept this need, it will be a blessing," says George.

"I'll get on the phone to each class member, and I expect a unanimous adoption of the help. I'll let you know after my calls, okay?"

"Good. I'm glad I reached out to you on this brotherly need."

Herman drops everything he is doing and begins dialing the phone numbers of class members. With each one, he explains the need, and within two hours, he has his unanimous yes votes to help Jake through his need. He asked the class to not mention this to Jake, and they would convene back in the classroom after the church service to surrender the needed cash to Jake.

This week goes by at a nice pace, and George picks Jake up from home on Saturday morning. They decide to pressure wash the brick on George's house and clean all windows on the outside. Their day's activity hosts a lot of kidding and laughing as they have some fun with the chores.

Sunday morning, they arrive at church on time, have some coffee and fellowship in the kitchen area, and make their way to the class area. The class teacher asks for any prayer needs and George offers, "You all know Jake. Weekly, we've all been in prayer for Jake. He's still going through a tough time without his vehicle. I would like for all of us to continue our prayers for Jake." Opening prayer is performed by Justin that again includes asking God to help Jake. The class then goes directly into the weekly study. After Bible study, everybody goes to the sanctuary.

This week, the pastor continues preaching in Matthew. Jake's mind is still wondering, thinking of problems in his life, with no transportation, his marriage that's on the rocks with his wife, and son living away. He manages to catch some of the sermon, especially the portions about Jesus Christ.

As church concludes, George, Carol, and Jake make their way toward George's car. Herman walks up. "George, could we see you in our classroom for a moment? Jake, you can come also."

George hands Carol the keys to their car so she can start the engine, turn on the air conditioning, and wait comfortably. He then tells Jake, "Come on. Let's see what's going on."

In the classroom, all the class members are standing as George and Jake enter the room. "Gentlemen, we have been in prayer and feel the good Lord is leading us to help a soul." Herman extends his hand. "Jake, the Lord has answered our prayers and is providing you with the $700 needed for your car repairs."

Jake is frozen in place. It's like he can't move. Herman is standing there with the funds in his hand, reaching out to Jake, and Jake is temporarily immobile for about ten seconds. Finally, his right hand reaches out and accepts the cash with tears swelling in his eyes. He attempts to maintain his composure, yet he then bursts out in tears, crying like a child. The class surrounds Jake with arms around him.

He continues to cry. He cannot stop. Herman pulls out a chair. "Here, have a seat." Jake sits with his elbows on the table, head cupped in his hands and continues his sobbing. Finally, he looks up the ceiling and wails out loudly, "Oh my God! Why have I been so blind? Please forgive me. Please accept me as Your son!"

The class members are now wiping their eyes. George has taken his emotions to the men's washroom.

"Jesus has just saved another soul," exclaims class member Lawrence.

It takes about five more minutes for Jake to regain his composure. By now, George makes his way back to the class and walks up to Jake, briefly puts arms around his shoulders, and says, "God bless you, brother Jake. Let's go enjoy lunch and fellowship, my brother."

Carol watches George and Jake approach the car. She immediately knows something is very different. *What in the world is going on?* she thinks.

The two are seated in the car and not a sound from either. *Absolutely quiet, too quiet,* Carol thinks.

However, she dares not ask anything. It's like a very calm air is around them, something abnormal. She looks at George, wanting to say or ask something. He just has this blank look on his face yet with a pleasant smile. George gets back out of the car, opens the trunk, and takes something out. He then opens the rear door of his sedan and hands Jake a new, recently purchased study Bible.

This time, instead of going to their home or going out for lunch, George drives straight to Jake's house. No words are spoken by anybody on the way. George pulls up in the driveway, and he gets out at the same time Jake climbs out of the back seat. They walk up to the door and face each other. Carol sees a conversation going on between the two but has no idea what is going on.

At the beginning of the sixth week of Jake's obligation to work, he continues with mild labor at George's property on Saturday and show up at 8:00 a.m. for church with George and Carol. Jake now continually asks questions after church. His interest level has skyrocketed. Weeks four and five Sunday afternoons have been question-and-answer sessions; on time, well into the evening. George can't believe what he is seeing. This hoodlum, Jake, has truly converted to a very different man. "Such a blessing," George mumbles to himself.

Early in the evening on Saturday, George is in the kitchen helping Carol with the dishes. George's cell phone rings. "Good evening, this is George."

"George, this is Jake. I hope I'm not calling too late."

"Oh no. You're fine."

"I have good news, George. My wife Sara and son Michael have been separated from me for over six months. We are now working toward reconciling our differences. This week, we've been talking daily and seeing each other almost daily. I have told Sara all about you and Carol. I've also talked to her about my experience at church. Last week during the service, when they were singing The Ole Rugged Cross, I had goose bumps running all over my body even on the front of my legs. It was like I was feeling the Spirit of God. I have never felt anything like that. Anyway, back on the reason for my call. Would you mind if Sara and Michael come with me to your house tomorrow and we all go to church together?"

"Jake! Are you kidding me? Jake, you bring them right on, and plan on lunch and fellowship here at our home afterward. Sara can attend Bible study with Carol. Michael will go to the children's class; he'll love it."

"Thank you, George. Thank you for all you have done for me. I guess good can come out of bad happenings sometimes, and I'm an example."

"And I thank you, Jake. You're a blessing."

"Okay, I'll see you and your family tomorrow even before eight o'clock if you wish."

"You know I'll be there."

Sunday morning.

It's 7:35 and the doorbell rings. Carol answers the door, and there stands Jake. He's early. Standing with him is his wife Sara and Michael, their son. "Come in. Come on in."

Jake initiates the introductions. "Sara, this is Carol and that is George, the best human beings I've ever met. And this is my son, Michael."

Carol welcomes Sara with a hug, then turns to greet Michael. "Sara, what can I get you and Michael to drink? I know Jake will have coffee."

"Do you have juice?"

"Orange or pineapple?"

"Orange."

"And you, Michael? What would you like?"

No answer. He looks to his mother, Sara. "If you have some drink with chocolate in it, he would love it."

"Michael, would you like hot chocolate?"

Bashfully, Michael nods, indicating his yes answer.

George speaks up, "We are so happy to have you folks join us today. I feel like I know Jake as a young brother, and we're looking forward to spending Sunday with you all, as a family. Thank you."

"Can we plan lunch here at our home, and then an afternoon of fellowship, just visiting and getting to know each other better? Will that be okay?"

Jake looks to Sara with a slight nod, then back to Carol. "That will be great."

George pulls his car from the garage and onto the driveway, allowing more ease for everybody to be seated. "Carol, why don't you ride in the back seat with Sara and Michael, and Jake will be up front with me."

"I would like that," replies Carol.

Arriving at church a few minutes later than normal, they missed the coffee, so George locates the youth teacher and introduces Michael. Sara accompanies Carol to class as George and Jake go directly to their classroom. The class is already seated as George takes his seat and exchanges verbal greetings. Meanwhile, Jake makes his way around the conference table, shaking hands and individually greeting each class member.

The class teacher asks, "Jake, I wonder if you would be comfortable with going to the Lord and opening our prayer this morning."

Without hesitation, he says, "I will do that. What I pray and how I go about it may not be what you're expecting. I may stumble through the prayer, but yes. I'll be honored to pray."

The class bows their heads and closes their eyes as Jake opens with, "Dear God, thank you for placing me around George Belten. Thank you for this class and its love for you, a love that rubbed off on me. Thank you for my family, Sara and Michael. I love you, Lord. Amen."

His prayer was far more substantial than the group anticipated. It was a simple prayer and obviously from his heart.

As the class broke for church service, the entire group individually renewed their welcome to Jake for becoming a part of this study class.

Carol had gone in advance and placed items in five seats so both families could be seated together. Weekly, Jake is becoming more and more comfortable as he joined in shaking hands with those around him. This time, with a big smile, he is busy introducing his wife, Sara. Michael is still in another area of the building, the children's church.

After the choir sings, the plates are passed through the seated areas. Without observing the plate's journey through their row, George's eye catches Jake tithing, and then Sara places her tithe in the plate. George thinks, *Man! The Lord is truly working in Jake. I am amazed at the changes. Thank you, Lord!*

After church and the drive back home, Jake is busy asking biblical questions to George until Sara speaks up, "Hon, you're wearing George out with so many questions."

"By now, he's used to it. This is nothing compared to last Sunday afternoon while we sat out on his deck talking, even well into the evening."

At their home, Jake and Michael join George in the family room. Sara immediately heads to the kitchen so she can help Carol prepare lunch. Carol had already decided to serve a country-style lunch of fried chicken, mashed potatoes, fresh zipper peas, and a garden salad. Sara volunteered to make the garden salad and serve the iced tea.

After less time than expected, lunch was served and on the dining room table. Everybody was seated, George prayed to the Lord, and they began eating. They enjoyed the wholesome food with little conversation.

"Now it's time for dessert," shouted Carol. And I have a fresh, homemade cherry pie. Any takers?"

Jake and Carol had already expressed how full they were, but now that cherry pie is in the mix, "I'm in. Bring it on," said Jake.

Carol cut the pie in equal pieces, placed each piece on a saucer, and added a scoop of vanilla ice cream on top. She served fresh coffee to those wanting coffee with the pie.

After eating, the men retreated to the family room. Carol rinsed the dishes and placed them in the dishwasher, with the insistence of Sara to help her.

Michael settles down to playing electronic games. The ladies now join the men in the family room. Conversations began with the work Jake and George have performed around the property.

Jake then shuffled and sat up very straight in his chair and turned to George, then Carol, and back to George. "I've got some news I want to share with you. I like auto-mechanic work. Even though I'm not a full-fledged mechanic, I'm recognized as a very good mechanic. Sara and I have been talking this week. We are getting back together as husband and wife, as it should be. I have discovered that I need to expect more of myself, and I plan to start helicopter mechanical school in two months. The extended range is that I may later get my helicopter pilot license. I'll work part time while in school, and Sara's income should allow us to live okay until I graduate. There is a high demand for chopper mechanics, and their beginning salary is above what I'll earn as an automobile mechanic."

George leans over toward Carol. "This guy is on fire! He's going places in life, his career, and the Lord. Something has happened, and it's all good."

Carol jumps up from her seat, swiftly goes over, and puts her arms around Sara. "Sara, do you realize what you now have here as a husband?"

Sara bursts into tears and wails out, "I know! Now I know!"

Carol returns to her chair and the room remains silence for a short time, time that seemed a lengthy period. Everybody regains their composure within a short time.

Jake walks over to Sara. "I love you, Sara, and I promise I'll become the husband and father that are beyond your expectations."

Everybody now seated and with emotions calm, Jake continues. "I've got one other announcement. I have been visiting with our pastor and have accepted Jesus Christ as my Lord and Savior. I will be baptized next Sunday."

Now George and Carol both show emotions as they allow the conversations to continue.

Sara now states, "I too have accepted Jesus and will be baptized along with Jake.

Again, silence. Tears fill everybody's eyes. This is far beyond the timely expectations of George. He knows that in no way he is responsible, even though this has been his prayer. The Lord has definitely come upon this man and his wife.

"Wow! What can I add to that? Carol and I are so happy for your decisions in Christ. You are a blessing."

Jake opens up again. "I rent that mobile home monthly, so Sara and I have discussed it in detail that I will be moving back home with my family next week.

"Now let's talk business for a moment. Next weekend fulfills my obligation to the court order. Unless you have a specific need in mind, I would like to rent a pressure washer and clean your driveway, and then spray the brick front of your house. I believe I can do that in one day. If not, I'll be back the next Saturday to complete the work."

"Really? Then I'll pay for the sprayer rental. And I'll be your helper with the spraying."

"No, sir, Mr. Belten. Your money will not be accepted! Consider this conversation finished. Next topic please."

George looks at his watch. "It's been a seven-hour day for you, or at least close enough. Why don't you folks spend the rest of God's afternoon at home, enjoying each other? Will that work for you?"

Carol speaks up, "Wait a minute! Little Michael is comfortable around George and me. He is enjoying the electronic games. Why don't you let him hang out with us for the balance of this afternoon? I'll feed him a dinner meal with macaroni and cheese, and a hot dog. All little boys like macaroni and cheese. Can we do that?"

Sara responds with, "Are you sure?"

"Absolutely. We'll take him to your home around 6:30, if that's okay. We know Jake's address, but we'll need yours."

"I'll write it for you. My house is at 1077 North Pine Street, and I'll jot down directions."

Jake then says, "We'd love to do that, not that we want to get away from you two, but we'd love to have time to enjoy the new decisions in our lives."

Walking out the door and to their car, Sara stops, looks back, and says, "Jake told me how wonderful you two people are. I now agree to the point that I can't find words to describe you and understand all the good things suddenly happening for us. Bye. We'll see you Sunday."

"Sara, have a great week!"

Back inside the house, Carol hugs George. "Do you remember the encouragement I gave you a few days ago? I said you're amazing and you'll get this done. You are even more amazing, George Belten!"

"Oh no. It's not me. I'm not smart enough to make this happen, not smart enough at all. It's God. He is just using me to handle his instructions. Praise God. Carol, I'm going to take a brief thirty-minute nap."

"And I'll join little Michael as he plays games. I'll even join in with him. Later, I'll cook our dinner, and we'll eat with Michael."

Finally, it's the Seventh Saturday of the court order; it's six o'clock in the morning. George has awakened to a loud, strange noise outside. He jumps up, still in his pajamas, and runs to the front window. Jake is outside with the pressure washer spraying the driveway. George then goes to the front door, opens it, and steps outside. Jake sees George and stops the engine. "George, I'm sorry to interrupt your morning. But I really needed to get an early start so I can complete everything. But I can stop for a while if you would like."

"Oh no. You go right ahead. I'll join you and become your assistant in about thirty minutes."

Jake starts the washer again, and George walks back in the house.

Carol is now awake, "What's all that noise? What's going on out there?"

"It's Jake with a pressure washer. He wanted to start early so he can complete his work today."

"I may as well get up now. I'd never go back to sleep after that," says Carol.

"I'll take a quick shower and get dressed in some old clothes to go out to help him," says George

"Okay. I'll brew some coffee while your oatmeal is cooking. It should be ready when you get in the kitchen."

It's 7:20 a.m., and Jake is busy cleaning the long driveway. *That will take a while, and afterward, he wants to pressure clean the entire front brick surface of my home? It appears to be a one-man job, but I'll make myself available to help if he can use me.*

Jake sees George walk up. He extends a big smile and without interruption, continues working. George ends up just standing around, not knowing what to do.

After another twenty minutes, Jake turns off the washer motor and walks over to George. "George, do you really want to help just a little? I'd like a big glass of ice water."

"Absolutely! I'll be right back."

Inside, he pours water over a large glass of ice and sets it on the kitchen counter. In the garage is a one-gallon water jug with its own spigot. Thinking, *I'll also fill that jug with some ice and water for Jake to have as he needs it.*

"Here you are, partner. And, here's an extra gallon of cold ice water reserve as you need it. I see little to nothing I can do out here, so I'm going to get out of your way. I'll be inside working in my office if you need me. Carol will let us know when lunch is ready, and I'll alert you. Don't work too hard out here."

The day speeds by. Its 4:25 p.m. George is standing nearby as Jake loads up the pressure washer in his car. "George, I'll leave now so I can return this sprayer before they close the rental agency. I guess I've accomplished everything I set out to do here today. I'll see you here again tomorrow morning. Sara and Michael will be with me."

"Great. We'll look forward to it," responds George.

Carol inquires, "How'd he do, George?"

"Marvelous, especially the driveway. It looks new. I have never looked at our brick on the front of our house as needing a good cleaning. Now I definitely see a difference. It looks much cleaner and brighter, but the driveway outshines the brick, I believe."

Sunday morning at 7:40 a.m., Jake, Sara, and Michael are all dressed in their best and ready to head out for church. George and Jake ride in front; and Carol, Sara, and Michael are seated in the back seat as they arrive at church just before eight o'clock.

Bible study class goes by real fast, probably because Jake has his mind on publicly accepting Jesus Christ and the baptism. George just notices, without purposefully looking, that Jake placed a twenty-dollar bill along with other bills in the class collection tray. It registers with George that Jake may be making weekly payments for the seven-hundred-dollar gift back to the class so it can be used to help somebody else in need.

The sanctuary is almost to its full capacity today. The choir was in place for about twenty minutes as they sang opening hymns. The pastor then preached on Romans. After the sermon, at 11:35 a.m., the pastor delivered his ending message, and while the music director sang a song, he asked for anybody that feels they need to be accepting Jesus Christ and be baptized to please come forward. As the song "Just as I am" is being sung, Jake and Sara walk down the aisle and up to the preacher and altar. They are welcomed by the pastor and two deacons.

The pastor then announces, "I am pleased to announce Jake and Sara Pinklier. Normally, we schedule a baptism in advance for an upcoming week. However, I have had a conference with Jake and Sara.

They have accepted Jesus Christ as their Savior, and it is their desire to be baptized today. So it will only take a few minutes to get everything ready, and we'll perform the baptism at this time.

The music director then sings two old gospel songs until the pastor signals they are ready.

After being baptized, Jake and Sara slip back into their attire and come back out to the sanctuary where they are greeted by Christian brothers and sisters. Afterward, they meet up with George and Carol, and head back to their home for lunch and a visit.

George talks during lunch, "Jake, I hope someday, you will have the loving experience, such as I have, to lead somebody to the Lord. I must say this has been, by far, the most rewarding experience I have ever had. You cannot imagine what this walk with you and God has done to and for me. It is truly beyond description, even imagination."

"George, you're no longer just a human being in my view. You're a special God-loving man of honor, character, and integrity."

"Thank you."

After lunch, George asks Carol to clear the dining room table and that everybody remains seated there. It takes only a few minutes to clean the table and for Carol to return to her seat.

"After God created the heaven and earth in six days, on the Seventh day, he said, 'It is complete,' and He sanctified that number Seven and He rested. My dear friend Jake, *it is done*!

"Several weeks ago, you wanted to condemn me for my use of the number Seven, remember? Now let's observe some contributes of Seven.

"You consistently worshiped in church, the first time in your life, for six consecutive weeks; and on the Seventh Sunday, you accepted

Jesus Christ as your Savior. You were short Seven hundred dollars toward your car repair. God met your need. You worked alongside a Christian for Seven weeks. You are twenty-eight years old (four Sevens) and decided on a new career (each of our brain cells refresh themselves in Seven years). You are now in your Seventh year of marriage and with a fresh beginning. Now it gets deeper.

"Sara's and your home is seven miles from the church you just joined. You drive down your street from home, and the speed limit is 35 (five Sevens). On the way to church, you're on the interstate briefly, and it's Seventy miles per hour (ten Sevens). Again, the quarter mile final stretch to your church is thirty-five miles per hour.

"Now let me see how this works. How much money is in your pocket right now?"

Jake answers, "It's $21. Why?" (Three Sevens.)

"Much of this list is coincidental. Don't you agree? Or is it coincidental and intended to apply in your case? One more expansion.

"I'll expand on a research article I read a few years ago. It said the human brain completely refreshes itself every Seven years. The brain completely generates new brain cells and none from the previous Seven years ago still exist. I am of age to tell you straight forward that I have experienced a, so to speak, refreshed brain cells and functioning throughout each Seven years. If you think about it, what I'll say has applied to you.

"When I was a child, up to seven years old, I was just that, a learning child doing childish things.

"At age fourteen, I began to change. My mind and body began to update, so to speak, use some of my childish learnings.

"At age twenty-one, I thought I knew everything yet knew very little. I had a mind of my own, making bad decisions.

"At age twenty-eight, I started to focus on a position rather than a job and to make better decisions.

"At age thirty-five, I had my first job of real responsibility and learned how to compete, how to excel.

"At age forty-two, I found out I still had more to learn in my people skills.

"At age forty-nine, I began to smell success, real success.

"At age 56, I was on cloud nine, competitive, climbing the income ladder.

"Each seven-year increments, as I look back over them, reveals refreshment, or maturity, in what I did, how I did it, why I did it.

"Jake, you're amidst your Sevens right now in your marriage, career change, finances. Don't let up. You now have God to lean on, so pray for His guidance."

*Seven is the number of God's perfection and creation. It's the mark of God's divine touch and authority. Go forward and pray as you seek more Sevens in your life.*

"Jake, Sara, Carol, and I have now established a Christian relationship of love for each other, and we're all united in our love for the Lord.

"It is *complete*."

# About the Author

J. Andy Welch retired early from the automobile finance division of a bank. He then owned Golf Masters Solutions, LLC until he sold it and, retired again.

Andy kept experiencing successes while unaware that the number Seven was his guide. He felt inspirations from God leading him to write about the number. With no outline to follow, Andy simply sat down at his computer and began writing. He never knew what would happen next as he wrote and, he was as much in suspense with upcoming events as the reader may be. While writing, at one point he laughed. At another point in his writing, his emotions led to near tears.

Some of Andy's personal experiences are handed off to George Felten, a fictional character in this writing. Leaning on prayer and God's sanctified and sacred perfect number Seven, a financial crisis is solved, an addiction is conquered, a marriage is saved, an overweight plan is initiated, along with other praises.